ONE LUCKY CHRISTMAS

REGINA BROWNELL

www.bloodhoundbooks.com

Print ISBN: 978-1-5040-8184-9

ALSO BY REGINA BROWNELL

The Two Week Promise

CHAPTER 1

*C*laustrophobic doesn't begin to describe the way I'm feeling right now. The red walls of the bathroom stall close in, looming over me. No way out.

Except. Maybe...

I hope there are no cameras in here to catch my sad attempt at escaping from a date. Steadying myself on the edges of the toilet seat, I check the window. It's small, but I might be able to squeeze through. Is this really what my life has come to?

Glancing up I throw one hand at the ceiling with a clenched fist as if I'm asking a higher power to come and save me. Instead of finding out, I spot mistletoe dangling. Who in their right mind would put mistletoe over a bathroom stall? I should question it. Instead, I panic when loud voices echo outside the door. I have to get out there before someone comes in here to find a woman with reindeer antlers peeking out over the top of the bathroom stall under a hanging ball of mistletoe. I don't need to end up as a viral video on the internet.

Stepping back, the heel of my red shoes slips on the slick toilet seat. My blood pressure rises, heat sinking into my cheeks. I try to grab onto something, but I lose my balance, legs wobbling. Crashing down inside the bowl, the water splashes all over my nude stockings.

"Shit, shit, shit," I mumble.

I should have never agreed to allow my mother to set me up on these dates. New York is filled with men I could find on my own, but I chose to do it to appease her. Stopping at date number two would've been the smart thing to do, but as the days and months passed, I had a hard time saying no to her. For as long as I can remember all I've ever wanted was for her to give me some indication she was proud of me. I wasn't my sister. I didn't have a fancy house with a darling husband and a growing family for Mom to love. I was just Kasey, her youngest daughter who worked at a small bookstore and made the *New York Times* bestseller list two years in a row. Nothing special.

Pulling my drenched foot from the toilet I hop onto the floor. My temples throb from the music pounding through the walls. Letting out a growl, I lean up on the stall and reach into my purse for my phone. It slips from my trembling fingers and sails straight for the toilet.

"No!"

I yell so loud that it echoes through the bathroom. Thank God we're in a bar with pulsing music beating against the walls. I hope he's not standing outside that door waiting for me. Number twenty-nine has proven to be clingy.

A loud thud causes my heart to skitter to a halt. My phone is face down on the floor. I smack my hand to my forehead, then reach to grab it. With shaking hands, I inspect every square inch.

I relax against the wall. My mind races, and for a moment I almost forget why I needed the phone. My thumb is slick with sweat and the thumb ID isn't working. Instead, I type in the passcode so I can text my best friend, Francesca.

#29 – The One That's a Stage-Five Clinger. 911!! Save Me!

It didn't occur to me at first, because things were going smoothly. When I initially walked in, I spotted him at the bar. He was already nursing a beer in his hand, long hair resting over his shoulder, red and white Santa hat on top. His eyes met mine and I actually thought wow! Movie star handsome. Maybe number twenty-nine was changing my luck. His muscular body turned in my direction as he stood from the barstool with a grin.

"Hello. I'm Daryl." Behind his smile were perfectly polished white teeth.

"Kasey. Nice to meet you." We shook hands and he led me over to a quiet table in the corner, where we ordered some wings and got to know each other a little better.

Our conversation had been drifting in the direction of the future but got super awkward when he mentioned engagements and that we'd make good-looking children. He kept telling me all the amazing ideas he had in his head and how I'm the girl he imagined. That fluttering in my stomach turned to ice. And panic. And maybe indigestion from the wings.

"How are you so perfect?"

I had a piece of chicken wing hanging from my half-open mouth. The hot sauce burned my lower lip as I just let it hang there. Yup, full-on panic now.

"I can't wait for you to meet my folks. The moment my mother lays her eyes on you she'll be planning our wedding."

I swallowed hard and tried to smile through the spicy mess sprawled all over my face. Pieces of chicken caught in my throat. Maybe I'd choke and spare myself the embarrassment.

"I mean, look at you," he said with a crooked little smile. "You would make a beautiful bride."

I wasn't sure what to say to that, but I did choke on a piece of wing that went down the wrong pipe. It took me several sips of water and him patting my back to the tune of "Jingle Bell Rock" to help it pass. It was at that point I got up to use the bathroom.

As I wait here in the stall for Francesca's return text, I put my phone on top of the toilet paper dispenser and reach under for some. I pat my wet tights and soaked shoes. But the only result is shreds of damp toilet paper sticking to me, a white residue of shame.

"Shit," I say again, like it's the only word I know. My brain can't move past it.

Just. Shit.

The dispenser vibrates with my phone, and I swipe it into my hand to check my message.

Already here, let me know when to run in.

I smile despite everything. It's like she knew this date would end horribly. Probably because they all have. Okay, not *all* of them. I did have a few really nice guys that I could have given a chance but couldn't find it in myself to go on a second date. There was just nothing there. No spark. No chemistry.

Number six wasn't that bad, only I'm not sure if he was actually into women. But we had some great conversations and he's sent a text or two since then asking how I am. Number twenty-three was pretty amazing, he had one of those sexy Scottish accents that curled my toes. For a moment I thought I'd found myself a Killian Jones – but he couldn't keep his eyes off the waitress's chest.

Not in a million years had I imagined playing along for this amount of time. But here I am in a pathetic attempt to make my mother happy. I shoot Francesca a text.

Ready!

With my wet foot leaving prints across the floor, I hightail out of the bathroom. The moment I swing the door open I spot him. Was he there the whole time? An unpleasant shiver runs down my spine.

"Oh, there you are." He looks around acting like he's forgotten that I'd gone to the restroom. I need to make up an excuse to get him to go out front.

"I'm sorry, I uh… my stomach is not agreeing with me. Must be the wings…"

"I just took a massive shit in the men's room, so I get it," he replies.

My mouth hangs open. I'm at a loss for words.

I'm about to say something when Francesca's high-pitched squeal pierces through the crowd. My savior in high heels.

"Kasey!"

Her loud voice is enough to cause people to cover their ears, even with the pounding bass of the DJ's speakers. I bet dogs a block away heard it.

Stage-Five Clinger, aka Daryl, takes another swig of the beer in his hand. Oblivious to the sound of her voice, he turns to me. "So, do you – uh – do you want to dance?"

Finally, words start to leave my tongue, but I'm interrupted by Francesca.

"Oh, thank heavens, there you are." She's using some strange accent I can't pinpoint. It's a mix between Australian and English, maybe a minor Boston accent planted in there too. Her Long Island drawl still comes through perfectly clear. Daryl gives her a funny look.

Tears that are faker than her nails spring to her eyes and roll down her pale freckled cheek. She looks from me to Daryl and blinks several times, then turns in my direction. "He left me."

"Oh, no. Again?" I almost laugh but hold it in.

"Yeah."

"I'm sorry, Daryl, I…"

He glances over at Francesca as she bats her brilliant long lashes at him. With a toss of her hair, he's caught under her spell. Francesca has this way with guys and it's not just the cleavage popping out from her low-cut tops, it's the sweet dimples when she smiles. I sometimes get caught up in it too.

Daryl redirects his attention to me. "You should go," he says, his face turning pale with beads of sweat forming near his temples. He grabs a hold of his stomach. "I think I gotta go again..."

He jets away from us and stumbles into the men's room behind Francesca.

"That was..."

"Unexpected?"

"Totally." She laughs then presses her ear to the door. I raise my brow at her gesture. "He's definitely going in there."

"Oh my God, you're gross. Let's get out of here."

She chuckles and backs away from the door. Slipping her arm in mine, we walk through the crowded bar.

"Are you supposed to be Rudolph or something?" she asks, as we reach the quiet of the main lobby.

"Hush, you, the theme of the night was Christmas."

She chuckles, holding me tighter, as we reach the front doors.

Outside, the cold moonless night surrounds us. My teeth chatter the moment the frosty air hits and I bury my face into the warmth of my fur-lined coat.

"I never want to go on another date again."

Her face lights up and she winks at me. "Never say never."

"That's easy for you to say."

She huffs. "Your mother clearly has no idea how to pick a guy. Where is she finding them?"

We turn the corner to a dark parking lot off to the side of the small club. It's still early, so the lot is full. People are hustling back and forth from the club to the lot.

"At first it was people she worked with, then some guys from the church she goes to. Now... I honestly have no idea."

Francesca chuckles as she beeps her red Toyota. I slide in, kicking the water bottles piled on the floor of the passenger seat.

They crunch under my foot as I settle into the seat. My shoe is still wet.

"Seriously though, why not let me try?"

Francesca leans over and reaches into the glove compartment. She tugs open a plastic bag of wet wipes and hands it to me. I raise a brow. "You've got a little something," she says, dabbing at her cheek.

Shit, wing sauce. I swipe the wipe from her, pulling the visor down to get a better look.

I shake my head and flip the visor up, curling the wet wipe into my fist. "I'm done after tonight. If I'm meant to find someone, they'll just appear."

"We can't all get as lucky as Julie from that phantom show on Netflix. Unrealistic expectations. Where can we find some sexy man ghosts?" Francesca snickers.

I shove her shoulder. We might be twenty-four, but our younger days aren't that far behind us, and we still love to indulge in silly teen dramas. Growing up I wanted my life to be a teen rom-com, one where my mom was on my side. This dating thing could have stemmed from a good place in her heart instead of being for her satisfaction.

I question whether I'm interested in finding someone. The wound from the previous Christmas is still fresh and it clouded my judgment when it came to making the decision to go on these dates. Finding my childhood love in bed with someone who I thought was my friend broke me to the core. Wanting to feel something again, I agreed, and now here I am almost thirty dates later with a soaking wet foot from a failed bathroom escape.

Francesca puts the key in the ignition. An up-tempo Christmas song blasts from the speakers, the sounds of the holiday season bringing a mixture of joy and sorrow. As we pull out of the lot, my phone goes off. I remove it from my small black purse, only to see it's my mother.

How was Daryl? she texts.

I roll my eyes and type a response.

You mean the guy who is currently blowing up the bathroom in the club? Wonderful.

I lay the phone face down on my lap and rest my head against the soft cushioned seat. It vibrates, and I growl out loud.

You are just too picky. In that case I have a few more guys lined up. I'll email you their contact info. You really need to prioritize your life. Look at your sister. Don't blow this. Who knows, maybe you'll actually have a man by Christmas. One can only hope. Your ovaries aren't getting any younger.

I throw the phone in my bag. It hits something hard, making a loud thump in my purse.

Francesca zeroes in on me. "Your mom?"

"Who else would it be." I sigh.

"You want my advice?"

I run a hand over my face, scrubbing hard, wishing I could just make this all go away. "Not really, but you're going to give it to me anyway. Aren't you?"

Francesca stops at a red light. The sound of the blinker clicks in my ear. "I think you should stand up to her. Tell her 'Screw you. I'm happy. The end.'"

"I've tried…"

"No. You say you have, but you haven't. I love you more than anyone in this entire world, but you can't let her control your life. You're twenty-four, it's time for her to just accept you aren't going to be Saint Piper."

I snort. Piper, my sister, is in no way a saint. Her teen years may have been all winning trophies and straight As, but that doesn't mean she didn't go behind Mom's back and sneak out to see her boyfriend, now husband, in the middle of the night. I still to this day have kept her secret.

Francesca shakes her head as we pull up at the curb outside of our apartment. She shuts the car off and turns to me.

"You don't need a man to define who you are. You're pretty amazing on your own."

I'm happy with who I am and where life has taken me, but there's always one thing that I will never have, that I want more than anything: my mother's love and acceptance.

My phone goes off again. It's like I'm Anne Hathaway in *The Devil Wears Prada*, and my mom is Miranda trying to mold me into something I'm not.

"You want me to order some pizza? And we can sing Christmas songs at the top of our lungs."

"As long as you wear your elf slippers with the jingle bells. Also, extra cheese on that pizza. Please."

"You got it! I'll call for delivery while you wash the bar smell off you."

I lift the fabric of my dress and smell it. She's right, the scent of booze lingers on my clothes.

"Sounds perfect."

CHAPTER 2

*A*nother man, another dud. The fiasco with Daryl should have been the last straw, but here I am jotting down what happened on the latest disaster of a date in my notebook, while thinking about the one I've set for this afternoon. I normally only go on one per weekend, but when Mom called me regarding number thirty-one, I was intrigued.

When Mom sent that text the other day about finding a man for Christmas, I'll admit it made me a little upset, but I tried not to let her get to me. Growing up I used to sneak Mom's holiday romance books under the covers so I wouldn't get caught reading them. I love the magic of the season and it would be nice to have someone to share that with. A year ago, I thought I had that, and, in the end, he hurt me. It's been hard to recover from the heartbreak, but a perfect Christmas romance has never been off the table. Maybe that's why I agreed to this date today.

The number thirty sits on the solid red line that runs across the page. Below that I've made a quick stick figure sketch of him in his underwear. The image causes a nasty shiver and not the good kind either. He was the one with multiple underwear ads. I scribble the words beside the number. The image of each picture burned in my mind for eternity. He really was quite the package.

Above his name are some of the previous dates I've had. The last four were:

#27 – Wyatt Kotch – the one who looked like Harry Potter (he was busy texting all night)

#28 – Lukas Pappas – the one with the ugly turtleneck (I think his ten cats were more interesting than me)

#29 – Daryl Hanson – the one who was a stage-five clinger

And finally…

#30 – Edward Smith – the one with the underwear ads.

I set the pencil down and allow my shoulders to fall.

"Are you slacking again?"

I clutch a hand to my chest to calm my racing heart. The manager on duty, Sam, comes strolling out of the stockroom. A lopsided grin forming on his neatly groomed face.

"Something like that."

Sam and I have been working together since we were sixteen. We both started off as part-time employees but grew to love our favorite bookstore so much we decided to stay. I'm only a full-time employee, but Sam managed to move up to an assistant. I love working with him and he doesn't treat me like I'm a step below him.

His lips part, but before he can speak, the tiny bell above the charming emerald door of Once Upon a Storybook rings. Lavender fills the room. I don't have to look up to know it's Francesca. Her heels click along the wooden floor and come to stop beside me.

"Best friend," she says. Then she turns to Sam. "Samuel."

Smiling, Sam points at her.

Francesca leans over the dark wooden counter and hovers above my shoulder. I slide the book away and she slaps her hand on it to get a better read. Sam's attention is focused on her, like always. Francesca bats her long lashes at him. She takes in his muscular build. He's one of those *I'm going to do pull-ups on the stockroom door during my fifteen-minute break* type of guy. Her favorite.

"So, the underwear guy didn't do it for you?"

Sam raises a brow but pretends to look busy by flipping through our inventory book beside the register.

"Well?"

Francesca bumps into my hip with a grin on her face.

I try to fight the images in my head. Mostly the tight black underwear around his hard muscular body. I won't deny his body was… wow! For me it was the way he spoke. Like how he droned on and on about the ads and how sexy he looked in each one. He had a very large ego, one I refused to contend with.

"That bad, huh?"

I groan. "The worst."

I rub my eyes with the palm of my hand to try to erase the memory. I hate that Mom won't give up trying to mold me into my sister. Piper had her whole life planned out by the time she was ten. The perfect husband, a white picket fence, and two beautiful children. I want love and maybe that's why I continue this crazy journey, but I don't expect it to be perfect or maybe I do and that is why this is so hard.

"Who's number thirty-one?"

Sam takes that as his cue to leave. He shuts the book on the counter and takes the five short steps to the stockroom door. Standing beside it he gives a glance over his shoulder. "You've got five minutes before Mr Ruppert arrives."

Mr Ruppert is the store manager. He doesn't know that Francesca visits daily. He would probably ban her from the store if he did. Sam, on the other hand, seems to enjoy them.

"Got it, boss!" I say, giving him a thumbs up.

With a coy smile, he checks out Francesca. "It was good seeing you."

A smug smile crosses her face. She blows him a kiss and he

pretends to catch it and put it in his pocket before vanishing into the stockroom. Francesca's face lights up. It's a look I've only seen around Sam.

She turns. "What?"

"Nothing." I laugh, shaking my head.

She stares off in a dreamy state. "Can you wrap him up and put him under our Christmas tree this year?"

Laughter fills my lungs. "I think you can unwrap that before Christmas."

"Oh my God. Kasey Johnson, where is your head?"

Grinning, she quirks a brow and clears her throat. "This conversation isn't about me. So, tell me, number thirty-one. Give me all the details."

I hate that she's turned her attention to me again. I hang my head. In retrospect, thirty-one dates seems like a lot. I could call and cancel, but I can't bring myself to do so.

"He's the pastor's son at the church Mom and Oliver go to."

Oliver is my stepdad, or was. He hasn't been around in a month at least, and Mom refuses to acknowledge it.

Francesca's eyes widen, and I know the wheels are turning in that pretty little head of hers.

"Don't give me that look."

She steps back, her mouth open. "I wasn't giving you any look. It sounds promising, that's all."

I'm so used to failed dates at this point that it feels normal to have doubts. "Help me get ready?"

There's a little bounce in her step as she hops towards me. "When do you get off work?"

I glance up at the old analog clock ticking away on the wall above the door. "Twenty minutes."

She reaches over and grabs a hold of my hand. "Meet you outside," she says with a squeeze.

CHAPTER 3

I should be a pro at picking out date clothes. I've bought a few new dresses but none of them fit my mood. Why can't something jump out and bite me?

Francesca holds a flowered quarter sleeve dress close to her body. I wore it on date number ten – the one who could burp the alphabet. The entire restaurant turned to stare. The embarrassment of that night seeps in, causing my cheeks to warm.

"No," I whisper.

I stick my head inside the shallow closet and let out a yell. Francesca's footsteps fall away in the opposite direction. I rest my back on the door frame and slump down against its jagged edge.

I want to enjoy this. Dating in my twenties is supposed to be fun. It was at first. The suspense of meeting someone new got me excited. While getting ready I imagined them in my head. Would they tower over me? Would I get lost in their sexy eyes? Now, when I go on a date, I make a note of where all the exits are.

Francesca's room sits beside mine. The closet door creaks open and the hangers scratch against the pole as she rummages through. For this date I imagine wearing something casual and conservative. I don't want to wear jeans. In my opinion, it's not appropriate attire for a date with the pastor's son. What if he takes me to church? I laugh in my head.

She saunters in with pants folded over her arms. I catch sight of skinny black jeggings. I jump to my feet, and start rummaging through my closet for the perfect shirt.

"Ah-ha!" I shout.

Reaching into the closet I grab a red sweater vest and add a white button-down shirt to go underneath. I undress and throw everything on, but there's still something missing. Francesca holds up a finger and rushes out of the room. She returns seconds later and wraps a Christmas green scarf around my neck.

"Very festive," she says, eyeing my choices.

"What about shoes?"

I scan the rack beside my closet door. I have quite a collection. The perfect pair has to be here.

"Black suede boots?" she asks, her brows raised.

I squeal as she holds up one of my newer pairs. "You're a genius! You should really quit your job and be a fashion consultant."

Francesca chuckles and kneels in front of me. Glancing up she smiles. "One fashion designer is enough in my family."

Francesca's mom is one, and there's no denying that Francesca definitely has a knack for it. For fun she used to make her own outfits, my favorites are the ones she makes for Christmas. She uses loud colors and designs, like candy canes or mini-Santas. One year she made me a dress designed to look like elves clothes, I loved it, but my mom – not so much.

Like I'm Cinderella and Francesca's the handsome prince, she slips the shoes onto my feet.

"Why can't we be the same size in shoes?" She groans. "These are to die for."

"You want giant feet?"

"It would be better than baby feet." She chuckles.

Francesca stands and bumps the closet door with her behind so I can check myself in the mirror on the back of the door. I sway on my feet trying to get a view from every side. My straight brown hair sticks up all over and no matter how much I press the pieces down they fly up. I'm convinced my hair has a mind of its own.

Francesca places a comforting hand on my shoulder. I lean into her, allowing my body to go limp. "You look wonderful, darling."

A soft blush crawls up my neck.

"All thanks to your inspirational jeggings."

Her laughter echoes through the room. She takes a few steps back to get a better look as I straighten myself and tighten my stance.

Francesca sighs. "I wish my dating life was as exciting as yours."

I roll my eyes. "It's only because of my mother and her insane notion that she can find the perfect man for me and that I'll turn into Piper."

I need to stop complaining. I'm the one torturing myself with these dates all because of some childhood dream that Mom will eventually see that I'm worth something.

"I'm sorry your mom sucks. Mine is probably gallivanting all over Italy, watching multiple fashion shows, and taking a relaxing ride in a gondola."

I should be thankful my mom shows some interest, even if it is negative most of the time. Francesca grew up being raised by a nanny most of her life. With her mother parading around the world designing fashionable clothing, she didn't have much time for Francesca.

"I'm sorry your mom sucks too."

She throws herself onto my bed fisting the white fluffy bed comforter in her hand. I settle down next to her. The warmth of my bed and my best friend by my side makes me want to cancel. I could watch rom-coms all day with her.

"You have that look in your eyes. I have a good feeling about this one."

I place my head on her shoulder and she leans her head over to cover mine.

"I wish we could have a double date then I wouldn't have to do this alone."

I pull away and she throws herself onto the bed. For a few lingering heartbeats she stares up at the peeling paint on the white ceiling above.

"Maybe one day. Who would I ask out?"

"Sam?" I tease, wiggling my brows.

She lifts her body just enough to smack my arm playfully. I smirk and she sticks out her tongue.

"Sam is quite the catch. And as much as I joke about wanting him. It would be weird dating your boss–"

"It's not like he's older than us," I say, cutting her off.

She lifts a finger to her lips and taps them with a steady beat. Sam has had a crush on her since the first day she barged into the store. She found out I'd gotten an after-school job and threw herself over the counter dramatically. Sam witnessed the whole thing. I remember the amused grin on his face.

I place my hand over hers and she squeezes hard. She's my rock, the only thing keeping me on my feet.

"If this guy works out, I'll ask him if he has friends."

"Oh." This perks her interest. "A nice religious guy. Maybe that's just what I need."

Laughter fills the space between us. Is it wrong that I'd rather spend my night with her?

"You should go," she says, reading my mind.

Francesca shoves me towards the edge of the bed and my behind almost lands on the floor. As I get to my feet, I stick my tongue out at her. I take a deep breath and check myself one last time in the mirror. Francesca's chin sits on the top of my shoulder, her mouth pulling into a smile.

"Go get him!" she says.

I close my eyes for a brief moment, shake out my body, and then stare at myself in the mirror. "Good luck number thirty-one."

CHAPTER 4

I'm not used to an early afternoon date, but he insisted on it. I was always under the impression that a lunch date put you in the "friend zone". Maybe that's all he's looking for, and like me, he wanted to please his parents.

My stomach thunders with hunger as the door to Merry's Cafe swings open allowing the scent of brunch to escape. I stand outside, the late November chill seeping through the light jeggings. My legs throb from the frosty nip in the air.

Red tinsel and mistletoe dangle from the overhang above. The holiday season is closing in quickly, and I'm not sure if I'm ready. How could my favorite holiday turn into my worst nightmare? Oh – that's right because my ex-fiancé was sleeping with one of my friends. Maybe number thirty-one is a lucky number. Here's to hoping this date goes well.

I prefer to meet the dates rather than having them pick me up at the apartment. I want to get to know someone first before I let them know where I live.

Lifting my phone from my purse I check the time. He's fifteen minutes late. If he's not here in five I'm leaving. I slip the phone inside my bag and lean to the left to get a view of the crowded streets.

"Excuse me," a deep rugged voice says from behind me.

I suppress a yelp by biting the inside of my cheek. I turn and come face to face with the most beautiful man I have ever laid my eyes on. *Kasey, get a grip!* My words are stuck.

"Are you Kasey Johnson?"

I'm mesmerized by his Adam's apple bobbing up and down. *Where on earth did that thought come from?*

"That's me," I squeak.

I glance up, my head barely reaches the tip of his chin.

"Tobias Scott."

His warm hand folds around mine in an intense shake. I lift my chin and stare up at the dark scruff that lines the edge of his jawline. Silence falls between us, while the rest of the town chatters on in the distance.

"It's nice to meet you, Tobias."

This man is like Christmas in a cup. A warm fuzzy feeling stirs up inside of me. His dark eyes find mine and my throat dries. Our hands are still softly shaking.

"We should probably stop shaking so we can go eat." The words tumble from my mouth like word vomit.

I fight the urge to slap my hand over my mouth to keep myself quiet. A hearty chuckle escapes his thin lips.

"We probably should." A soft flush of pink tickles his cheeks.

We've only spoken for thirty seconds and already this date is off to a better start than approximately ninety percent of the ones I've been on.

"After you," he says quietly.

He steps out of the way holding the door. Only one other date has held open the door for me and that was number five, the one who couldn't stop talking about his ex. I sure hope this one is different.

His presence lingers over me as I walk into the cafe. A soft melodic tune of a familiar Christmas carol plays overhead. The yellow walls and bright lights give off a warm summer morning vibe, perfect for this cold winter day. The holidays are alive at Merry's. There's something in the air, making me feel light again. Maybe it's the lit tree in the corner of the room, casting a glow upon us or it could be the strikingly handsome man I'm on a date with who's allowing a family of four to go through before him.

The scent of crisp bacon hits my nose. There's steam rising from the chafing dishes at the far end of the room. I peek over at the tables scattered in the center of the small cafe and there aren't many open seats, I sure hope he made a reservation.

Tobias falls into step with me as we stop at the lectern placed in the center of the waiting area. A hostess in a bright yellow dress comes sauntering over with a smile on her wrinkled face.

"Good afternoon, folks, two?"

Tobias doesn't skip a beat. His smile is so radiating that even the hostess's cheeks flush by just looking at him.

"Good afternoon, ma'am. I have a reservation for two under Scott."

She pushes up the round clear glasses that slide down her nose as she inspects the list. While the hostess checks for our reservation, I take a moment to get a good look at Tobias. The side of his cheek twitches while he waits, he shifts a few times back and forth and his hand fidgets at his side.

The hostess glances up through the top of her glasses, her smile directed at Tobias.

"Here you are. Right this way, sir."

"Thank you," he says, kindly.

I'm far too smitten for my liking. He throws a look at me, and my cheeks burn. I'm not sure what it is but I don't peg Tobias as a brunch type of guy.

"What?" he asks, laughter filling his voice. "You have that look on your face."

As if he knows me, Tobias focuses on me with a wide grin.

"I was thinking that you don't look like the type of guy to do a brunch date."

He holds his hand out for me to walk first, I do some kind of weird curtsy thing, *oh God I probably looked ridiculous*, and start following the hostess. I turn my attention to him as he walks beside me. The corner of his eyes wrinkle. I really need to stop swooning.

"I would do dinner, but we have plans at four."

We stop at a small round table in the direct center of the room. A quaint red and white checkered cloth covers the table, with a beautiful floral centerpiece in the middle.

"Here's your table. Enjoy your meal."

"Thank you," we both manage at the same time.

An awkward beat of silence passes between us. I take this as an opportunity to remove my jacket. He notices and immediately steps behind me to help. Tobias places it over the back of the chair in front of us.

He leads me to the rear of the room where we hop on the line for our meal. There's only one older couple in front of us. Tobias grabs two warm white circular plates and hands me one. The tip of his finger grazes my skin, zapping me to life.

"Have you had the muffins here?" He reaches for the tongs and sets down one cranberry and one blueberry onto his plate.

"The cranberry ones sure are the best. Are there any left?"

He turns to look in the basket, pursing his lips as he scans over the muffins. I browse around myself, but there aren't any more. Without hesitation he takes the one on his plate and places it down on mine.

"Was that the last one?" I ask.

"Yeah. It's no big deal. Just one muffin?" He smiles with his eyes, and I'm immediately directed to the wrinkles again. He's attractive and thoughtful, two qualities I was convinced had died out with our generation.

"Yeah. One is good." My voice comes out shakier than I expected.

Putting the tongs down we move over to the next chafing dish. Instead of filling his plate first he turns to me at every station. He's such a gentleman and I'll have to remember to thank his parents if I ever meet them.

My entire body heats up, sweat pools at the nape of my neck. There hasn't been a date where in my mind I could even contemplate meeting his folks. Now I sound like Daryl the clinger. My pity party is interrupted by his free hand resting on my arm. I lift my gaze to a smile.

"You all finished?" he asks.

"Yes. You?"

"Definitely, but I'll be back for more."

"I'm not even sure I can fit all of this in my stomach." I chuckle.

He scans my plate and scoffs. "I have to confess this place is my weakness."

"Well, if we're confessing then I have to be honest, it's mine too."

That gets him to give me another sparkling smile. I'm sold. Cancel number thirty-two and beyond, because my God this man is... dare I say – perfect?

When we reach the table, he puts his plate down and comes to my side, pulling the chair out for me to sit. My cheeks hurt from the power of my smile as I settle down in the chair.

I take in his appearance. He's more underdressed than I imagined, but it suits him. I love the casual black crew neck T-shirt set under a checkered button-down shirt that's slightly pulled open.

A waitress, in a uniform matching the hostess, comes over to our table.

"Can I get either of you a drink?"

Tobias averts his attention from the steaming plate of food in front of him and smiles. "Fruit punch, please."

She turns to me, and I stumble over my words in an attempt to order some orange juice. I've never had a guy order fruit punch on a date before. Tobias grows quiet as he takes a few bites. His leg moves a million miles a minute under the table. I casually play with the ends of my hair. What if he's the one contemplating escaping out the bathroom window? I set my fork down to get a hold of myself. It would be ironic if it happened since I've bailed on dates before, karma for sure.

Not wanting this date to go downhill, I decide to grow a pair and speak up first. He could be just as nervous as I am. I clear my throat and he lifts his attention to me.

"My mom says your dad is the pastor at church?"

As I ask the question the waitress returns with our drinks. She sets them down in front of us and Tobias takes a quick sip before thanking her.

"Yeah. Have you been to any of the services?" he asks the moment she walks away.

"No, I haven't." I grimace, shifting in my seat. Did I just screw that up? "My mom was baptized when she married Oliver Keller. My sister and I stayed with our dad from Sunday through Tuesday when my parents got divorced. So church was something she did on her own."

He drinks a little more, but keeps his focus solely on me.

"That's a shame. I hear the five o'clock service has a kick-ass guitar player." He grins.

I sink back into my chair. Crisis averted. He's not upset that I don't go to church. "I assume that guitar player is you?"

His face lights up and it's hard to control my smile. I let go of the hair from my death grip and grab my fork instead.

"Yes, ma'am."

I laugh a little, no one except the older men who come into the store have ever called me that.

"Can I let you in on a secret?" he whispers, leaning forward partially over the table. He curls his finger towards him for me to come closer. I lean in too.

"I read comic books during church. I hide them under my guitar." His dark brown eyes sparkle.

It's nice the way he's slowly opening up. He's reading the cues I give, and when "awkward Kasey" shows, he pulls a trick from his sleeve that helps me relax.

"I won't tell. I promise." I give a wink that in my head is sexy, but probably made me look silly.

He sits back with a satisfied grin. "Good, because my dad would kill me."

I laugh. "These comic books have nothing to do with God, do they?"

He shakes his head and stabs some eggs with his fork. "I try to save Thor for the service."

For the first time in thirty-one dates a real smile shines through. I find myself mentally checking off all my favorite things about Tobias Scott.

1. He orders fruit punch with his meal instead of coffee or OJ. (Child at heart.)

2. He reads comics during church – Thor to be exact. (Handsome, yet nerdy.)

3. His ability to read me. (Not even my ex could do that.)

His quirks are intriguing, and I find myself wanting to see if he has any more. They are what makes him who he is, and I love that he's not afraid to share them with me. I'm looking forward to the second part of our date, this is going far better than I ever could have imagined.

CHAPTER 5

obias stands to throw his black bomber jacket on as we prepare to leave. He had two hearty servings of food and I find myself wondering where he puts it all. His body is that perfect mixture of muscular with probably a few pounds of beer gut he's trying to let go of from his college days.

I loved listening to him talk about his family while he consumed the second part of his meal. His older brother is in the army and stationed in Georgia and his sister lives in Hawaii with her well-off husband and their children.

His face lights up the most when he describes what music means to him. He started in the church choir at six but didn't play guitar at church until he was fourteen.

We exit the warmth of Merry's and venture out into the cold. The town is crowded with Christmas shoppers enjoying the holiday festivities. It's the end of Thanksgiving weekend so the streets are filled with people taking advantage of the sales. Our local businesses thrive this time of year.

"What do you do for a living? Are you going the pastor route like your dad?" I ask as we walk side by side.

A soft chuckle escapes his luscious lips. Heat creeps up my

cheeks the moment it hits me. *Kasey, you've officially lost your mind.*

"I could never do what he does, it takes a special person to do something like that. I'm a music teacher. This is my second year teaching elementary music."

Tobias's body collides with mine as we hustle through a small crowd of people walking in the opposite direction.

"What about you?"

I catch him watching me. I kick the tiny pebbles on the sidewalk. My stomach sinks. Answering this question shouldn't be hard, I love what I do and who I've become, but my mother's condescending voice echoes in my head.

His hand gently grazes mine as he keeps himself close even after the crowd thins out.

"I work at Once Upon a Storybook. I've been there since I was sixteen."

"Oh. Really?" His voice jumps up an octave and immediately I want to shut down.

"I feel like I've seen you around. I should remember, especially with how beautiful you are."

I shift to check his expression. His cheeks flush, and the smile he gives is to die for, and I love how his eyes twinkle like Christmas lights. I'm hooked.

"I'm an author too. I wrote a YA fantasy titled, *The Beauty of Frost and Flames.*"

His mouth falls open. "That's why you look so familiar. I thought my mind was playing tricks on me. I was at the signing last April for book number two."

I scan his face for recognition. How hard would it have been to spot someone as handsome as him?

"You were there?" I ask, blinking several times.

There's a soft flutter low in my belly, while I wait for him to answer. I don't get many attractive men in their twenties at my signings. My readers are mostly teens and middle-aged women.

"My mom is an English teacher at the high school, and she reads all the books teens are into. Yours is one of her top favorites. She had to miss the signing for a conference, so I went to get the book signed for her birthday."

My brain is fuzzy with admiration for this man. Someone pinch me. I must be dreaming.

"I'm more of a comic guy, but maybe I'll give your book a read."

He holds my stare, and I can't control the smile that fights its way to the surface.

We walk farther up towards the park at the end of Main Street. The small lake in the center is used for ice skating this time of year. We lean against the fence enjoying the view of the skaters, silence falls between us. The sound of skates gliding on the hard ice along with the laughter of children echoes around us.

Soft voices begin to sing.

"Christmas carolers," he says, pointing to the group. It's mixed with both children and adults. The women are dressed warmly in old fashioned red and green dresses, and the men are wearing large black coats and top hats.

They are making their way closer to where we're standing. Everything about this date is setting up perfectly, almost a little too much, but I'm not going to fight it. I'll let it happen.

"I haven't seen carolers in so long," I say.

"Same. You know, back a few years ago we went caroling with some church members. It went well, actually."

"Sounds like something out of a movie."

He laughs. "You've never had carolers come to your home and sing for you?"

"Nope, never."

We quietly watch the carolers. I take in the scene around me, and it feels like home.

"What's your favorite Christmas song?" he asks.

"Um… probably, 'Have Yourself a Merry Little Christmas'."

He pushes himself off the fence and faces me. "Why?"

"My dad used to sing it to me when I was younger. Things with my family aren't great, never have been, but every Christmas Eve after he'd read me a story, he'd sing it."

Stirring up some good memories from my childhood is a little painful, but not at the same time. I miss my dad. He's not around as much, because Mom pushed him away.

"What about yours?"

"That's easy, it's 'The First Noel'. My dad taught it to me. It was the first song I learned how to properly sing. Funny, we both have musical memories with our dads."

Tobias reaches out and grabs hold of my hand. "Come with me."

My brows crinkle in confusion, but I follow him, because I'm curious. We leave the skaters behind and find ourselves standing in front of the carolers while they are taking a small break. Tobias walks up to one of them and whispers in the young gentleman's ear. He pulls away, and the two smile at each other, then he goes and whispers to the others.

Sucking in a deep breath he begins to sing the song I told him I loved. While he's singing, the carolers begin to sing the song *he* loves. Somehow it links together, and their voices mix in a beautiful harmony. I'm beyond impressed by his vocal ability, and I can't help but sing and sway along to the music.

He reaches out for my hand. I take it and he twirls me around the open space on the sidewalk. With the snow flurries, the music, and the energy of the moment I'm transported into my very own romance movie. In and out of his arms I twist and turn. For once I'm not stumbling over my feet, it's a Christmas miracle for sure.

When the song ends, an applause erupts around us. Tobias thanks them as they set off to sing in another location.

"That was amazing. Your voice, it's really something."

"A good thing or a bad thing?" he asks.

"Good. Definitely good." I chuckle.

Tobias covers my hand with his and my knees grow weak. I hope he doesn't notice them buckle when he tightens his soft grip.

"Would it be okay if we walked to part two of our date? It's right around the block."

I swallow hard, still aware that his hand hasn't let go of mine.

"Yeah. That's fine with me."

The soft tiny droplets of snowflakes increase with every passing second.

"Mother nature, she sure knows when to bring the magic, doesn't she?" he says.

For a moment he looks to the sky, allowing the droplets to fall along his handsome face. I do the same lifting my chin to enjoy the fresh clean snow falling. I stick out my tongue and his shoulders shake from his wholesome laughter.

"Shall we?" he asks.

I try blinking away the wet droplets of melted snow on my lashes. Tobias lifts his hand and without a single ounce of hesitation wipes my lash with his fingertip. The gesture causes my blood pressure to skyrocket, warming my entire body.

My phone buzzes in my bag followed by a soundbite of Shawn Mendes, "Stitches". It's Francesca's ringtone, but I let it go to voicemail. I expect her to get the message but instead it starts again.

He bumps into my hip when I don't answer.

"Is that your 911 bail call?"

My mouth hangs open. How did he have any idea that I was that girl who waits for a fake emergency? Do I give off that kind of vibe? Oh God, he probably knows about my thirty something dates.

"Hey." Stepping in front of me, he reaches for my hand.

He's got my full attention and I can't look away.

"I got one too if that helps," he says.

I exhale and my shoulders fall. He bends so he can lean closer. Our noses are almost touching. An amused chuckle leaves my lips.

"Was hoping we'd try this again sometime, but first we should get to part two because that will make or break this whole thing."

He presses a finger into the side of my cheek attempting to lift my fallen smile. "No time for a frown. Part two might not be something you're used to, but I hope you'll give it a chance."

"Of course," I say.

"We should go or we're going to be late."

Tobias releases one of his hands from mine before falling into step beside me. Holding on to him sends an electric charge through all my nerves.

"Here we are," he says, as we round the corner of Main onto Chester.

I can't help the grin forming on my face. We're at church. It's one of the oldest buildings in this ancient little town. Light filters into the church from the beautiful stained-glass windows. In the front there is one on both sides of the large wooden doors.

"Tobias Scott! Are you taking me to church?" I giggle.

I face him and find his lips turned up into a perfect smile.

"Picture it like a Shawn Mendes concert. I could pass for him, couldn't I?"

I lean into him, pushing gently. I'm surprised by my action and how easy it was to fall into the motion. A low gentle laughter rumbles through him and the sound warms my body all over.

"After you," he says.

CHAPTER 6

I've never stepped foot inside the church before, but I've always admired the building from the outside. It's a huge staple in our town, one of the oldest we have. They did a small renovation a few years ago due to some structural issues, but it didn't take away from its beauty.

The scent of burning candles and potpourri hits my nose. It's soft and inviting. I'm in awe of the shimmering stained-glass dome that sits high above the center of the main church. It brightens up the room even on a gray snowy day like today. Francesca loves artistic things. She would probably appreciate the artwork that went into each pane of colorful glass.

As we walk up the red carpeted aisle a few kids skip gleefully towards us. Tobias lifts a young girl with chocolate brown pigtails and gives her a giant bear hug. She giggles as he sets her down. A boy with floppy blond hair steps forward and he and Tobias do some silly little handshake that leaves them both laughing.

Tobias turns to me. "Abby, Charles, this is my friend, Kasey."

They greet me with wide smiles, reminding me of my niece and nephew. I miss them so much it hurts.

"It's nice to meet you both."

"Will you sing with us?" Abby begs.

Tobias nudges me while giving an encouraging grin. The last time I sang in front of anyone was in the high school choir. I was someone who tried to blend in with the crowd, but I did get chosen for a solo when we sang a *Rent* medley junior year.

"Uh... I... I don't know any of the songs."

Singing with the kids, I'll stick out like a sore thumb. I can create every excuse under the sun, but under Tobias's watchful glare I wouldn't want to ruin this amazing date.

"Please." Abby and Charles press their tiny hands together. How can I say no to that?

"Sure. I'd love to."

Beside me Tobias shifts on his feet, his body softly colliding with mine. I glance up to find my favorite eye-wrinkling smile. My stomach does several flips before returning to normal.

I don't have a chance to say another word as Abby and Charles grab hold of my hands and lead me towards the risers. The choir sits to the left of the beautiful raised platform. Other than Tobias there are two more adults, one on the piano, and another staring at sheet music on a black stand a few rows up.

We stop in front of three other kids who are on the second row of risers.

"This is Clair, Ian, and Heather. Guys, this is Kasey, she's Tobias's girly friend," Abby says, wiggling her brows.

I can't tell how old Abby is, probably around eight or nine but she is sure intuitive for such a young girl.

Clair hides behind her beautiful platinum blonde locks, but she waves. Ian and Hannah both wave with enthusiasm, their light gray eyes and sharp facial features are so similar they could be twins.

"Sit with me," Abby chides, tugging on my arm.

"Of course," I tell her, with a smile.

She leads me over to the first tier in the direct center. Sitting beside me she begins fidgeting with the music on the stand. I run a hand through my hair, tugging at another strand.

People begin filtering into the church and sliding into the wooden pews. Dressed in her Sunday best I spot Mom settling down in the front row. She plays with her bouncy curls, fixing them so they sit in front of her shoulders. Her intense hazel eyes meet mine and a satisfied grin crosses her face. I hate the way my blood boils. Letting go of my hair I grip the edges of the chair and squeeze. The cool metal calms me.

Tobias walks over with a guitar in hand. He turns one of the chairs round and sets his guitar beside him as he sits facing us. I try my hardest to focus on him, but my mother's glare distracts me. Could she have known that I would be here tonight? She knew I went on the date, but how much does she know? And had he been the one to talk to her or was it his father who set it all up? I have so many questions, but I will never ask them.

"Are you guys ready to practice?" he asks the kids, but his attention is all on me.

I lower my head, my cheeks burning.

They all shout at the same time, their voices echoing through the church. Tobias smiles, grabs his guitar, and begins playing a song. Abby points to the music in front of us, at the song we'll be singing, and I try to follow along.

Another older woman about Mom's age comes over and taps Tobias on the shoulder.

"The service is starting," she kindly says.

He thanks her for reminding him and takes his seat at the front.

As the service begins Abby tugs on my sleeve wanting me at her level. I sink down in my seat and give her my attention.

"You have a very pretty voice," she tells me.

I smile. "Thank you. Yours is lovely too."

She sits up straighter with a proud grin plastered on her face. Abby is such an amazing little girl. Their voices are so well rounded and each of them brings something different to the choir.

I'm enjoying myself more than I imagined. I lose track of time and mostly forget the fact that my mother is out there.

We all take a seat as Tobias's father walks up to the front. It's almost like looking at an older version of Tobias. Their resemblance is uncanny. Their noses are almost identical, both sticking out and slightly curved at the end. His voice is soothing, and everyone is glued to him the same way they are when Tobias sings.

As we all listen to his words my sights land on Tobias. He lifts his guitar that he placed over his lap, flipping a page of his comic book. I suppress a giggle by covering it with a cough. He turns and I incline my head towards the book on his lap. A grin forms on his handsome face as he places a finger to his mouth. I rub two fingers together at him and faintly whisper, "Tsk, tsk."

As the entire congregation begins to stand, his father's dark eyes land on him. Tobias was so caught up in the moment he almost forgot it was time to sing again.

Abby grabs my arm and I lean down again.

"Tobias likes you," she whispers.

My face warms as I turn to her. "Aren't you a little too young to notice that?"

"I know because he's never smiled at anyone the way he's smiling at you," she tells me, before belting out a high note not even I can reach.

Tobias is fully engaged in the song with the congregation. His voice fills the small full space, and the entire room sings along with him.

CHAPTER 7

I'm not surprised that when it's over Mom is the first to grab hold of Tobias. She doesn't even acknowledge my existence. My heart sinks. No matter how many times she snubs me it doesn't get any easier. I hate being her biggest disappointment.

Tobias saunters over with her on his tail. Underneath her sparkling eyes are a pair of judging ones that only I can see. My chest aches and I try not to wrap my arms around myself. I want to stay in one piece.

"Hi, sweetheart," she says, pulling me into a hug.

I take several deep breaths and pat her back lazily. She pulls away and looks lovingly over at Tobias. If only he had a clue he wouldn't be smiling back.

"Tobias was just telling me how well your date is going." She smirks. "I'm so happy to hear. I'll catch up with you two in a few, but there's someone I have to say hi to first."

As Mom excuses herself Tobias stiffens beside me. A woman short like myself is heading right for us. For church, she's dressed rather inappropriately if you ask me. Her breasts hang out of her red festive top, although I'm not sure anything could hold them back.

"Tobias." She calls his name with a purr.

His cheeks are blazing red, and his shoulders are taut.

"There you are, you handsome devil." Her intense green eyes are devouring him by the second. It's as if she doesn't even realize where we are.

"Roxanne." He scowls at her.

Her smile is like Mom's. It's on her lips, but her eyes are saying a whole different story. She's focusing on the small space between Tobias and me. I'd reach out for him to make sure he's okay, but I don't want to stir up drama. I wish my mind didn't drift to all the exits in the room. I like this man, but something tells me that this woman has an effect on him that could make or break this date or relationship if it goes anywhere.

"Oh, Tobias. Who is this sweet little thing?"

Who is she calling little? We're the same size, only she's bustier where it counts.

I stare at him, nudging his side. He doesn't budge. When I'm certain he's not going to introduce me, I do it myself.

"Hi. I'm Kasey."

"Cassie?"

"Kasey."

"Oh." She smiles through her bright red lips. "That's a beautiful name."

"Thank you."

Tobias is bothered by this woman. He's glaring at her, either like he wants to rip her head or her top off, I can't tell. I hope it's not the latter. I don't have the urge to run off and find a bathroom window to crawl out of, but I do wish he'd say something.

His hand slips into mine, and I gasp at the warmth of it. He squeezes gently. "I'm so sorry," he whispers.

I study him. It's easy to see the pain in his eyes, with how they shimmer. I know the feeling all too well. He's been burned by this woman.

"I'd really like to meet your dad," I say, attempting to defuse the situation and get us out of here.

"Oh. Yeah. Of course. He'll be thrilled to meet you too." Tobias's attention lingers on me for a few more seconds.

"Roxanne, if you don't mind, Kasey and I have somewhere to be." His tone is sharp, and not the least bit friendly.

"Don't let me stop you. I can see you two are on a date. It was nice to meet you, Cassie."

"It's Kasey," he says, sternly.

"Sorry." She holds up her hands and slowly backs up.

Before leaving she gives a wave. I watch her walk away and give a saucy glance over her shoulder at Tobias. He's quiet and hasn't moved yet. I'll let him decide when we do, give him some time to go through whatever happened. Something is keeping me here when normally I'd be up and running for the hills.

"Kasey?" His tone is soft now. I can feel the weight of his stare on me. "I'm so sorry about that." There's a genuine gleam in his eyes.

He tucks a finger under my chin, so I face him. My mouth grows dry. His warm eyes captivate me. I'm on the most amazing date I've had in a while. I can't let the run-in with Mom, or that Roxanne woman, ruin that. This date has been the most pleasant one I've been on.

"Are you okay, Tobias?" I don't want to push him, but I hate that downcast look on his face.

He breathes in deep and then releases it. "Yeah. I'm so sorry, Kasey. I–"

"There's a lot there I can tell. No worries. You don't have to explain, it's only our first date. Okay?"

His lips part as he bows his head. "What did I do to deserve a date as amazing as you?"

I can't help the smile that crosses my lips. "You're pretty amazing yourself."

He leans down, placing his free hand against my cheek, then plants a soft kiss to my forehead. "Thank you for being understanding."

I don't know what else to say.

"Come on, looks like Dad is already waiting."

Mr Scott is already looking in our direction. Tightening my grip on Tobias's hand I tug him forward.

When the people before us step away, his father turns to us. His smile is inviting and it's easy to give him one in return.

"So, you're the famous Kasey I've heard so much about."

A blush creeps on my cheeks, what is it with the Scott men making me blush? "Well, not sure how famous…"

"Nonsense," Mom says, out of nowhere. She's standing behind me, a fictitious smile on her face. "She's a well-established author. Although her next book could be more Christian based."

I glare at her, my mouth wide open. I wish she would stop pretending that she's actually read a single page of any of my novels.

"My wife certainly loved them." He chuckles.

"Tobias was just telling me that he was at my signing last year."

His warm eyes meet mine. "I do hope you'll join us for dinner one day, she would love to meet you."

"Don't scare her away," Tobias interjects.

Mr Scott's laughter fills the room, and he puts his attention on me. "I'm sorry, Kasey, it's not every day my son gets distracted at church by a beautiful young woman."

I'm officially a ripe tomato at this point. Tobias hooks his arm around my lower back, and I sink into his touch.

"I'd love to have dinner sometime," I say.

He glances up and waves towards someone behind us. "I'm

sorry, Kasey." He reaches out to shake my hand, takes both of his and holds on to mine. "I have some more members to greet."

"It was so nice to meet you, Mr Scott."

"Likewise," he says, before retreating.

Mom gives a wave then turns to us. "I should go too. Tobias, it's a pleasure as always. I do hope I'll see you again."

I clench my fists at my side digging my nails in deep. I can't wait for her to walk away. She gives me a curt nod as Tobias wishes her well.

He loosens his grip on my waist and turns to check on me. It's as if he can feel the tension bubbling between Mom and me. If he has questions, he doesn't ask them, and I'm grateful for that.

"Do you need me to drive you over to your car?" he asks.

"My friend dropped me off, my car can be temperamental, especially in the cold weather."

"Oh, then I'll drive you home. If that's okay with you of course."

He reaches out and gently touches my arm, his fingers grazing my skin. I hug myself to hide the shiver that rages through me from his light touch.

"Are you sure?" I ask.

Normally I wouldn't allow it, but this date has exceeded every expectation. Plus my mom knows his family.

"Of course, it's dark and cold and I'd never forgive myself if something happened to you."

I swallow hard. Where is this man's flaw? Everyone has one, but so far tonight I've seen none. It's only the first date, but the more I learn, the less it seems he has one.

"Thank you."

He stretches his arm out allowing me to decide whether I want to hold his hand. Our fingers slide together so easily. I'm not even sure this man is real. I'm not ready for our date to end, but I also need some time to process the whole thing. After so many disappointing ones I don't want to rush right in only to get my heart broken again.

We pull up to the apartment. It's only a few blocks over and thankfully the snow has stopped, leaving only a light sprinkle of white on the frozen ground. He idles his red Ford F-150 truck in the driveway.

"May I walk you to your door?" he asks.

"I'd love that."

Not one guy has ever walked me to the door before. My ex would drop me off in front of the house and then zoom away. Tobias gets out first while I gather my bag. The passenger door opens, and he stands there, his arm outstretched to help me down. I take it and we walk together hand in hand to the door.

"I had a really nice time, Kasey. I hope you did too. I'm sorry about what happened at the church."

His eyes flutter in different directions and his body shifts from side to side. Is he as nervous as I am?

"No worries. I get it. But to be honest, this was the best date I've been on in a while." I bat my eyes and pray that I don't have a lovey-dovey look in them.

"Most girls would probably think I was crazy for taking them to church."

Our laughter swirls together like the tune of a Christmas song. I could get used to this.

"It was different. I wouldn't mind going back."

"I'm glad to hear that." His lips press into a straight line. There's something he wants to say but can't quite get it out.

"Well, it's been fun. Goodnight, Kasey."

He stands in front of me like he doesn't want to move and now I know there's something more on his mind.

"Goodnight, Tobias. Thank you for brunch and for introducing me to the people in your life."

"Yeah. Sure."

He turns to step down when something catches his eye. I suck hard on my bottom lip. I'd forgotten that Francesca had hung mistletoe on the awning. He points to it and then closes in on me. His soft lips land on my frozen cheek, warming it up.

"Goodnight," he says, softly.

I squeak out another goodnight and enjoy the view from behind as he struts down the walkway, adding a happy skip to his stride. Before he gets to the truck, he gives a quick glance over his shoulder. A sweet smirk planted on his face. My sight doesn't leave his truck until it rounds the corner.

Tobias Scott, number thirty-one, was the one who took me to church and captured my heart.

CHAPTER 8

Outside the frosted window of my second-story apartment, I watch Christmas shoppers trek along the sidewalks with large shopping bags in hand. The house overlooks the busiest roadway that leads into town. It's very active for a Monday. Let the holiday season begin.

This time of year is so hard, and I want to enjoy the little things. Like Christmas cookies and decorations, and Tobias kind of opened that up for me again. I press the heel of my hand into my eyes trying to forget what Lloyd did, but he was my first love, and the open wound is still raw.

Snow lightly falls onto the frozen grass below. I love the wintry mix, but I'm hoping it will be gone before I have to go to work tonight.

The dating notebook is open on my desk beside my keyboard. An uneasy wave of nausea forms in my stomach. It's weird, usually the day after a date Mom has a few potential bachelors lined up. It's possible that she's got something up her sleeve. It's that or she's run out of men. I want it to be neither. It's only been less than twenty-four hours and I've been glued to my phone, hoping for a sign that yesterday's date wasn't a dream.

Needing a distraction, I turn on reruns of *Friends* and attempt to dish out the last few chapters of the third and final book in my Fae series. I'm so close to the end but my mind is anywhere but on the blank page in front of me.

Last night I relived the entire date with Francesca over Chinese takeout and large homemade sundaes. She despises my mom for stringing me along the way she does, but that didn't stop her for being giddy with me over Tobias. She may disagree with my reasoning for going on these dates, but Francesca truly just wants me to be happy.

My phone vibrates, shaking the pages of the date book. I peek over to find Mom's picture pop up. It's an older one, from when I was a kid. She was all decked out in her usual holiday attire, very sophisticated and nothing too flashy. I chose that picture because she actually smiled. A smile I remember from before she expected me to be perfect.

"Hi, Mom." I try to sound upbeat, but it falls flat.

"What are you doing on Sunday?"

Her question takes me by surprise. We don't get together often. Holidays and some birthdays, but mostly we speak through text or on the phone when I'm willing to pick up. She never has anything nice to say, so ignoring her is usually best.

"I'm working until noon. Why?"

The nausea returns, she's got something cooking in that head of hers and I'm not sure I can stomach much more.

"That's perfect!" Her peppy tone leaves me uneasy. It's close to her – *I'm setting you up*, voice. Only, I don't want her to set me up. This is it, I'm ready to tell her I'm done. Even if Tobias isn't the one, I had that one perfect date and I don't want to ruin it with fifty more unruly men.

"I want you to come over for brunch."

I choke on my saliva. "You what?"

As far as I'm aware Mom has never gotten the family together for brunch. Brunch reminds me of Tobias. The way he sipped his juice like he's still young at heart. How he offered each item to me first out of courtesy. The date was almost too perfect. What if this is a setup?

"I'm making brunch. Kasey, can you hear me? Is your connection bad."

I shake my head. "No. No, Mom, it isn't. A brunch? You're going to host a brunch? For whom?"

Mom scowls at me through the phone. "Just because I haven't doesn't mean I can't. I want to get the family together before the holidays."

We didn't have Thanksgiving as a family this year, instead Francesca and I had our own Friendsgiving. My sister went to her in-laws and Mom had some secret dinner she refused to talk about.

"Piper is bringing Marabelle and Ryan. They can't wait to see you, Kace."

I contemplate whether to decline the invitation. I could use work as an excuse, which wouldn't be a total lie. My book is my main focus. My editor has been patient and my deadline is quickly approaching. Unlike what Mom believes, writing is a job and it's as good an excuse as any.

"Okay."

I hang my head. How hard would it be to just say no? Then there's Marabelle and Ryan. My niece and nephew mean the world to me. I haven't seen them in over two months. Piper and John lead busy lives – both working in the city. They spend their weekends going on daycations or weekend long excursions with the kids.

"Why do I not believe you?"

I sigh. "Mom, I'll be there."

I stare at the blank screen in front of me on the computer, the cursor blinks, mocking me.

"What's the matter, are you mad because I haven't set you up on any dates? Was Tobias not–"

"God, Mom. No! That's not it at all. I had an amazing time yesterday. I don't need to date a new guy every week to be happy. I don't really need a guy at all." I pause. "Never mind." I shouldn't stop myself, but I do. "I have a deadline for book three. I'm sitting here staring at a blank page trying to figure out how to end my entire series. As a pantser, writing a series has been very hard."

"I hope you're writing with your pants on, Kasey."

I snort, not sure why I find her amusing. Sometimes I forget she doesn't understand writer lingo.

"I have my pants on, Mom. It's a writing term meaning flying by the seat of your pants. In other words, I don't plot my stories. The characters kind of tell it to me while I'm writing."

There's silence for a few moments on the other end. "Oh," she finally says. "Well, that's a new vocabulary word. To tell you the truth I'm pantsing this brunch."

I hold back a laugh. So why is she having one now? I want to ask, but don't. Tobias crosses my mind again and I'm tempted to ask if the Scott family will be joining us. Why do I sound so obsessed with this guy? I've had one date with him.

"Mom, I hate to cut this short, but I have to write at least a thousand words before my shift tonight."

"Okay, I'll see you Sunday at noon. Also, you can invite Francesca if you want." Mom's tone tells me she doesn't really want her there, she's just doing it to get me to show up.

"Okay. See you Sunday."

She hangs up and I have to take a few moments to regain my sanity. I rest my elbows on the table and cover my face with my hands. *Deep breaths, Kasey.* I shake the conversation out of my head for now and stare at the computer screen. With a wiggle of my fingers, I set them down on the keyboard and allow my characters to tell me their final story.

CHAPTER 9

*F*rancesca nearly throws herself on the counter, a daily occurrence that doesn't faze me anymore.

"I still can't believe we're having brunch at your mom's tomorrow."

Her push-up bra lifts her breasts so far that they are almost fully exposed. I stare at her, but she's zoning out. At least the store is empty. Sam left a little while ago to go grab lunch and there haven't been many customers today. Francesca's on lunch break herself, so it's not unusual for her to show up randomly during the day.

"Do you think church boy will be there?" she questions, as she thumbs through my first book. It's displayed on the counter with a small handwritten sign that Sam doodled on that says: *Written by our very own Kasey Johnson.*

Watching her flip through the book sparks an anxiety unrelated to my mother or Tobias. There's still so much more to write and I've got a whole shift to finish tonight followed by tomorrow before brunch. Completing the book seems like a distant goal.

I've spent so much time on these pointless dates instead of writing. The thought brings me back to Tobias, and that woman.

I don't know why it's bothering me, clearly, he's not ready for a relationship. He would have called if he was. The date was perfect, he twirled me around in the freaking snow. What did I do wrong? Am I that unlikeable where men cheat on me or don't like me enough to ring? I'm not so innocent attempting to crawl out of bathroom windows, but I can't help the negativity that floats around in my head sometimes.

"Earth to Kasey. You okay?"

I dip my head. "Yeah. Sorry. My head is spinning a little."

She puts the book face down, open to one of the pages. Reaching forward she takes hold of my hand.

"He hasn't called, tomorrow will be a week. Why do I get the feeling this whole dating debacle and me not finding someone, is because of me?"

"Oh, Kace. It's not. Anyone would be damn lucky to have you. Hell, I'll take you." She grins.

I playfully shove her hand away and chuckle. "It was too good to be true. I actually liked him. There was that woman though, she seemed to get under his skin."

She sighs. "Well, if he decided that he was still attached, maybe you're better off."

"You're right. I'm just letting my mom's voice get in my head again. It sucks having those negative thoughts drilled into me."

"I know. You'll always have me, and who knows, maybe you and I are just meant to be single for all eternity. There's nothing wrong with that. You're easy to live with, we love each other, we both have good jobs, hell, you're semi-famous. I think with or without men, we've got it pretty good."

"Look at you." I chuckle. "Being the voice of reason."

She leans against the counter and looks at me with her quirky smile. "I try."

The bell rings on the door and Sam walks in. Francesca pulls away from the counter and adjusts herself as he strolls towards us. In his hand is a brown bag from the Meat Market across the street. He sets it down near the register and swings around behind the cash wrap.

"Frannie," he says, in a smooth teasing tone.

Francesca leans again, pressing her chest to the counter. She's not as oblivious as I thought. I shake my head, this time feeling the grin stretch out my cheeks.

Sam throws her a flirtatious look. It starts at her beaming face and draws down to her bouncy breasts.

"Samuel. What's for lunch? More beef?" she asks, wiggling her brows.

I snort through my nose, sounding like a deranged pig. Sam slides the bag over and pulls out my roast beef sandwich. I eye it almost drooling, not even realizing how hungry I'd been. A Pop-Tart for breakfast while rushing out of the house wasn't the best way to keep my stomach full before work.

I snatch it from him before he can drop it between the small space separating us. He's so busy making googly eyes at Francesca my sandwich would have been garbage if I hadn't intercepted it when I did.

"I've got some inventory to check," he says. "Are you good on the sales floor by yourself for a while?"

"It's really slow today. I'll be good."

"Excellent," he says, a broad smile lining his long face.

"You ladies behave." Sam grabs a book from under the counter. His attention falls to Francesca when he lifts his head.

"I always behave."

I hold in a second snort with a cough. They turn to me. I ignore them and open the wrapper to take a bite of my sandwich.

Francesca watches him leave. She blinks as if she were in a daze. Even as the door closes, she stares. She jumps when her eyes land on me again.

"You should date him," I say.

Her cheeks glisten under the fluorescents above the cash

register. "He's so out of my league," she says, returning to my book.

I scoff at her. "Have you not noticed the way he looks at you? Well, you and your chest."

Her cheeks turn a darker shade of pink. "Nah. My man will always be Brythan. You broke the mold when you wrote him."

A deep laughter fills my chest, somehow making me lighter. "He *was* my favorite character to write. He's my perfect man."

Writing is great like that. Without even knowing it you can create the ideal man of your dreams. One day he's in your head, the next you're searching every street corner looking for that fictional man. There have been so many readers that have told me they've met their Brythan and they are never letting go. It gives my stomach butterflies to know that people have found a way to relate to a character that stemmed from my imagination.

"I thought the church boy was your perfect man."

Warmth creeps up my face.

"I'm telling you I'm positive he'll be there tomorrow."

I want her prediction to be right. I would have reached out to him this week, but doubt creeped in before I could try. I've put my heart out on the line many times, only to have it crushed. Letting it go again frightens me.

I straighten my shoulders. For my sanity, if he's not there tomorrow I'll put my big girl panties on and text him myself. My mom may have a handle on my emotions and part of my dating life, but I'm the one who should be in control.

Starting tomorrow, I, Kasey Johnson, will take my life back, because in the end I deserve to be happy.

CHAPTER 10

I returned home from work a little while ago and immediately slipped into something more comfortable. I'd love to take a nap, but there's no time. I have to be at Mom's within the hour and I'm procrastinating for as long as I can. I barely caught a wink of sleep last night leading to a slight throbbing behind my tired eyes. I'm convinced this is another one of her setups. Even at work my mind wandered and Mr Ruppert had to call my name several times to get my attention.

"Would Mom freak out if I showed up like this?"

I stand in front of Francesca wearing my favorite soft purple and white checkered pants and a ratty old boyband T-shirt. Francesca is sprawled out on the couch covered in her favorite blue penguin blanket. She lowers her round reading glasses to get a better look.

"She'd flip her lid, but it would be fun to watch."

I snicker at her comment and slide into the spot beside her. She places her *Twilight* bookmark into the page she's reading and sits up.

"You think he'll be there?"

"Anything is possible when it comes to your mom."

It's true. I hope that whatever she has cooking isn't anything that's going to destroy my dating life for good. What if it is Tobias that is there? The way my family behaves is embarrassing. He'll never want to step foot in that house again. One brunch with my family could destroy everything.

"I should be thankful my mom is in my life, but I'm never going to live up to her expectations until I quit my job and marry a charming prince."

Francesca's hand covers mine as I sink further into the couch, wishing it would just eat me up so that I wouldn't have to suffer through brunch. Mom didn't mind me working at the bookstore when I was sixteen, for all of two seconds she was proud of me for taking initiative. She loved that I had a job. My sister didn't because she was too busy with Advanced Placement classes. Once I graduated from one of our local colleges Mom's hatred for my job started. I was an adult, and I should have an adult job.

"If it means anything I'm proud of you. I mean how many people can say they topped the bestseller list twice. You're a goddess in my mind."

Laughter fills the tiny space between us. Francesca adjusts to sit up and I rest my head on her shoulder. My heart weighs more than usual.

"Let's get dressed," I mumble into her neck.

Francesca holds my face in her hands. Her gentle eyes finding mine. "If at any time you want to leave just say the word and we're gone."

"Yeah," I exhale. "Sounds good."

There are so many things I want to say to my mom today, but the moment I come face to face I'll lose all integrity and fail. I talk a big game, but when it comes down to it, that little girl inside only wants one thing. Acceptance. Is that so hard to ask?

CHAPTER 11

$\mathcal{I}$n the end I decided to change into something more suitable. I found a cute quarter sleeve red dress that still had the tags attached. Between all the dates it must have gotten shoved to the far end of the closet. I match it with my favorite brown leggings and toss a tan-brown plaid scarf to match. I'm a scarf enthusiast and will find a way to match them with every outfit.

We arrive at Mom's in Francesca's car and pull up behind Piper and John's shiny gray Honda Odyssey. The little stick-figure family sticker mocks me as she puts the car in park. Even their van is perfect and looks just as new as the day they bought it.

All the emotions building up come rushing in and the air in my lungs deflates, the pressure strangling me enough to cause a lump in my throat. I grip the soft cushioned seat below me, holding on tight wishing I didn't have to let go. *Just breathe*, I try to tell myself.

I look to Francesca for comfort and concern passes through her scrunched-up face.

"Maybe this was a bad idea. We could turn around and go, right?"

Panic climbs up and I'm afraid I might explode from the pressure.

"Look on the bright side, the kids will be happy to be with their favorite aunt. You can't deprive them of that. They love you."

She's right, those kids mean the world to me. Seeing them will negate any of the bad that today will bring. The pressure lightens when I imagine their smiling faces.

I don't bother to knock on the freshly painted red door. Once inside, voices murmur from the dining room. Pots and pans crash around in the kitchen and laughter fills the house. Visiting your folks shouldn't make you nauseous.

I shimmy off my coat and look around the familiar entryway. Mom always had a knack for house decorating. She would have made a great interior decorator, instead of spending her life stuck in an office all day. Everything is so perfect that I'm pretty sure I've never even spotted a speck of dust in her house, ever.

The scent of bacon meets pine wafts through the air. The pine is stronger as I note a small bowl of potpourri on a random table beside the wall near the mudroom closet door.

"I'm still in awe of your mom's house, it's always so tidy."

I scoff. "It's like the *Hallmark* channel threw up."

Francesca snorts loudly and it echoes in the nearly empty entryway. The ceilings are high, and Mom only has the right amount of furniture to not make the area overcrowded, so there's always a slight echo.

Mom already has Christmas decorations up. They are always so… "proper", I guess that's the word I'm looking for. They're strategically placed in what truly resembles the set of a Christmas movie on *Hallmark*. When Francesca and I moved in together and we started buying secondhand decorations and dollar store tinsel, it made the holiday feel more magical. Like it should be.

We hang our jackets inside the closet to our left. The minute I shut the door two sets of feet stampede towards us.

"Aunt Kasey!"

I come face to face with quite honestly the most beautiful children I know. Marabelle has her dark hair pulled into a high ponytail. She's gorgeous. Sometimes she reminds me of myself when I was younger. The little guy Ryan is three and he stands next to his sister making silly faces at me.

I kneel and scoop them up into my arms. They attach their sticky hands around me, but since it's them I don't mind. I hold them at a distance to get a better look. They've grown since the last time we were together.

Marabelle and Ryan both have matching holiday shirts. I look up at the sound of clicking heels on the freshly polished wooden floor. Walking into the hall dressed in business attire is my sister. Her hair looks like it was just redone, dark on the bottom light on top. Her face is caked with concealer, and I pretend I have to squint to find the real her behind all of it.

"Mom was ready to go on a witch hunt to find you. She was going to take heads in the process. What took you so long?"

"Hello to you too, Piper."

"Hi," she says. "Your boyfriend's here too."

My what? I stare at her. Has she lost her mind? Is he really here?

Francesca bounces into me with her hip. She lifts her chin in the direction behind my sister and sure enough Tobias is standing there dressed in his Sunday best. I'm at a loss for words and mostly it's because my sister had to use the term "boyfriend", especially since we've only gone out once.

"Hey," he says, stepping forward.

My sister gathers the kids and ushers them out of the hall, leaving just the three of us alone.

Francesca takes in the man standing in front of us. He looks amazing. I don't think there's anything he could wear that would make him look bad. His dark hair stands stiff with gel and pulled back nicely, a few stray strands falling over his warm eyes. I'm in awe that he's here. Part of me wants to actually hug my mother, the other half wants to hide, because this can't end well. Family gatherings never do.

"I'm Francesca, and you must be the church boy," she says.

I'm thankful for Francesca stepping in first. I'm not ready to speak just yet, my throat is dry and hoarse. Whatever comes out of my mouth at this moment would be gibberish.

"Francesca, it's a pleasure." He holds out his hand like a gentleman and she stares at it, then up at him.

"You said church boy," she says, emphasizing the word boy. "That, my friend, is a man." She winks at him.

His laughter takes me by surprise. My entire body quakes inside from the sound. It's that joyful feeling you get as a kid on Christmas morning. He's the present you open that you can't get enough of.

"Kasey," he says, nodding.

"Hi," I manage to squeak.

His magnetic eyes land on mine. I'm warm from the inside out. My hand twitches at my side, wanting to tug on the front strand of my hair to relieve the anxiety building. I thought for sure he'd written me off, to be with Roxanne, but here he is standing in my mom's house with a gleaming look in his eye.

"I wasn't expecting you to be here, did my mom put you up to this?" My voice is still a higher pitch than usual.

"My parents are here too, she invited us over for Sunday brunch before the service."

I open my mouth just as Mom comes barreling to the room.

"Oh, there you are."

She looks well knit, but there's no denying the crazed look in her eye as she heads towards me.

"You two! In the kitchen to help, now! And you." She points to

Tobias, shaking her finger. "Go make sure your parents are taken care of."

Tobias isn't afraid of my mom and her crazy antics. He's polite and offers one of his killer smiles. I clench my teeth. Him not seeing her for what she truly is bugs me. I pump my hands like they are holding on to a stress ball.

"Yes, ma'am."

Francesca jumps in, grabbing a hold of Mom's arm before she can swipe him from my view.

"Love what you've done with the place, Stacy," she says, attempting to hook her arm in Mom's.

She turns back and points to Tobias; he's starting to walk away. I grab onto his arm. He jumps at my touch, and I pull away.

"It's really nice to see you again," I tell him.

I'm being clingy. In my head it sounded like the right thing to say, but when it left my lips, it didn't quite come out the right way.

"I thought–" I start to say but stop myself.

His round cheeks pop with a sharp grin. "I hope you don't think I forgot about you."

Did he read my mind? I shake my head, pretending that I wasn't pathetically waiting by the phone all week.

"No, I was really busy this week with work…" Technically that's not a lie. I did have work and a lot of writing to get done.

"I hope I didn't mess things up between us. I went down to Georgia to visit my brother for a few days, and I lost my phone on the flight."

Duh, Kasey. Of course, he had a good explanation. I could tell he wasn't the type of guy to ditch someone after one date. Oh wait, that's me, I'm that type. I shake my head, attempting to pull myself together. My chest warms at his intense gaze, making me smile.

"How was your trip? Aside from the loss of your phone. RIP phone."

He chuckles. "It was really nice. My brother had some time off, so he took me sightseeing. I just picked up my new cell yesterday and haven't had a chance to upload your number."

"It's no problem, I…"

"Kasey Anne Johnson, get your butt in this kitchen. Now!" Mom's voice echoes through every room. I close my eyes and nibble on my bottom lip. A warm hand reaches out. I blink at his touch.

"I'll save you a seat next to me?"

C'mon, Kasey, say something! I'm struck with silence again. "Sounds good."

He smiles. "Great. Now get in there before she comes out and drags you in."

I laugh. "I'm sorry, she's a little… intense?"

His face is still lit up as he swipes his hand in front of him. "Nah, if you want intense, you should meet my sister."

"You have met mine, right?" My voice lowers an octave as I point over my shoulder to the dining room.

"She's not so bad."

"You just wait." I laugh.

Mom's loud voice echoes through the house again and Tobias squeezes my arm gently, before releasing his grip. I give a quick smirk and then rush off to the kitchen before she can embarrass me even more.

CHAPTER 12

I help Mom finish preparing some of the food. She went all out for this brunch. Between the eggs, homemade bagels, and potatoes my stomach is full just from the scent of it all. In her head she's probably picturing this being a yearly occurrence with his family. It's obvious she's already plotting our wedding.

I cringe. It's not that Tobias isn't marriage material, any girl would be lucky to marry him. For me, I just can't fathom how someone could know that from the first date. Maybe I'm a little bitter too, because marriage is the only way Mom will show me any kind of love.

I try to erase that nonsense from my head, and for a brief moment allow myself the satisfaction of her being proud of me, because I know it won't last.

An unfamiliar woman enters the kitchen. Her pointed nose and soft brown eyes remind me of Tobias. Her face lights up when she spots me.

"Oh my gosh," she says, clasping her hands over her mouth. She steps forward. "My son told me you were beautiful, but I was not expecting this." His mom is glowing.

After today I'll permanently have flushed cheeks. She crosses the room, past the center island, and stops right in front of me.

"I'm sorry. I didn't mean to gush. I'm Sarah, Tobias's mom."

I stare up at her gorgeous young face. She doesn't look a day over fifty. The sweetness radiates off her, nothing but fake lies behind her smile.

"It's nice to meet you."

"I've read all your books, Kasey. I have to say you have quite a way with words."

I smile at the memory he shared of the signing. Her being a fan and enjoying the books means a lot to me. I'll never get tired of the outpouring of love I've received from readers over the last few years.

"Please tell me book three is coming out soon. I'm dying to find out what happens to Brythan and Halia."

Everything negative falls away like a distant memory. It happens when I dive into my fantasy world. It's one of my favorite things about writing, nothing beats skipping out on reality for a few hours. I love being able to discuss my characters with others. Sometimes fans have a better idea of where they envision my character going and I try to incorporate their ideas with my own.

"I truly hope you kill off the Fae King, he needs to be put in his place."

I can't fight the smile pushing its way to the surface.

"He's terrible. He and I have these intense conversations about behaving and he just doesn't listen."

Now I've got her holding her stomach from laughing so hard. She touches my shoulder. "I knew I liked you from the moment Halia and Brythan kissed in book one."

I smirk. "I'm writing book three now. Writer's block has a hold on me. Please feel free to give me all your suggestions. Maybe I'll give you an early preview."

That sparks an interest in her glittering eyes. "I'd love that."

She is literally fangirling. Her enthusiasm melts my heart.

"Kasey, could you please get the home fries for me?" Mom asks, her voice on edge.

She can't stand any conversation involving my books. She'll pretend to brag to her friends, but when we're home, writing doesn't count as a job or anything for that matter.

"It's okay, dear," Sarah says. "We can talk later."

She pats me on the shoulder and then rushes over to help Mom. I give myself a moment to cool off. I pump my hands in and out, the motion calms me. I don't want to cause a scene in front of Tobias and his family.

"Excuse me," Tobias's voice fills the room.

I open my eyes and turn to him. He's making his way through the kitchen as Mom and Sarah head for the dining room with some dishes.

"How hard did Mom fangirl over you?"

He's so close I can almost taste him. The idea heats up my core, and I shake my head to clear my dreamy state. He makes me both nervous and excited at the same time.

"She wasn't too bad. I asked her if she wanted to take a peek at an early draft."

I turn my attention to the home fries waiting to be brought in. If I don't get my ass in there, Mom will freak.

I lift the skillet from the stove and realize I've forgotten a potholder to place under.

"Could you grab a potholder? Second drawer on your left."

"Oh, sure." Tobias turns round to find one for me.

"I bet my mom loved the idea," he adds, as he sifts through the drawer.

"She definitely did."

"This one okay?" He holds up a knitted potholder that my Nana Jean made. She passed away many years ago, but I always remember the bright orange and yellow colors she used to make it.

"Perfect."

I carry the pan in while he follows behind with the potholder. We reach the dining room and it's like a circus. The kids are chasing each other around the table, my brother-in-law is having an intense conversation with Dad. Dad? I nearly drop the pan. He hasn't been to a family event that involves Mom since their divorce.

He looks up as I set the pan down on the holder that Tobias brought in. I give him a quick thanks, before my attention lands on Dad. His hazel eyes find mine and he excuses himself from talking to John. John, perfect as always with his knit sweater hiding his ridiculous muscles from his workout obsession. He gives me a small wave and I return one to be nice.

"Hey, sweetie." Dad comes over and kisses my cheek. I lean in and give him a side hug.

"Dad? What are you doing here?"

The light throb in my head intensifies as I try to process my father being here in the same room with Mom. The last time this happened there was a huge blow-up at the table that led to him packing his bags and only returning to gather his things. Having the memories I've suppressed resurface causes my stomach to twist.

"Your mother invited me. Said something about you finding the one."

I close my eyes and exhale. Dad smiles knowingly.

"You know how she is," he says softly.

Of course I do.

Mom calls everyone to sit and I search the room for Tobias. His presence is like an anchor holding me in place. He's on the side closest to the large bay window, opposite of the kitchen entrance. He pats the chair beside him with a smile. I make my way over and he pulls the chair out for me. A lazy smile forms on my face.

"Thanks."

Dad takes up residence in his old spot at the head of the table. The tingling in my nose catches me off guard. I quietly try to relieve it by sniffling softly. Images of family dinners play in my head. I blink away the tears and scrunch my nose to clear the tingles.

Piper and John are across from Tobias and Francesca slips in next to me. She scoots her chair and inspects the food before turning her attention to Tobias and me. We're sitting closer than I realize.

Two little voices pull me out of my head. In the corner of the room near the wall Marabelle and Ryan are sitting munching on muffins and eggs. Most of Ryan's food isn't making it into his mouth. Marabelle has a disgusted look on her face as she stabs her scrambled eggs with her fork.

"Shall we pray, William?" Mom glances over at Tobias's father, who is sitting on the opposite end of Dad. His wife, Sarah, sits to his right.

"Of course, Stacy." He smiles.

Pastor William clears his throat and clasps his hands together. "Let us pray."

We didn't start praying before a meal until Mom married Oliver, who isn't even here. As a kid I used to dread dinners at her house, because all I wanted to do was eat.

"Lord, we thank you for this meal we are about to have. We also thank you for bringing our two families together. Please keep our son, Dawson, in your prayers as he continues his journey in the army. And please watch over all these wonderful new people who have come into our lives. Amen."

A round of amen circles the table as each of us says it. Everyone starts to dig into the food placed in the middle of the table. Tobias grabs some items for both Francesca and me before he fills his plate. The motion takes me back to our first date when he gave me the last muffin.

"He's so perfect for you," she whispers. I check in on him and he's busy having a conversation with Dad across the table, discussing music.

"You think?"

She leans over further to whisper. "He can't stop looking at you."

I shake my head in denial. I'm sitting right next to him, of course I'd notice if he were. I check, and sure enough while conversing with Dad he can't help peeking over.

"So, how did you two meet?"

My eyes dart up to Dad as he chews and observes my reaction. The food I ate sloshes around in my stomach. He knew I went on blind dates that Mom was setting me up on, so his question catches me off guard.

"Oh, it was all me." Mom chimes in long before Tobias and I have a chance to tell the story ourselves.

I drop my fork and grasp the sides of my chair. Mom starts from the beginning. Instead of looking at Dad to tell the story, she turns to Tobias's parents. When she mentions my ex, Lloyd Hammond, waves of vertigo hit me, the intensity enough to throw my heart into a frenzy.

Tobias interrupts Mom well before she's even to the point of getting to our date. "Your daughter was surprised when I brought her to church on our date."

I release a shaky breath from my trembling lips.

"Church?" Dad asks, almost choking on his eggs.

Tobias kindly smiles at Dad and laughs. "Yeah, I thought she might want to see what I love to do in my spare time. She got a kick out of it, right, Kasey?"

Tobias stares at me, and when he says my name my heart flutters. He reaches below the table taking my hand in his. I can't hide the gasp that escapes as he tightens his grip.

"It was different."

I swallow hard attempting to keep my brunch in my stomach where it belongs, instead of on this table in front of everyone.

"We really hit it off," he says, glancing over at me. "In fact..." He stops talking to everyone and turns his entire body towards me, never letting go. "I'd really love to plan our second date. I'm thinking maybe your choice?"

Beside me Francesca elbows me in the ribs. I grunt. I don't know why this man gets me all tongue-tied, but he does.

"I'd love to."

From her seat Mom claps her hands happily. All these years I imagined what it would be like for Mom to look at me the way she does Piper. Now that she has, it makes my blood boil more than satisfies me.

"John and I have some exciting news too!" Piper jumps in. All eyes land on her.

It's not a family dinner without my accomplishments being overshadowed by her.

"We were going to wait for Christmas, but..."

But she couldn't handle Mom discussing something exciting happening in my life. The dinner when I told them I was going to be a published author played out the exact same way. Mom seemed slightly interested, heck I was only in my junior year of college, so it was a huge accomplishment. I made my announcement and Piper couldn't handle it and announced that Ryan was a boy.

"We're expecting number three," she says.

I rest my elbow on the table and rub the bridge of my nose.

As if she's done nothing wrong, she smiles at everyone, then glances at John. He looks up at her lovingly. He's not a bad looking guy, I guess. He was cuter in high school with his long hair. He started losing some and decided to shave it down. I perceive him as someone who acts like they're the best thing known to man, and I've caught him several times watching himself in the mirror in our living room.

Mom jumps for joy. She loves being a grandma. Dad doesn't look as thrilled, being a grandpa threw him in the old man age category and he hates it. He puts on a fake smile for Piper and gives her a hug.

She babbles on about a gender reveal and the exciting milestones on the horizon. All of which include a sprinkle. Like she needs more of a reason for us to celebrate everything Piper.

Instead of indulging in the chaos that's erupted over my sister's big announcement, Tobias turns to me. "So, where do you want to go next week?"

"Francesca and I still need a tree for our apartment, we had planned on getting it next weekend. Maybe you could join us and then you and I could do something after?"

Something flashes in his eye, and he smirks. "Why don't we do a double date?"

I furrow my brow. "With who?"

"I've got a guy. He'd be a great fit for Francesca."

Francesca is listening in beside me. She places her chin on my shoulder and stares over at Tobias. "You got a guy for me?"

A sly smirk plastered on his face like this is a plan that he's conjured in his head prior to coming here. That's impossible because all he knew about Francesca was that she was just the 911 text.

"I do. You're going to love him. What do you think, Kasey?"

"It sounds perfect."

Francesca and I have never been on a double date. We didn't have many boyfriends growing up and if we did it was never at the same time. Francesca dated two guys during high school and one during college. I had one boyfriend in ninth before dating Lloyd. Saying his name, even in my head, leaves a twinge of pain in my heart.

While Francesca babbles on trying to get Tobias to spill his secret date, I zone out. All the conversations around me blur together, minus Piper's voice that is somehow louder than the rest. The only thing keeping me planted in my seat is Tobias's hand still relaxing over mine. He squeezes to get my attention.

"Are you okay?" he asks.

"Yeah. I just need some fresh air."

"Mind if I join you?"

I'm caught off guard by the sincerity in his voice.

"Sure."

I'm not going to say no to being alone with him.

CHAPTER 13

*a*t the back of the house sits a closed porch. Mom lives up against a wooded lot, so the view is usually nice in the summer. Now in the colder months the trees are empty of leaves, in its place, ice crystals hug the branches. Mom's property is huge and houses an in-ground pool that I spent many lazy summers in. It looks sad now covered in a black tarp with some tiny pools of ice scattered along the surface.

The heat is never enough to warm this room, leaving a slight chill in the air. Tobias retrieves a soft white blanket from one of the other chairs and places it over me as I go to sit down.

We sit together on a floral-patterned wicker couch. My mom has had this set since she moved in. I'm surprised it's lasted this long since it doesn't match the other decor in the house. It squeaks as we settle into it.

"Sorry, I had to get out of there."

"That's okay. Family gatherings can be overwhelming at times."

My chest is lighter out here and him understanding the need to escape helps the tension in my muscles relax. "Your folks seem okay."

He stares off into the backyard and then returns his attention to me again.

"Yeah, they're good. Kind of weird having them on a date with me." There's a playful tone to his voice.

"Oh, so this is a date now?" I tease.

Tobias chuckles and shifts so that he's closer to me. I feel bad taking the entire blanket, so I lift an end and offer it to him. He raises a brow at my offer, and I slouch, maybe I need to dial it down a bit.

"Well, half a date," he says, taking the other side of the blanket. He scoots a few inches closer to me. His body is so warm there's no need for a heater here.

"Is that even a thing?"

His laughter shakes his shoulders, causing the blanket to shift and for our bodies to touch. Before coming here today the idea of him being here worried me. What if he saw how terrible my family was and decided it wasn't worth it? I'm not getting that vibe. He's more interested in what I have to say over the shenanigans that went on around us. Unlike my ex who egged Mom on, making me out to be the bad guy.

"Let's make it a thing."

There's not much space between us now. His leg is pressed close to mine. I fight the urge to rest my head on his shoulder.

"You're different." The words are out of my mouth before I can stop them.

"Oh, really. How?"

I lift the blanket up to my chin wanting to crawl under it and hide. Tobias adjusts it slightly with an amused smirk on his lips.

"Well, um…" I fidget with the blanket, our fingers gently collide, a shock zaps me to life and not from static electricity.

"Out of all the guys I've dated, you're the first one I haven't wanted to find a bathroom window to climb out of."

His laughter fills the room. I bump into him with my arm, and he pushes against my weight. His face is lit up, cheeks a little flushed, but he looks happy. A flutter low in my stomach catches me off guard.

"I guess I should consider myself lucky then," he says. "You're different too. You're the first girl I brought to church."

"Why me?"

He shrugs. "I'm not sure. I had a good feeling."

I open my mouth to say something when my sister's head appears in the doorway. All the excitement I felt a mere second ago vanishes with her scowling face.

"Mom wants you inside."

I bite back the choice words I have for her. "We'll be there in a few."

Piper doesn't respond, just pulls away and disappears. I ball the blanket into my fists but release it before he catches me having another moment.

I turn to him. "Sorry about that."

"It's okay. We've got plenty of time. At least I hope we do." He lifts his hand and pushes the random strand of hair that has fallen over my eye, behind my ear. I shiver from the touch of his finger grazing my earlobe.

"Yeah," I whisper. "Yeah. We definitely do."

He softly rubs a spot near the corner of my lips with his thumb before dropping his hand. Standing he pulls the blanket gently placing it over the arm of the couch. He reaches an arm out.

"Let's get back in there."

His tongue moistens his lips and I find it hard to look away. With my hand in his he tugs but overcompensates enough so that I fly into his arms. My body sits flush against his hardened chest. For a whole two seconds he stops breathing, before releasing a stuttering breath.

Without letting go we walk back into the dining room together. Eyes fall upon us as we enter the room. Everyone is engrossed in conversation, minus Francesca, she's busy stuffing her face with all the good food. We haven't had a sleepover at Mom's since we were teens, and her favorite part was always Mom's home fries. Francesca's savoring it all because who knows the next time we'll have them.

When Tobias finally pulls away to eat, my entire body goes cold like it's missing something. It scares the crap out of me but gets my blood pumping at the same time.

I hand Tobias his jacket as he and his parents prepare to leave. He takes it from me, our hands brush underneath the rough fabric and for a second, he stops. I'm probably imagining it, but I swear he wraps his pinky around mine. I pause to catch my breath.

"So, should I come pick you and Francesca up on Saturday?"

"I have work till noon. Could you swing by the store and pick us up from there?" I ask.

"Sure, that would be fine."

"Great. I can't wait." I give him my best smile.

"Same here!"

Francesca comes bounding over and only then do I realize the warmth of his hands are gone as he throws the jacket over his shoulders. My face is probably tomato red at this point. There has never been a guy that has made me blush as much as he does.

"Goodbye, church man," she says. Francesca is that friend who never listens to that inner voice inside her head. She usually just says whatever comes out.

He chuckles. "Goodbye, Francesca."

His eyes travel from her and land right on me. "It was really nice to see you again today, Kasey."

He leans in and I'm half expecting him to go in for a kiss, but instead he wraps me in a hug and I gasp from the contact. It takes me a second to register the gesture before I finally hold on to him too. He pulls away, his eyes meeting mine.

"I'll see you on Saturday."

"Saturday," I repeat.

His mom comes over next and she wraps me in her hug. It's as warm as his. Home is what I feel when I hug her. My mom's hugs always felt forced, and void of any emotion.

"It was such a pleasure meeting you, Kasey. Let me know when I can help read your book. The girls in my class will probably go crazy when they find out I was here with you this weekend. They love you."

"I could come to your class and do a lecture on the writing industry. If the school allows."

Her face lights up with excitement at my offer. "You'd do that?"

"Of course. I've done a few libraries and reading groups outside of town. I wouldn't mind."

"I'll check if I can get that set up with the school. I'll be in touch. You'd make some students very happy."

Pastor William comes over and places a loving arm around his wife. Together they look like a prized couple. Even with the grays peeking out of his short once-dark hair, his face is just as handsome as Tobias. His mom is also gorgeous, she's not all done up and her natural look makes her even more beautiful.

"It would be my pleasure."

She has more to say, like she could talk to me for hours. Pastor William gives me a polite smile.

"We should go if we're going to prepare for the five o'clock service," he tells her.

"Right. Sorry. It was a pleasure, Kasey. Please don't be a stranger."

They all gather at the door and say goodbye to my parents. Piper and her husband are off in the other room being their usual snobby selves. The hairs on the back of my neck stand up. I turn to see Tobias at the door, his hand on the knob ready to go. He gives me a smile and I return it. My entire body tingles.

The door closes and Mom turns to me. I'm already playing with the strand of hair Tobias tucked behind my ear. The way my entire body sparked with electricity replays in my mind. I focus on that rather than my mother's glare from behind me.

"He's the one, isn't he?" Her smile brings me back to childhood before she turned on me. I've waited years for this moment, so why is it not what I expected?

"It's been one date. I can't know if he's the one."

Out loud, I will never tell her the truth about what he does to me. She doesn't deserve to be let in on my little piece of happiness.

Her scowl makes me retreat a step or two. "Dear, if you mess this up, I've pretty much lost all hope."

The walls are closing in on me and my chest squeezes tight. I'm losing air like I'm drowning. I've been saved before but I'm not sure how to recover from those words.

Dad overhears her comment and comes strolling right over to me. "Stacy, please. Our daughter will find the man she's meant to be with when she's ready. I like Tobias, but these things take time, and we can't push it."

Mom makes a strange noise in the back of her throat. The only thing that will get her off my case is if Tobias gets down on his knee during our second date. Dating to find the right person will never be enough for her, it never was. It's marriage or nothing.

"She should be more like her sister," she says, and rolls her eyes.

Mom stomps away probably to go be with her golden child. Dad takes a step forward and Francesca places a hand on my shoulder.

"Don't listen to her, I love you just the way you are," Dad says.

I hate that she's pushed me to tears. She's witnessed me cry more times than I care to admit. Showing her it affects me has done nothing and now I'm at my breaking point with her.

73

"I'm fine. I think I'm going to go." I should thank him, but I can't find the words.

I turn to Francesca. "Are you ready?"

"Of course, let me get your coat."

Dad reaches out as she walks away and pulls me into a hug. He and I weren't super close, but he was always the one to give me confidence with the things that Mom would always put me down for. I wasn't a prom queen or the head cheerleader, I was just me.

"Tobias seems like a good man, but you do what feels right in your heart. If he's not the one, then he's not. You're twenty-four with your whole life ahead of you. You don't need to be your sister, getting married before she was even legally able to drink and pregnant on her twenty-first. You are your own person and I love you for that."

"Thanks, Dad," I sniffle, wiping some more tears.

"I wasn't expecting you to be here," I say.

"Yeah, neither was I."

The way he speaks about Mom, makes me wonder if there's something happening between them. I try not to dig too much. I can't handle any more drama for today.

I give myself a few seconds to wipe my eyes, then put on my jacket. I say a quick goodbye to my sister and John. Marabelle and Ryan throw their arms around me and look sad when I wave goodbye. I hate that I don't get enough time with them. I don't bother to give a formal goodbye to Mom, I yell at her from my spot in the dining room. From the sound of the water running, I can tell she's in the kitchen doing dishes. Piper gives me the stink eye like she's disgusted by my behavior, but I can't be bothered to worry.

In the car I slide into the passenger seat and let out a frustrated growl as more tears follow. I wipe my face with my sleeve, and I don't care how gross it is. Francesca leans over and hugs me the best she can in the small space of her car. I cry into her jacket, tears, and snot galore, and she doesn't care.

"Let's get home. We should watch all the Candace Cameron movies on *Hallmark* and drink every time they say Christmas."

Laughter fills my lungs. The sensation lessens the blow.

"We'd probably need our stomachs pumped, but I am down for a Christmas movie marathon."

We've been watching holiday movies since the summer when *Hallmark* has Christmas in July. It's something to look forward to and part of our own countdown to our favorite time of year. I don't like that there's so much sadness and hard times associated with the season, but with Francesca by my side she makes my spirits brighter.

"Awesome! Chinese or pizza?"

"Chinese."

"Dah Li Kitchen here we come."

CHAPTER 14

I'm in the middle of helping a customer when the door to Once Upon a Storybook opens. Standing there with her arms spread and a huge smile is Francesca. She's all bundled up, yet still somehow, she's dressed sleek and sexy.

She always makes quite an entrance, even the young dad I'm helping turns to gawk as she struts forward. He's got two toddlers tugging at his jeans, while I ring up three picture books that his wife sent him on a mission to find.

He focuses on me and the cranky kid whining at his feet. He looks utterly exhausted with heavy bags under his sky-blue eyes. In the calmest voice he can muster, he pleads with toddler number one that he needs to wait until they get in the car to read the book. He lifts the second boy and sets him on the counter. The boy sticks his tongue out and makes a silly face.

I love the shirt the boy is wearing. It's got a picture of a Santa hat and cookie crumbs, and in big green lettering says, "I ate Santa's cookies". I snicker.

"Santa and his elves left some Christmas stickers behind, do you boys like stickers?" I ask, hoping it will give them something to occupy their time before they reach the car.

"Did you meet him?" the one below the height of the counter asks. His tiny hands curl around the edges and he jumps up to see me.

"They are very sneaky. I came to work this morning and they were right here. They spilled this jar of pencils too," I say, gesturing towards a container we have sitting beside the register. "The pencils were all over the floor."

Both boys chuckle.

"We like stickers," they say.

The dad gives me a tired yet appreciative smile. I reach under the counter grabbing the roll of various holiday stickers and hand one to each child. I slide the bag in his direction, and he thanks me silently as he lifts the one boy into his arm while reaching for the other one's hand.

"Have a nice day," I call after him.

Francesca's eyes follow him right out the door. She turns to me with a lazy grin on her flushed face. "Oh my God. DILF," she says, a little too loud.

I attempt to shush her but realize that the store is empty.

"Sorry, I had a tiny smidge of wine before I walked here." She stumbles a bit, and cracks herself up. "Where's Sam, by the way? I need to brag about my date."

I shake my head at her, but smile. Her nerves got the best of her. Francesca's college breakup was a messy one, so it's not unusual for her to have a glass of wine prior to a date.

"He's off today. Tanya is here to release me from the sales floor."

The stockroom door opens and Tanya saunters out. Thankfully it's not Mr Ruppert coming to check what all the racket is about. Francesca's outburst probably would have cost me my job.

"You look like a lumberjack," Francesca notes, eyeing my outfit.

I've put together something comfortable, yet date worthy, with a hint of Christmas. Her lumberjack comment comes straight from my red and green plaid button down and tan work boots.

"I wanted to look nice, but heels and Christmas tree shopping didn't sound too appealing."

"You look amazing," Tanya pipes in as she comes around to clock into the register.

She's a few years younger than us and graduated high school this past spring. She started working here last fall. Her biggest surprise was that one of her favorite authors would be working by her side.

"Thank you."

Tanya adjusts her oval glasses and smiles. "No problem. Where are you ladies off to?"

I open my mouth to tell her about our double date when the door opens. Two male voices carry through the store.

"You didn't tell me we were..." a familiar voice says but stops before he can finish.

Sam's eyes widen as they meet mine. Beside me, Francesca's jaw goes slack. I lean over and close it with my finger. It drops again, I snort, and push it closed.

"Francesca..."

"Samuel," she says.

"Oh hey, Sam. Thought you were off today," Tanya cheerfully chimes in.

"I was going on a double date with my buddy, but he failed to mention it was with my work-wife and her best friend."

I wink at him. "Work-wife, I like that. It fits."

He glares up at his friend, who just happens to be Tobias Scott. He rolls his eyes up to the ceiling as if he had absolutely no idea. He glances over in my direction and smiles. I had a strange feeling he was up to something when he said he had someone in mind during brunch.

"How do you two know each other?" I ask.

Tobias looks at Sam. "College." They say it in unison in that low guy voice, like when they have a kick-ass memory that they are both reliving at the same time.

"Should we be bothered by the way you said that? You two aren't together or anything, are you?" Francesca wiggles her brows. "I mean that would be–"

"We were in the same frat," Sam interrupts.

"Oh, church man was a frat boy. The plot thickens. Dun dun dun."

Francesca has had far too much wine. Her actions around Sam are normally silly. She does it to keep him at a distance, but also wants him to know how she feels. Her mind must be reeling.

"Are you guys ready?" I ask.

"Yeah. My truck's parked out front."

Tobias holds his arm out allowing Francesca to leave first, then Sam follows. It's easy to step into the space beside Tobias. He curls his arm around the lower half of my back and tightens his hand around my waist.

My legs wobble like jelly as I exit the store in his grasp.

CHAPTER 15

*I*nside the truck Francesca and Sam sit behind us in the small cab. Their bodies are close together, both are enjoying the lack of space between them. Their giggles carry through the truck.

Before we even pull out of the parking space, they make comments like, *Are we there yet?* And *Mommy, he touched me.* Their playful banter is calming my nerves. I'm not afraid to be with Tobias but being that this is our "third" date, I'm nervous to find out where it goes from here.

I check on them in the rearview mirror to find Sam's eyes glued to hers as she babbles on.

Tobias turns to me. "I found this really nice place about forty-five minutes away, hope that's okay."

"Perfect. We were just going to check one of the lots around here, but that sounds much better."

"That's because you wanted a Charlie Brown tree," Francesca sings.

As Tobias pulls out of the spot, he glances over at me with a smile. Leaning in he says, "Does it feel like we're the parents and they're our children?"

"It does. Should we punish them when we get home?"

Francesca leans forward, sticking her head between us. She smirks, then plays with the radio dial turning it up. It's the station that plays Christmas music from Thanksgiving straight through to New Year's.

"Sorry, Mariah is my jam," she says, before Sam pulls her into her seat.

Tobias bobs his head and starts to hum the melody. Out of nowhere he belts out the chorus to "All I want for Christmas". I'd forgotten how smooth and lovely his voice was. He hits all the right notes.

"Come on, Kace, sing it like we do when we're decorating!" Francesca yells.

"Yeah, Kace, join us," Sam parrots, reaching forward to give my arm a squeeze.

Tobias nudges me. "I heard you at church and I know you've got stronger pipes than that," he teases.

Laughter fills my lungs as he tickles my sides. I love how playful and encouraging he is.

Sam starts singing way off tune which makes it easier for me to blend in. He and Francesca are watching each other as they sing. Their notes are way off-key, but Tobias doesn't seem to mind.

"Hey, Kasey, can you check the map on my phone for me. I know where I'm going but this area seems off."

Tobias detaches the phone from his belt clip, unlocks the screen, then hands it to me. He's concentrating on the road ahead, his eyes darting in all different directions. We've been driving for a little over thirty minutes. The road is finally winding down to one lane as we head further east.

I scroll through his apps for the map.

"It's Bob's Christmas Trees," he says.

As my finger taps the map application a message pops up vibrating the phone in my hand. The name Roxanne lights up on the screen and I mistakenly click that instead of maps. A gasp gets caught in my throat and comes out as a cough.

"I'm in the app now," I say, hating the lie on my lips.

I'm glad you're coming, is the newest message on the screen. Some old ones show up too from a few days ago.

I want to see you tonight. Please.

Tobias, can you come over and help my father with something? Please.

Out of all the messages, he's only replied to the one about her father. He asked what was needed, but there was no response. My hands clench around the phone. I know I need to go into the map, but I can't stop looking at her name on his screen. Flashes of what happened between me and my ex play over in my head like a broken record, causing every muscle in my body to tense.

"Any luck?" he asks.

I click out with trembling hands, nearly dropping the phone on my lap. He reaches over with one hand and rests it on my leg. "Are you okay?"

"Mmm, yeah."

Finally, my fingers work, and I've got the map pulled up with the farm. "You're on the right road. It's a few miles up on our left."

"Thanks, Kasey," he says, squeezing my leg once before returning his hand to the wheel.

I rest his phone on my leg and stare out the window. The singing has died down and there's a stillness in the car. I catch Francesca's hand in Sam's. A brief smile crosses my lips at the sight. As I return my attention to the window, the phone in my lap vibrates again.

See you tomorrow. Dad says thanks. Should I make you your favorite dinner as payment? Or maybe I can be your…

"Here's your phone," I say, a little too loud, causing everyone in the car to turn their attention on me.

"Oh. Can you hang on to it for me? I'll grab it when we get there."

"Yeah, of course," I squeak, turning the phone face down so I don't have to look at any more incoming messages.

Tobias pulls into a small tree farm parking lot. It's been some time since I've been to the east end of Long Island. It's a whole different world compared to our small town in Western Suffolk.

The gravel driveway jolts us around as Tobias pulls into a spot not too far from the entrance. Before I'm able to gather my bag off the floor, he has the door open for me.

"Here's your phone." I try to keep my voice steady, but there's a little bitterness there.

"Thanks for holding on to it for me." He takes it, lifting it to check something. His eyes widen at the screen, then with ease his gaze meets mine. If I knew him better, it would be easier to gauge his response to knowing what I saw on his phone.

"Kasey, I can…"

"No worries. Let's go find a tree. Okay?"

"It's stuffy back here, let me out!" Francesca says, interrupting whatever cold moment is happening between us.

He clips his phone into place, then reaches his hand out for mine. I hate that I love how our hands fit together nicely. My feet hit the ground and our eyes meet again. His lips part, and he's searching my face, trying to fix the tension rolling between us.

There are so many things left unsaid hanging in the air around us. I squeeze his hand, because I do believe that Tobias is truly a good man, and whatever is happening between him and that woman is none of my business. This is only our second date. There's no reason I should be upset, we're here to have some fun.

"Come on, Sammy boy," Francesca belts out. "Let's go find the perfect tree."

She places an arm around him. His cheeks glisten from her

touch. Outside the four walls of our little store, he looks happier. It's easier for him to show his affection out here. Before she tugs him away, Sam checks in with me. His eyes hold steady on mine like he's asking me for permission.

"Go," I mouth.

Tobias and I watch them disappear into the trees. Turning back to him I can see the war going on in his head.

"This is a nice tree farm," I say, moving myself closer.

We watch each other. I want him to know that we have time to discuss our past, but for now we're here to enjoy each other's company.

"We used to go tree shopping here when I was younger," Tobias says. "We haven't come back in many years. With everyone living their own lives it's been kind of hard."

"It's so nice here. Much better than the ones in town." I laugh.

A smile lights up his eyes, another eye crinkle has me swooning. That's better.

"Well, I hope we can find something you both like out here. I love the east end."

"Me too."

"In the summer we should go wine tasting out here. My favorite place is ten minutes up the road."

As his words slip out, his cheeks turn a shade of pink. The sight of his flushed face makes my heart stammer. He wants to make this work, wants us to plan things. I push the thoughts about Roxanne out of my head, and smile.

"It's a date," I say, grinning widely.

Under the sign at the entrance is a large red barn filled with Christmas merchandise that overflows out into the entryway. In a frosty window beside the barn doors are beautiful wreaths and trees all decorated.

The scent of manure catches my attention. On the left side of the entrance kids are feeding some sheep and goats. A donkey brays, it's in the back past the other animals. As we walk further up a pine fragrance filters through the manure, giving off an odd mix of odors.

Next to the barn there's a small line of children waiting to meet Santa. He's sitting in an old rickety looking wooden chair. An alpaca stands behind him, someone stands beside him with a leash. Some kids are lining up to take pictures and pet the beautiful fluffy animal.

"You're quiet," Tobias says.

"I'm taking in the scenery. My parents never did these kinds of things with me. Mom always had a fancy fake tree. One year she got one of those ugly white ones. It was bad."

He laughs. "Those are awful."

We step further into the swarm of trees. Francesca's voice echoes through the lot. I shake my head, but smile, knowing she's having the time of her life with Sam.

"I'm debating on getting a fake tree for my classroom. It would be a fun activity to decorate for the holidays while having them sing carols. I've already gotten the Menorah," Tobias says.

"That sounds great. I don't remember music class being so much fun. I do remember annoying my mother with my recorder. She actually went down to the school and demanded that they not allow children to bring them home."

Tobias laughs. "My parents hated those too. In fact, my brother and I used to use them to annoy my sister. She'd get so mad at us. We'd stand outside her door while she was on the phone with one of her boyfriends and loudly play 'Hot Cross Buns'. It was literally the only song we remembered."

There's a glow on his face while he talks. His story makes me laugh, but it leaves my heart a little heavy with envy. His siblings sound amazing, I wish I had that kind of relationship with Piper. I was her annoying little sister who used to steal her clothes and try to hang out with her friends. I wanted someone to look up to and all she wanted was to be an only child.

"Your brother sounds like fun." I glance down at the gravel for a second to fight the building sadness squeezing on my heart.

"He's coming up for Christmas for a few days, I'd love for you to meet him."

Maybe this is more than feeling each other out. The way his dark eyes find mine and hold on, that alone tells me that he's serious about what is happening with us. The voice in the back of my head, the one that fears long-term relationships, and worries about loyalty, keeps trying to slip past. Holding strong, I push it back. Not every guy is out there to cheat on me.

"I would love that." The words finally surface, and I mean each one of them.

We stand there for a few moments lost in each other's smiles. This man is so sexy, I don't think I'll ever get enough. I could honestly stare at him all day. Part of me is shocked that he's viewing me the same way.

"Kasey, is that you?"

CHAPTER 16

*M*y knees buckle and not in a good way. Lloyd's voice pierces through me. What are the odds that we'd be in the same place, forty-five minutes from the comfort of our little town? Life is clearly trying to test me in more ways than I can handle.

The weight of Tobias's stare catches me off guard. Now he's the one questioning my intentions. It takes me counting back from ten in my head, along with several deep breaths, to finally turn and face Lloyd. Standing beside him is someone who I considered one of my best friends. Quinn Long, Francesca, and I grew up together. We cried on each other's shoulders and obsessed over boy bands. Never in my wildest dreams did I imagine she would betray me in the worst way possible.

I glance down past her long auburn hair, to find her belly popping out from her jacket. My eyes dart back between them. She doesn't smile, but Lloyd has all his attention on me. I catch him sizing up Tobias, like he's the competition. He lost the right to fight for me when he slept with my friend.

Being the bigger man, Tobias reaches out to shake his hand. "Hi, I'm Tobias."

"Lloyd." He flips the dark strand of hair hanging from his long drawn-out face, then takes Tobias's hand in his. Their shake holds firm and is over in a matter of a second.

"It's a pleasure, Lloyd." Tobias stops and looks at Quinn. "I'm sorry, I didn't catch your name."

She stutters like she's smitten with him too. Her eyes rake over his entire body and I want to pounce on her for even glancing at him. The last time she looked at the guy I was dating I found them under the covers of his bed – way too cozy to be just friends.

"It's Quinn."

"Nice to meet you."

She responds too, but then zips her mouth into a straight line.

"What brings you out here?" Lloyd asks me.

I try not to look him in the eye, so I stare at everything else. I look for anything to distract me, the trees, his shirt, her belly, the ground. It's childish, but I don't want to answer his question. It's none of his business what we're doing here. Is that wrong? Does it make me a bad person?

"Uh. Francesca and I are looking for a tree for our apartment."

Stupid mouth, stop talking. He doesn't deserve your time. I'm still bitter, even with the most amazing man by my side. The pain of what happened still suffocates me, no matter how much time it's been since he broke me.

"Oh. I assumed you and…" He glances towards Tobias.

"I uh…" I can't form the words.

"We're moving in together after the holidays," Tobias cuts me off. It's his turn to save me.

My heart races as he throws an arm around me. I look up at him and find his eyes locked on mine. He winks at me, and it takes effort to focus my attention back on Lloyd. I wrap my arm around the lower half of Tobias's back and squeeze at his side. I rest my head against him, and it fits perfectly in the crook of his shoulder. I smile as if it were true. I'll admit the image in my head brings me a joy I didn't know I needed.

"Oh, wow. That's great. Congratulations. We are getting married in the spring after this little babe is born. We should go though. It was great seeing you, Kasey."

I bury myself deeper into Tobias's grasp. His warmth blankets around me, calming my heart to a slow and steady pace.

"Yes, you too," I lie. It's hard to be happy for someone who betrayed you.

Tobias holds me until the two of them disappear around a group of trees. All the tightness in my chest ceases and I let out a harsh breath like it had been stuck.

"Thank you," I choke.

He turns me around to get a better look. Knitting his brows together he watches me as if he understood every inch of pain that was coursing through my body.

"Are you okay?"

I clench my fist. *Don't let him get to you*, I repeat to myself a few times in my head. Seeing Quinn pregnant pulls all the air out of my lungs. For the man who didn't want to settle, he sure has settled. It took him three years to tell me he loved me, another three to even talk about commitment. We were young, so it made sense. For so long I imagined him as the one. I guess that's what happens when you're young and stupid.

"I think I am."

Tobias takes my hand, and stares intently as my fingers glide naturally into his. I catch him shivering when they meet.

"It hurts like hell. I know the feeling all too well. I've been kicked so many times by the same person. It was always at my lowest point when she couldn't kick me down any further, she still managed to somehow do it."

I wonder if that someone is Roxanne.

"People suck," I say, through a building sob.

Fresh tears prick my eyes and bubble at the edges.

He lifts a finger and gently wipes them away. "I can't promise to take away all the pain from your past relationship, just as I know you can't promise me the same. I can make a promise for however long we are together that I will try to make you laugh to numb whatever it is he did to hurt you. You've already done that for me in ways I could never have imagined."

His confession reminds me of something written right into the pages of a book. The words echo in my mind. I worry that I'll lose whatever this is I'm starting to build with him. Clearly, we both have a past that we can't push behind us. This is all new and maybe I shouldn't be so dead set on us being open so soon. I swallow hard to move forward and push the negative energy far back in my mind. There's something here, and I'm not ready to let it go yet.

He leans forward and places a soft gentle kiss across my cold wet cheeks. I stop breathing until he pulls away.

"Do you wanna take a break from tree hunting?" he asks. "Those animals look a little hungry."

I laugh and shake my head. "Yeah. That sounds good."

I'm thankful for the distraction.

The goat in front of me devours the food in my hand, its tongue is wet, weird, and sloppy. I lift my attention to find Tobias reaching over to pet one of the goats, the goat bleats at him. He chuckles and dumps some food onto his hand. He scrunches his face at the feel of the goat's tongue.

"This was much less gross when I was a kid," he chuckles.

I laugh as he feeds another little guy walking up.

"Right? I used to beg my mom for quarters at the ecology park. She'd always tell me she didn't carry change with her. Dad would let me. She hated that place. Anything that doesn't smell like fancy potpourri was not her cup of tea."

"I remember that place. My favorite part was feeding the goats too."

I wipe my hands down and we head over to the sinks to wash up. As I grab a paper towel from the dispenser, a spray of water hits my face. His eyes are full of mirth as he leans over in the sink. I take my paper towel and scrunch it into a ball. It smacks him square in the head, and the giggle that comes from my mouth makes me sound like a young girl in love.

With his wet hand he sprays me again and I throw my hands up. He picks the towel up off the floor, throws it away, then grabs one for his hands. He copies me, balling it up in his fist, then throws it, smacking me in the forehead. I cross my legs out of sheer caution of peeing my pants and continue giggling.

He closes the distance between us and brushes the speck of water rolling down my face. My breath catches in my throat. His gaze is intense, like I'm his everything. The crazy part is, I'm not afraid.

"I found a tree!" Francesca's loud voice interrupts us.

Tobias clears his throat and glances at Sam and Francesca.

"Come on, you two, it's so perfect!"

Francesca waves us along. Sam gives Tobias an apologetic look, then turns to follow her. Tobias stares back at me for a moment and gives a quick smile. I follow quietly behind him as we weave in and out of the trees. As we walk, I can't help but stare at the back of his head. There's something about him that reels me in. I've never felt such a strong surge of emotions over someone I literally just met.

He stops next to a sorry-looking excuse for a tree. The branches have turned mostly brown, and some are even missing. I halt a few inches beside him, and he reaches out for my hand. I inhale as our hands link together as if they were meant to be that way.

As we round a group of trees we finally catch up to Francesca. She's right about the tree. She and Sam stand in front of it, their arms wide as if they were presenting a prize. Sam's dimples show and I know from working with him that getting him to smile in that way is no easy feat.

"That's by far the best tree in the lot. Look how green it is."

I find myself letting go of Tobias's hand, but immediately regret it. I run my fingers over the needles of the tree and breathe in its scent. I love the smell of a real tree.

"Francesca, it's perfect."

"Right? My buddy, Sam, spotted it from a mile away," she says, elbowing him playfully.

The two go back and forth with the gesture a few times before he takes her hand. I want to squeal out loud over this new development.

She lets go of Sam and skips over to me, connecting our arms together. "Can you boys take care of the tree, while I steal this beauty away for a few? I saw this really cool tree topper in the barn I want to check out."

Tobias and Sam look at each other, then turn back to us.

"Yeah, of course," Tobias says.

Francesca pulls me away, but I can't help staring back at him. He shoves his hands deep in his pocket. Sam starts saying something but I can't hear the words as we skip around the trees.

Francesca asks, a little out of breath, "So? How's it going? You two look so good together it hurts me to watch."

"Us? What about you two?" I ask, nudging her.

She giggles so loud that a family a few rows down glances up from their private conversation.

"He's just putting up with my shenanigans, as always," she says.

"Are you kidding? He's so into you!" I squeal, making her cheeks blush.

She bumps her hip into me and smiles down at the ground. As we trudge forward, I catch an unwanted glimpse of Lloyd and

Quinn leaving the tree farm. A soft gasp tumbles from my lips. Francesca's eyes widen.

"No way. Is that? Did you?"

I hate the way he still has power over me. It's been a year, this is ridiculous. Why do first heartbreaks hurt the most? Tobias kept me grounded and here I am slipping away ready to cry at any moment.

"She's pregnant," I whisper. "Apparently they're getting married in the spring."

Francesca stops short and grabs me by my arms. "Oh damn. I'm so sorry, sweetie."

My attention wanders back to them holding hands and smiling at each other as if I never existed. If I want my relationship with Tobias to work, I need to be stronger. I bite the sides of my cheek to keep the tears at bay, but they don't want to listen. They are doing their own thing.

"Damn it!" I yell, stomping my foot.

Francesca throws her arms around me and holds on tight.

"He shouldn't make me feel like this. I'm here with an amazing guy, so why does it still hurt so much? Why is my heart on fire all over again?"

Francesca sighs. "He was your first love, darling. Of course he's still going to have some impact on your life."

I pull away from her and gently wipe along the bottom of my eyes.

"It's so stupid to let him get to me. Mom always said he left because of me, because I wasn't serious enough. Maybe she was right?"

Francesca shakes her head. "Absolutely not. I'm sorry, but your mom can be a bitch. That's not how it went down. I would know because I was there. You tried to get him to talk about those things and every time he skirted around the subject."

I hate that I'm throwing a pity party for myself when I should just be thankful that I'm a healthy young woman, but I can't help the overwhelming sadness that consumes me, especially around the holidays.

"Hey. You're not pathetic. You were trying to get your mom's approval."

"Pathetic," I say again.

"Kasey, you're not. Look at all you've accomplished. Who would have thought that the nerdy *Twilight* fan fiction writer would one day have two published books, and one on the way? Seriously, you are living your dream. We may not have steady men in our lives, but you and I are where we always wanted to be. Living together, loving our careers. Your mom can't dictate your life forever."

I sniffle and continue wiping my eyes. She's one hundred percent right. "It's hard to give up on something you've fought so long to have."

"Yeah, but you've got us. I mean, did you ever imagine we'd be standing in the middle of a tree farm with two of the hottest guys we've ever seen?"

Laughter filters through my lungs and the high from it helps dry my eyes.

Francesca continues, "She may never accept who you are, but there are other people who love you more than anything, who already have accepted you."

Tobias catches me watching him. His smile makes my stomach flutter. Warmth spreads along my cheeks. I've never felt such an intense pull towards anyone before.

Today was like one of those pinnacle moments in life. I've been torn down by my mother and sister and have had my heart stomped on. Looking around and catching a glimpse of the two new men in our life coming around the corner with our tree in hand gives me hope.

CHAPTER 17

$\mathcal{E}$verything is right in the world when I have my best friend and Christmas music to dance to. I'm putting everything that happened at the farm in the back of my mind, because I need some fun in my life, and this – this is more than fun.

The guys are here with us too, they helped set up the tree in our small living room. We found a spot in the corner near the window. We've got the lights and some tinsel on and are slowly putting up the ornaments. I especially love the new ones we picked out at the tree farm. The secondhand decorations will always hold a place in my heart, but I think buying the topper was kind of like starting a new chapter of our lives. Even though Christmas is at the end of the year, it's the perfect time to reevaluate life. I need to move forward because if I don't, I'll be stuck in this endless loop of being down on myself.

I pull out the topper from the packaging and hold it up to get a better look. A thin sliver of light from the window across the room causes the star to twinkle. It's magnificent and the meaning behind it makes my eyes tear a little. I look up at the tree. It's average size, but still too tall for me to reach the top.

"Need a little help?" Tobias asks, a playful tone in his deep voice.

I try to wrap my head around the fact that he's here, that both are. This whole scenario is oddly comforting.

I turn and smile. "Being short is the worst."

He chuckles, then bends down slightly near the couch.

"How good is your balance?" he questions, looking up through his lashes.

Sam lifts his attention to us. He's squatting on the floor helping sort through the massive collection of ornaments Francesca and I own.

"It's pretty terrible. I once sprained my ankle in school falling off a balance beam, and almost did it several times after, they eventually had me do another activity instead."

Francesca snickers from the kitchen. She peeks her head around the entryway. "It's true. She could never be a gymnast."

"Oh hush, you!"

She giggles, winks at Sam, then disappears back behind the half wall separating the living room from the kitchen.

"Trust me?" he asks.

"Don't trust him, Kasey, he once dropped me in the pool while carrying me around on his shoulders," Sam says.

Tobias shoots him the finger with a Cheshire grin. I've come to the conclusion that Sam and Tobias are Francesca and I in male form.

Francesca pops her head out again. "Do I want to know?"

"It was a frat thing," Tobias answers, chuckling softly.

"Sure it was," she teases.

I love the easy banter between Francesca and Tobias. It was never that way with Lloyd, every time she'd say something utterly ridiculous, he'd roll his eyes. Tobias plays around like they've been friends forever. Seeing how they interact makes me giddy.

When she disappears back into the kitchen the oven door

squeaks open and the scent of chicken nuggets waft through the room.

Tobias turns his attention back to me. I stare down at him wide-eyed. "I'll hold you up."

"Don't do it, Kace," Sam jokes.

Ignoring Sam, I walk over to the couch.

Tobias taps his own shoulder, and I carefully slip each leg over him and grip tight on his neck. He chokes a little and I loosen my hands, only slightly. He holds on to me and stands.

At first, he's wobbly on his feet, but then steadies himself. My head just narrowly touches the ceiling. It's been a while since I've laughed this hard. Tobias is like my Christmas miracle. I can't help it, around him every moment feels full of possibilities.

Sam stands to get the star that I left on top of its box. He reaches his arm up and Tobias falters, my heart leaping into my throat.

"Wait! Hold that pose!" Francesca shouts.

He's trying his hardest to not drop me and I'm surprised he can hold me steady on his shoulders. His muscles tense under my weight.

"Alright, put it up!"

I stretch for the top of the tree as the camera shutter on Francesca's phone clicks several times. My laughter and hesitation are not helping, I keep missing. Tobias is becoming unsteady, his soft warm laughter shaking his shoulders.

"Got it!" I lift my hands in the air, only to realize it throws him off balance.

Sam's behind the two of us before I can blink, as Tobias slowly bends so I can hop off. Sam holds his hands out to keep both of us from falling as I retreat from him. Tobias rolls his shoulders and stares up at the tree, rubbing the back of his neck.

"It's so crooked." I burst out laughing.

Tobias steps towards the tree and reaches his arm up. He adjusts the star, then pulls me into his arms. I love the way it shines like a real star. The camera clicks again, but I ignore it and focus on the sensation of Tobias's body against mine. He holds on to me tighter, then presses his lips to the top of my head. I close my eyes and exhale slowly.

"These came out great." Francesca skips over to us, interrupting the quiet moment between Tobias and me.

She holds out her phone, showing us each photo that she took. The ones on his shoulders are hilarious. Tobias's expression makes him look constipated, and I resemble a pug with my face all scrunched up in fear. The pictures are priceless.

"So, who's ready for dino nuggets and French fries?" Francesca sings, as she slips her phone back into her jean pocket.

Sam raises his hand. "Oh, me!"

Tobias chuckles. "I haven't had dino nuggets since I was a kid."

"Well, today you get them, because Kasey and I pretty much live off of them."

I suck at cooking and Francesca isn't any better. Our diet consists of salad, chicken nuggets, grilled cheese, and pasta. It's not the best, but whenever we try to cook anything remotely hard it ends up burnt or too salty.

Our table is set in the back of the living room, beside the entryway to our kitchen. It's not meant for the four of us, but we make do. Being this close to Tobias is nice. He makes it a point to bounce his leg into mine every few seconds. The conversation flows easily between us, making this one of the best days I've had in quite some time.

"I must confess. Chicken nuggets are my all-time favorite meal," Sam jokes, while ripping off a huge chunk of his dino nugget.

Laughter fills the room. I love how these two have brought such joy into this tiny apartment.

"You're like a carnivore ripping off his head." Francesca bats her flirty eyes at him. He takes another huge bite, his eyes never leaving hers.

Tobias sits quietly next to me smiling and shaking his head at the ridiculous conversation going on between two grown adults. I peek over at him, and he pushes into me with a sly smirk on his handsome face.

He opens his mouth when his phone vibrates. I can't help wondering who is on the other end of that message. He lifts it up to check and his shoulders fall.

"I'm sorry to do this, but Dad needs me at the church."

Tobias's eyes meet mine, and I don't know what it is about the way he's staring, but I believe him.

"Oh, that's okay. We really appreciate the help," I say.

He slips his phone back into his pocket and gives me a sad smile. Sam stands, since he and Tobias came together.

"Come on, Sam, let's go get your jackets," Francesca says, with a flirtatious tilt of her head.

Francesca pushes out her chair and stands beside him. I'm pretty sure she's pulling him away to give Tobias and me a chance to say goodbye. Either that or she's going to attempt to make a move on him.

"I had a really great time today," he says, interrupting my thoughts.

Her bedroom door clicks shut, leaving Tobias and me alone. We are standing in the center of the living room facing each other. Neither of us make the first move.

"Me too. The most I've had in a while," I admit, fire blazing on my cheeks.

"Yeah," he whispers. "I can't remember the last time I've looked forward to spending the holidays with someone."

I feel my eyes widen as he pulls me close and holds on tight. His breathing falters. I rest my head on his shoulder, as he bends forward to plant a kiss on my head. I melt into his arms. I like that he's taking things slow, but I'm curious to find out how his lips would feel on mine. I've imagined it every night since our first date. My toes curl inside my socks.

"I'll call you this week, okay? I promise." His soft tone makes me want to melt.

He holds me at a distance but doesn't let go. Through his eyes I can sense that the same picture is mulling around his mind.

I nod. He leans forward and places another soft kiss on my forehead.

"You ready?" Sam asks, standing near the door.

I was so wrapped up in Tobias's warmth I wasn't aware that they had come out of her room. He gives me one last squeeze before letting go.

"Bye, Kasey, see you at work tomorrow."

I give them both a wave as they leave.

The second the door closes Francesca screams loud enough for them to hear on their way down. "Did we just have the most perfect double date of our lives?"

She flops down on the couch and releases a dreamy sigh. I sit beside her and do the same. Staring up at the ceiling, I allow my brain to process the day we had. It really was mostly perfect, minus the run-in with Lloyd and the texts from Roxanne.

"I think we did," I say quietly.

She has a dreamy look in her eyes, as she rests her head on my shoulder gripping tight on my arm.

"I wish we could go back in time and tell those two nerdy girls, who fawned over boys we could never have, that they will get their chance one day."

I laugh so hard that my sides hurt.

"If only those girls knew."

She laughs. "If only…"

CHAPTER 18

I'm finally getting somewhere in my manuscript, but things aren't falling into place the way that I hoped. I can't concentrate. I'm okay when I'm at work doing things or when I'm hanging out with Francesca, but today I'm by myself and my mind refuses to shut off.

I thought I could push past it, but my mom has been messaging me daily about Tobias. She keeps asking me how things are.

Tobias has been quiet for a few days and hasn't responded to many of my texts. Between the doubt in my mind over that woman, and then seeing Lloyd last weekend, I'm trying to hold myself together.

The text messages I read on Tobias's phone replay in my mind because they are so similar to the ones that Lloyd received when he was off gallivanting with someone else.

I can't focus anymore. I'm ready to call it quits for the day and cuddle up with a good book. As I start to shut down, my phone goes off. As if he'd known I was thinking about him, Tobias's name flashes across my screen. Snatching the phone off my desk I press the green icon so fast that I almost drop the phone.

"Hello?"

"Hey, Kasey. I'm just checking in on my lunch break. How are you?"

I briefly close my eyes. "I'm okay. Trying to write and the magic isn't happening."

"That sucks. Anything I can do to help?"

"It's just hard to write when my characters are mad at each other and one is locked in a dungeon thinking the other forgot about them, when really, he's been searching this entire time."

He chuckles. "That's rough. Wish I could help, but my creativity only comes in the form of song lyrics."

There's a light tug on my cheeks from smiling. "No, that's okay. I'll get something eventually. Trying to beat my deadline."

"This week has turned into a crazy mess. I've been so busy running around after school helping an old friend, so I'm not sure if we can get together."

Old friend. Roxanne. My excitement fades. The pressure of being the perfect match for someone, and my mother's words hang over my head, dangling like bait.

"Don't worry about it," I say, peeling a random piece of tape that's stuck to my desk.

"Hey, why do you sound upset?" he asks, and I can't help but hear a little edge to his tone.

My mom's voice plays on repeat in my head. *Don't mess this up, Kasey.*

"I'm not. Really, it's fine. I've got some things going on with my mom and–"

"This is about the messages, isn't it?"

I'm convinced this will be our last phone conversation. Is it wrong that I'm curious?

"Maybe a little. I don't really know what to think. As you saw at the tree farm, I don't have the best track record of men being faithful to me."

Tobias releases an elongated breath. "I'm not trying to be

deceitful. Everything I've said I've meant. You've brought this light back into my life that I didn't realize I needed. I wish you'd trust me," he says dryly. "I can't be in another relationship where trust doesn't exist. I just can't do it." The agitation is clear in his voice.

My fingers stop picking at the tape. A silent stream of tears builds up behind my eyes. Releasing them I feel defeated.

"I shouldn't pry. It's not my place to do so. I'm sorry. I should really go." Sniffling, I wipe my face with my arm.

"Kasey, we should talk about this…"

"I really have so much work to get done. I'm so sorry."

For a second, silence falls between us and I hate it, it feels wrong. I'm allowing my mother to infiltrate my thoughts and I shouldn't. Why can't I be stronger?

"Goodbye, Tobias."

I don't let him say a word before I hang up and have myself a long ugly cry.

CHAPTER 19

rancesca skids across the floor, frolicking around the store, and singing, while I ring up books for a customer. The woman waiting for her items glares at Francesca. The woman's older, her hair filled with curlers under a handkerchief. Her wrinkles wrinkle further as she scowls at Francesca.

The woman pushes her credit card into the machine all while keeping a side glance on Francesca. Her voice carries over the entire store as she hums a tune from *The Little Mermaid*. I smirk, while handing the woman back her bag. She's not too pleased with Francesca's antics. I thank the woman for shopping, and she says nothing more than a humph.

When the woman leaves, Francesca takes it upon herself to flatten her body over the counter. Her arms hang over the side. She releases a soft breath as a dopey grin forms on her lips.

"Someone's having a good day." I smile despite the dark cloud hanging over me.

After my conversation with Tobias, I shook it off, and wrote an intense scene in my book. It reflected everything I was feeling and poured out so beautifully. I'm almost afraid it's too good. After that scene I've finally reached seventy thousand words. I've nearly made it to the final battle scene between the prince and his brother, the king. I can't screw this up, my readers have been so patient in waiting for book three.

I turn my attention to Francesca. She's in a dream state as she stares at the back door waiting for her prince to exit. Like he senses her presence he walks out of the backroom with the same grin. His brows are raised as he passes her by, causing her to jolt up from her spot on the counter.

"Scaring away my customers?" Sam teases, in a voice he only uses around her.

"I'm waiting on your sorry butt to get off work so we can go have that dinner you promised me."

He strides over to the front windowsill, placing some Christmas titles on the book stands that sit over the fake fluffy snow.

"Was that tonight?" His lips form a straight line.

She takes a few large strides across the sales floor and hits his arm playfully. His eyebrows knit together as he laughs and cries out in pain at the same time.

"I'm off at six," he tells her, through laughter.

"Oh, damn. That's two hours. Whatever will I do now?" She pretends to be over dramatic, throwing an arm over her face.

Sam closes the space between them. He removes her arm, and holds her face in his hands, smirking like a mad man. The gesture is so intimate that I look away.

"You could work for me for a few hours. The children's section needs to be organized."

She cackles. "Oh hell no. Put me in the smut section and I'm your girl."

A smirk hides under his pursed lips. I love how he embraces Francesca's bluntness. Most guys just roll their eyes and walk away or give her weird looks, but not Sam.

I giggle at her response. Francesca knows how to make anyone uncomfortable and laugh at the same time.

"That's not an actual category," he informs her.

Francesca tilts her head and taps her lip with her finger. "Romance?" She wiggles her brow at him.

"What, this isn't enough for you?"

My eyes widen as he points to his body and smirks with a devilish grin. It's only been a few days since we had our double date and so far, she and Sam have spent a few minutes of each day with each other. Something changed that day between them and their endless innocent flirting has turned into something more.

Watching them makes me miss the connection I felt with Tobias. I haven't spoken much to Francesca or Sam about what happened, and I'm grateful they haven't asked. Francesca knows that I need time to process some things before hashing them out, and when I'm ready I know she'll always be there.

"I'm going to freshen up anyway. I've got sweat in places I didn't realize I could sweat. They keep the heat blasting at the bank."

Sam chuckles and plants a sweet friendly kiss on her cheek. Her face turns a bright shade of pink. She doesn't allow him to pull away. She grabs hold of his black collared shirt, balling it into a fist, and pulls him close. I love how our date the other day brought them to this point.

I don't want to intrude on their private moment. I avert my attention to the list of new releases on the counter. There's a slight pressure behind my tired eyes. I blink several times to clear the haze that builds.

"Sam, I'm going to go work on the sales floor and maybe prepare some new releases."

There's a nagging pull in the pit in my stomach, throwing me off balance today, and I can't tell if it's the whole thing with Tobias or if there's a storm about to blow in.

"Go ahead, I've got the front."

I give Francesca and him a wave. "Laters," she calls out, as I walk away.

I head over to the backroom and rummage through the new release box. Flipping each book over, I read the back covers. Genre doesn't matter, I like getting a glimpse of how the blurb is written. I separate the pile of new releases in order of where they need to go on the shelf.

It's nice to sometimes hide amongst the stacks of books. I love to lose myself in them, even if it's for a short while. This place is surrounded by the scent of new and old paper, it will always feel like home.

Back out on the sales floor I go through the aisles looking for books that belong on our winter endcap. I kneel, grabbing a few titles from a lower shelf. From my position on the floor, I stand with several books in my hand. Moving forward I bump into a familiar warm body. Some books tumble to the floor. His hands steady me. My pulse jumps as his fingers graze the bare skin of my arm, goosebumps rising all over my body. Tobias.

"Woah there," he says, holding on tight.

I wasn't expecting him to show up, but now that he has, a fire inside of me ignites.

"Kasey," he breathes. "I'm sorry to bother you while you're working, but I couldn't think or concentrate on anything else. I needed to see you."

I put some space between us to capture his feelings. The forlorn look in his eyes says it all.

"There's a lot I should tell you, but I can't right now. It's too fresh. It's years of my life I can't ever get back, and I'm still working my way through this mess, figuring it out. If I haven't destroyed my chance with you, I'd really like to take you out. Maybe get some coffee when your shift ends?"

I'm tongue-tied. The words are there, lingering on my lips, but refuse to come out.

"I understand if you don't want to. Maybe I already screwed

this up." He runs a hand through his dark hair. "I haven't really dated much because of my past relationship, but, with you, it's different, and for the first time in a long time, I'm happy. There's something amazing going on between us, I'm not sure I want it to end. Please let me fix this."

Seeing him frustrated and worried somehow makes me feel better, because I wasn't the only one panicking that this whole thing might be over before it's even started. I'm almost relieved.

"I'm sorry I got upset. I understand what it feels like to be burned. I guess my insecurities got the best of me. I'd love to go get coffee with you. Or dinner is cool too." I grin. "I'm off at six."

"Really, Kace?"

He raises his dark brows, the question lingering over his soft features.

I don't know what it is about the way he says my nickname, but it ignites a fire so hot inside of me, that I almost need to find a way to relieve it.

"Yeah. Really." The smile I feel tugging at my lips is so full of relief that I almost cry.

His arms tighten around me, and he pulls me close. "You're amazing. Here, let me help with those books."

He bends down to grab a few books that dropped. When he stands up his eyes are drawn to my face. Tingles race through my body as I squirm around under his intense glare.

"After you," he says, a calming simper shining across his face.

CHAPTER 20

*W*e take the books to a display of holiday and winter books at the front of the room. In my pocket my phone vibrates. I pull it out, my sister's name flashes across the screen. I hit the ignore button because I'm not in the mood.

I lead him over to the endcap where I'm placing these books, and he sorts them into the piles on the floor beside the stack I had. As I'm about to thank him my phone goes off again.

"Sorry." I hold up my hand for a moment.

I turn the phone over. Piper's name appears again. She never calls me more than once. In fact, she rarely even calls me at all. This is the second within a few minutes. The pressure from the tug in my stomach intensifies.

"I should probably take this," I say. As much as I don't want to, something doesn't feel right.

"Yeah, of course. I'm just going to look around."

There's no one aside from Sam and Tobias on the sales floor, so I decide to take the call in the backroom. I answer it before I reach the threshold. "Hello?"

"Oh, thank God. I need a huge favor." Her voice breaks in a way that I've never heard before. My sister rarely cries, but just from the few words she's spoken I know she's on the verge of letting go.

"I need you to watch the kids. I have to go to the hospital, because I think there's something wrong with the baby."

Her breathing is unsteady and her voice shakes with each word. Her calling me means that I'm her last resort, I would never be the first.

"What about your sitter?"

I don't mean to say it, but it slips out.

"She's got some kind of really awful flu and Mom is off gallivanting with Dad."

My heart stops. She's doing what? I fight the urge to question Piper and decide that whatever is happening between Mom and Dad can wait. There's something wrong with Piper, enough that she's relying on me. It's a natural reaction and I hate that it pops into my head, but maybe if I do this favor for her things will be different between us.

"Kasey, are you still there?" The urgency in her voice pulls me from my thoughts.

"I didn't bring my car to work. I'd have to find a ride. I'm not sure how long–"

"It's fine. John is home now, but I need him here with me," she says, cutting me off. A second later Piper cries out in pain. Getting to her house is my number one priority. I will find a way, even if I have to Uber my ass there.

"Right. Okay. I'll figure it out, tell John to sit tight."

With a shaky hand I hang up. Neither of us say goodbye. I stand still for a moment in shock. Tugging at the ends of my hair I pace around the backroom. How will I get to her house? Will I get there in time so that John can go be with her? Piper is strong and I know she can handle things on her own, but I'd never forgive myself if something happened and he wasn't by her side. I hope Sam is okay with me leaving. I tug harder at the strand, so much that it hurts a little.

"Sam," I call out, as I burst through the door. My voice has a high-pitched squeak to it. He turns right away at the sound of it.

"I need to go. My sister is having problems with her baby, and I need to watch her kids... I..." My words get stuck. I blink several times to try to clear the wetness building in my eyes.

"Hey." Sam rests a hand on my shoulder. "Kace, just breathe, okay?"

I attempt to take deep breaths. I hold a tight grip on the counter for a moment to center myself. I don't do well under pressure. There's a lot riding on my shoulders. I can't mess this up.

"Hey, what's going on? Kasey, are you okay?"

Tobias jogs over, placing his phone into the case on his belt loop. He stops on the other side of the register and takes in the scene before him. Everything from the look on my face, to the way Sam's trying to keep me from falling apart on the sales floor.

I turn to Tobias. I hate to ask, but he's my only option if I want to leave now.

"I..." I swallow hard. "Can you drive me to my sister's? She's. There's. Something might be wrong with her baby. I'm sorry about our date." I'm babbling, not even sure I'm making sense.

"Yeah, sure, of course. Rain check on the date, no worries. Okay? Family is more important."

There was no hesitation or asking why, he was just right there ready to jump in to help.

Sam steps aside so I can grab my bag. I curse under my breath as my shaky hands defy me while trying to open the combination of the locker. Sam reaches in and pulls out my bag and jacket.

"Hope she'll be okay," he says, sincerely.

"Thanks, Sam. I'm so sorry."

"No worries."

I move around him and almost trip over the stupid step between the counter and the sales floor. Tobias is there to catch me. I squeeze my eyelids closed and take a moment to gather my thoughts.

"Come on, let's get you to your sister's," he says, wrapping his arms around me.

I glance back briefly and give a small smile to show my thanks.

Tobias leads me out to his truck. Once inside I give him the directions. It's a bit of a drive, but he doesn't mind.

"So, I was wondering if you'd like to come to my classroom the Friday before Christmas break? I want to do that singing/decorating thing we talked about at the farm, and I'd love for you to join me."

I'm stuck in my head, and I barely register what he's asking.

He apologizes. "I'm sorry, that was stupid of me. Your mind is unraveling before me."

"Oh. No. Tobias, I'm sorry. I would honestly love to do that, it sounds fun."

He glances over quickly, before checking his mirrors to switch lanes. I'm glad he's trying to distract me. I need it.

"The kids will be excited. They love having guests in the class-room." He grins.

"I have some extra ornaments if you need. They were older ones that we were going to toss, but they are still in good condi-tion," I offer.

My leg shakes with anticipation as he merges onto the expressway.

"That would be awesome. Oh, and my mom wanted me to tell you that after the holidays she wants to set a date for you to come and speak to her class."

"Definitely. I have some swag I can give away too." I give him the best smile I can muster.

A long-drawn-out silence echoes around me. I need a distrac-tion to keep my mind off my sister and the fear of watching her kids.

"So, can I ask you something?"

"Yeah, of course."

"How did you know to set Francesca up with Sam?" I ask.

Tobias's laughter fills the cab, just the sheer warmth comforts me.

"I put two and two together after talking to you about where you work. I had a feeling Francesca was the girl he'd been talking about."

We arrive quicker than expected, and our conversation comes to a halt. Tobias parks at the curb in front of my sister's house. John rushes over before I have the chance to get out.

"I'm so sorry. They've already eaten dinner, um…" John stumbles over his words, as if trying to remember everything. "Marabelle knows the nighttime routine and where all of the diaper supplies are."

I've never seen John this frazzled. The sight makes me dizzy with worry.

"Okay."

"Emergency numbers are on the fridge. I really appreciate this, Kasey."

John is sometimes easy to tolerate. My sister might have him roped in, but overall John tries to stay out of the family drama.

He speeds off down the road to be with Piper at the hospital, leaving us standing outside. Tobias and I glance at each other. I'm not sure what expression crosses my face, but whatever it is it causes him to rush to my side. My knees wobble, almost bringing me to the ground.

"Let's get you inside with the kids."

He helps me stay on my feet. As we enter the house, we are greeted by two emotional children. Tears stain Marabelle's cheek and Ryan's eyes start to water at the sight of his sister in tears.

I get down to their level and scoop them up in my arms, attempting to reassure them their mom and new sibling will be okay.

CHAPTER 21

The combination of fear and worry over my sister, mixed with not eating for the past few hours, led me to almost passing out. With some water and a hearty bowl of what might be fruit loops but tasted like cardboard, given to me by my niece, I feel much better. She brought it over with dimpled cheeks on her gleeful face, and every awful thought in my head instantly vanished.

"You're the man that does magic," Marabelle says to Tobias.

I love how she remembers him from brunch, I must have missed the magic tricks. We are all sitting at the dining room table. My sister's house is the spitting image of Mom's. The entire place has her influence written all over it. There's not one toy out of place, it's so clean you'd never know children lived here. The only thing I like is how the sparkling white walls give the room a light and airy feel. Other than that, it's way too perfect, and that's coming from someone who lives with the neat queen, Francesca.

Tobias slides organic apple juice boxes towards the kids, then settles in beside me. I crack a smile and roll my eyes, of course it's organic.

"Oh, you mean this kind of magic?" Tobias leans over across

the table and pulls a coin from her ear. The red in her eyes from all the tears are replaced with amusement, and sparkle in the glow from the lighting above.

"How did you do that? Do you just have random coins hiding up your sleeve?" she asks.

For an eight-year-old, Marabelle is pretty in tune with the world.

"A true magician never reveals his secrets." He winks.

"What else you got?" She props her head in her hands and stares at him, a dreamy look in her eyes.

Tobias chuckles and reaches into his jacket pocket. I hadn't realized he was still wearing it. He tugs and reveals a deck of cards in his hand.

"Do you just randomly keep a deck of cards in your pocket?" I ask him.

I'm smitten by how sexy the nerdy side of him is. Between the comic books under the guitar and now the magic tricks, I'm even more turned on by this man. The only other guy I dated who liked those things was number eight. He showed up looking as if he'd just stepped out of *Lord of The Rings*. He even wore tights. I was attracted to him, until he spoke to me in elvish and expected me to understand.

Tobias brushes his arm, and it comes in contact with mine, a sexy eye-wrinkling smile dances across his face. "Never leave home without it," he says. If he doesn't stop, I might melt into a puddle of goo right here in the middle of my sister's dining room.

"Just like your comics…" I tease.

"Never leave home without those either." He shoves his hand back inside his jacket pulling out a ratty old comic book. From across the table Ryan's eyes light up. Tobias notices right away. "You like comics, little man?"

Ryan's head bobs up and down with excitement. Without hesitation Tobias slides the comic over to him. He holds it in his hand and flips through the pages. His eyes widen with each turn of the page.

"He can't read, but he loves the pictures," Marabelle tells us. She points to something and starts quietly reading some of the words to him.

"I've got two of those, it's yours, little man," Tobias offers.

Ryan looks up. "Mine?"

"Yup."

I love how Tobias keeps his eyes focused on him while he talks. He's a natural when it comes to kids. My ovaries twitch. He will make a good dad someday. I can see why he went into teaching.

"Yes!" Ryan does a little happy dance as he continues to look through.

Marabelle quietly waits for him to perform another trick. Tobias turns his attention back to her. He dumps the cards into his hands and begins to shuffle them. Her eyes widen in amazement as he fans them out, then slides them against his fingers making a loud clicking noise as he passes each one. He spends another few seconds shuffling before holding the deck out to her.

"Pick one."

She wiggles her fingers and scrunches up her little nose. Humming, she swings her head back and forth, analyzing her move to pick the perfect card.

"That one," she says, as she pulls it.

She brings it to her chest and in one stealthy move checks it, then stares up at Tobias like she's battling him.

"You're holding the seven of hearts."

Marabelle purses her lips, checks her card again, and lays it face up on the table. She's intrigued and angry that he figured it out so fast.

"Me try?" Ryan asks, closing the comic book, but keeping it near him.

"Sure," Tobias says, shuffling the deck once more.

He holds it out and Ryan takes one. Marabelle helps hide it. Tobias gazes at them for a long moment. He scrunches his brow. Marabelle leans over and whispers something to Ryan. He giggles. I love how caring she is for her brother. I've seen pictures of Piper and I when we were around their age. There are ones of her holding me and smiling. I wish I could remember the good memories, but the only ones I have are where she wanted nothing to do with me.

"The king of..." Tobias pauses. The sound of his voice brings me out of my thoughts. "Diamonds."

Marabelle takes Ryan's card and places it on the table. She knits her brows together trying to pull the answers from his head.

"How do you do that?" Ryan questions.

"Magic of course." He smirks.

"More, more, more!" the two of them shout.

"Before you guys start, does anyone want to make Christmas cookies?"

A shocking memory finds me. I'm not sure how I remember, but I was probably four. It was Christmas Eve and things were good. Mom had the radio turned on with Christmas songs. Dad picked me up, put me on the kitchen counter and sung along with me using the spatula Mom was about to use to mix the batter for cookies. She grinned, batting him away and stealing the spatula back. I blink to leave the memory behind and tears fight to break the surface.

Their hands shoot into the air. "I do!" they say in unison.

I rest a hand on Tobias's shoulder then slide out of the chair. "While Tobias shows you another trick I'll see if your mom has all the things I need first."

You would never know that just under an hour ago we were all huddled together in the doorway in tears. Seeing them happy again warms my heart. I'm sad that I don't get more time with them.

CHAPTER 22

Once I get in the kitchen, I call Mom. I figure John is going to be preoccupied with keeping Piper calm. I don't want to upset her any more than she already is. Mom picks up on the first ring.

I don't bother to say hello, all I'm calling for is to find out if there's an update. "Have you heard from Piper?"

"She's doing okay. They don't think it's anything, just observing her."

I search around Piper's updated kitchen trying to find where she keeps the baking supplies. It wouldn't surprise me if I found coconut flour or something fancy to replace sugar. There's not even goldfish or those teddy graham snacks I used to love.

I browse through the small island in the center of her kitchen. The green marble shines as I pass over the black wire fruit basket sitting in the center. It's looking less and less like I'm going to find something to make a sweet treat with.

I pad across the room and reach up over part of the countertop that hugs the outer walls and find what I'm searching for. I pull one of the stools that sit at the center island and drag it over.

Balancing the phone between my ear and shoulder, I stand on the chair and reach into the cabinet.

"Not sure when she'll be released, but I don't think they are keeping her," Mom finally says.

I breathe a sigh of relief. "Okay good. Let her and John know the kids are doing fine."

There's silence on the other end.

"Mom?"

I slide around some of the supplies and grab the ones I need, placing them on the counter below me.

"She asked you to babysit?" she squeaks.

I'm surprised John didn't say anything to her. I'm offended by the tone in her voice. In her head I can't handle something with this amount of responsibility. It feels like I'm the biggest regret of her life.

I step down from the chair and press my hands on the counter to steady myself. I blink away the moisture pooling in my eyes. I'd blame it on the dusty cabinets, but Piper's house is so spotless she's probably killed every single dust bunny.

"Yes, Mother, she did. And for your information we're doing just fine." My voice wobbles, and I cough to clear the sadness behind it.

"We?"

"Tobias and me."

"Oh, good you have help."

I open my mouth to tell her off, but I hold back. This night is not the right time to argue, it's about Piper and the baby making it back home safe. That's the only thing on my mind.

I can't handle talking to Mom anymore tonight. "Mom, I've got to go."

"Tell Tobias I said hello."

I hang up without saying goodbye and keep a grip on the counter. *Five-four-three-two... Come on, Kasey, breathe. All that matters is your sister's fine.*

"Hey, you okay?"

I jump from the sound of his voice. Before I can open my eyes, he's standing behind me. He places one hand on either side of mine on the counter. His breath tickles the nape of my neck. A shiver starts at my neck and works its way down low enough to cause me to squeeze my legs.

I turn and I'm trapped inside his arms. The tight tug in my chest loosens at the sight of his eyes bearing down on me. His mouth parts and he leans forward. He's so close I can almost taste him.

"Cookie time!" both kids shout as they enter the kitchen.

Tobias jumps back. My body burns hot under my clothes.

I clear my throat before I speak. "I think we have everything. Are you guys ready?"

In the corner of the kitchen sits what looks like a booth at a restaurant, not a kitchen table. The kids slide into the soft turquoise seats as I bring over the ingredients. Little by little I grab everything I need and set the oven. Each of them gets a turn dumping in ingredients. They are so thrilled when I let them roll out the dough and make them into flat circles. It's almost as if they have truly never baked cookies with my sister before.

"Can we listen to Christmas music, Aunt Kasey?" Marabelle asks, rolling a ball of dough in her hand.

"What song is your favorite?" Tobias asks.

"Hmm... I like the one from *The Grinch* movie, the one with the real people."

Tobias softly hums a tune. If I remember correctly, it's the one the little girl sings. Marabelle belts out the words, while Tobias hums. Her little voice cracks trying to reach all the notes, but Tobias guides her along by singing.

Like the Grinch, my heart is growing with each passing second of them singing together. For once I'm here living in the moment, not caring about evil voices in my head. Maybe that's what happens when you're around people who truly like you as much as you do them.

Tobias helps the kids clean up in the bathroom, while I set the cookies in the oven.

Around twenty minutes later he comes back into the room, without them. I glance up from my spot near the sink. I'm cleaning up the dishes so that my sister doesn't have a fit when she finds the mess we made.

The closer he gets the faster my heart beats. I shut the sink and turn. With a determined look on his face as he crosses the space.

"Where are they?"

"Watching a Christmas movie." He smirks.

"Thank you for driving me here and for helping me with the kids. It means a lot that you stayed to help."

"It's no big deal. It's actually kind of fun."

His tantalizing grin captures me, holding me into place. He leans in, brushing his soft wet lips along the tip of my ear. "You got a little flour right here."

He lifts his hand from behind his back and runs it down the side of my face. Instead of wiping anything off, he's making the streak of flour worse.

"All you did was make more of a mess." I wipe at my cheek, and he chuckles as he poofs another small splash of flour at me. Laughter fills me as it floats down to the floor.

"If that's how it's gonna be." I stick my hand inside the flour and cover his face with it. The white gets stuck to his scruff, making him look like Santa. My hand lingers.

His eyes tighten and focus on my lips, they've gone dry. Never have I wanted a man to kiss me as badly as I want him right now. He lowers his head, and I study his handsome face, and swoon over the tiny dimple that is barely noticeable underneath the hair on his cheek. He closes the space between us without leaving any gaps. His bulge presses into my middle.

"Are they done yet?" Marabelle asks from the doorway.

I slap my hand right over where my heart's beating like crazy. Is this what it's like to have children? My cheeks burn.

"Almost," I say. "Do you know if your mommy has any icing to decorate them?"

Tobias turns to face the opposite direction as he adjusts himself.

Marabelle shrugs. "No idea."

I step away from him and climb the chair again to search. There's no frosting, but in the back behind some brown sugar I find a small container of rainbow sprinkles. I place them on the table and hop down.

Marabelle peeks in the oven. "They smell so good."

When the timer beeps, I take them out and place the pan on the stove top. Ryan comes waddling in and we all sit at the booth in the kitchen. Tobias finds us some cups and milk and together we all decorate and eat cookies. I'm happy that the kids are laughing and forgetting what happened earlier. Even I feel a little lighter.

By the time we finish I check the time and notice it's after ten.

"Alright, you two, it's time for bed."

Two sets of lips pout at me, but if my sister comes home and finds them awake, she's going to flip her shit.

"Daddy says you know the bedtime routine?"

"Yes, ma'am. It's easy peasy."

Marabelle slides out from the table and stands straight. Her shoulders roll back at attention. A proud grin forms on her lips. "I can help Ryan get dressed. Mommy and Daddy always read us bedtime stories. The books are on the shelf in the playroom. Then we read in the big comfy chair."

"What about brushing your teeth?" I ask.

A blush forms on her cheeks. "Oh. Right. We do that too." She smirks.

She stands quiet for a moment, her eyes rolling back like she's contemplating if there is anything else.

"Well, I think we can handle that, can't we, Aunt Kasey?" Tobias asks in a playful tone.

Marabelle holds out a hand for him to take it. Tobias slides out from his spot at the table and takes her hand. Ryan gets to his feet and joins them.

"I'll clean up and Tobias can help you both find some good books to read. Marabelle, you help your brother with getting dressed."

"Aye, Aye, Captain Kasey!" Ryan says, using his free hand to salute me.

Laughter fills the room.

As the three of them march off together, Tobias takes an extra moment to look back. The corner of his lips pull into the smile I've grown to love. I have to control myself, but all I want to do is stroll over there, take his face in my hands, and press my lips against his. The almost-kiss flashes in my head. I hold on to the edge of the table to calm the desire.

CHAPTER 23

When he disappears along with the kids, I start cleaning. I shoot a short text to Mom, instead of calling. I don't want to ruin my good mood. Talking to her will put a damper on things. I wish it didn't have to be that way, but unfortunately it is.

I'm surprised by how much fun I'm having, despite the circumstances. I'm not going to lie, the idea of having kids of my own still scares me to death. One night of babysitting is not going to change that. I remember when Marabelle was born, and my sister asked if I wanted to hold her. I was only sixteen. Holding something that tiny was frightening. I worried that I would hold her wrong, but something strange happened the moment John placed her in my quaking arms. My heart melted. I couldn't believe the amount of joy something so small could bring.

I place the last dish inside the drying rack and shut off the sink. Laughter erupts from all three of them. Tobias is making up a crazy song with a monkey who ends up having to fill in for Santa Claus. I shake my head and laugh.

I shut off the lights in the kitchen and make my way upstairs to the playroom. Sounds of joy and laughter radiate out into the hallway. Quietly, I peek my head around the doorway of the play-room. I take in the sweet sight before me. He's a pro. Tobias is nestled into the dark blue rocker. The kids are piled into his lap as he hums a Christmas tune for them; this time it's not about a monkey.

Marabelle and Ryan stare up at him as if they are in a trance. He smiles at them as he sings. With all the nagging my mother did I never imagined finding a man I could picture myself having kids with. It crossed my mind with Lloyd, but it never felt real. Standing here observing Tobias with my niece and nephew, I realize the perfect man is right in front of me. The desire to marry and have kids grabs hold of me like a giant lasso. I can either run from it or move forward, I choose the latter.

Tobias's face flushes a light shade of pink when he realizes he's been caught. The kids notice me too and both hop off his lap. Marabelle heads for the bookshelf where she picks out a book for us to read. I step forward into the room and we all settle on the floor beside the blue chair.

"You be Piggie!" Ryan tells me.

Marabelle hands me the book and I stare down at the smiling pink pig on the front cover.

"Elephant!" he says to Tobias, pointing to the large gray elephant standing beside the pig.

By the end of the book, not only are the kids cracking up, but we are as well. Tobias and I act out each part. The book is hilarious. I make a mental note to add writing a children's book to my list of writing goals.

When we finish reading, I take Marabelle to her room, and he brings Ryan to his. Marabelle gives him a big bear hug before retreating with me to her room. Inside is dark, but the ceiling is lit with glowing stars from above. She settles into her twin bed in the far corner of the room. A soft glowing light from the moon above reflects off the windowpane.

As I pull the dark navy-blue comforter up over her small body, she stares up at me, tears lingering in her beautiful eyes.

"Is Mommy coming home tonight?" Her lip quivers as she asks.

I don't want to lie to her, nor do I want to scare her. It's been a hard day for them, and they don't need the burden of worry on their shoulders.

"Grandma says things are going well. Mommy might be home by the morning."

Marabelle grabs her sheets in a tight fist. In her head she silently mulls over everything that's happened tonight. Her little mind is working overtime. I hope it won't keep her awake and she gets some rest.

"I'm really happy that you and Tobias are here, Aunt Kasey. I've missed you." She watches me with a twinkle in her eye. Kids can sense when things are off and Marabelle has for quite some time.

I rest my hand over hers and smile. "I'm happy we came over. I wish it would have been under different circumstances. I've missed you both too."

She sits up and wraps her arms around my neck, pulling me down. I hold on to her, blinking back tears so she doesn't notice how much the situation affects me.

"If I'm not here when you wake up, I'll see you at Christmas. Okay?"

She pulls away and wipes at the fallen tears. "Will Tobias be there? I really like him. His magic tricks are cool. I think he likes you too, Aunt Kasey."

I let loose a bubbly laugh. "He might be there." I wink.

With a satisfied smile, she lays back down. I fix the comforter, resting it over her again. Her words give me hope. I don't know how many times I've said it in my head, probably hundreds, but I really like Tobias. There's something there that makes me hopeful that whatever is happening between us will last.

My body jolts at the sound of a soft knock at Marabelle's door. I turn and find Tobias smiling down at the two of us.

"Ryan's in bed, the monitor is on," he says, holding up the video monitor. "He's waiting for you to say goodnight."

I give Marabelle one last squeeze and kiss her forehead. When I reach the door, Tobias holds out his hand to stop me.

"Meet you downstairs?" he questions. His somewhat mischievous voice makes my toes curl. I allow his fingers to graze mine and suck in a breath from the touch.

"Yeah." I clear my throat, my voice coming out a bit gruff.

By the time I get to Ryan's room down the hallway, he's almost fully asleep. I don't want to disturb him since he's neatly tucked into his superhero toddler bed. I tiptoe into the room and kneel beside the bed, leaving a soft kiss on his forehead.

"Love you, buddy," I whisper.

I leave the door open a crack then head downstairs. Tobias is sitting on the couch flipping through channels. I settle down next to him and sigh. I'm exhausted and hungry for real food. My stomach is so loud it makes him laugh.

"Good thing I ordered us a pizza while you were cleaning," he says.

I throw my head back and sigh. "Oh, thank God. It felt like my stomach was going to try to eat itself."

"Figured as much." He chuckles as my stomach gurgles.

He snakes his arm around my midsection, pulling me into him. I want him in a way I can't quite describe. The feeling becomes more powerful as his fingers tease along the hem of my shirt. I breathe his ivory scent, like he's fresh out of the shower.

I hum in enjoyment as his fingers dance further up my stomach. We find each other and are lost in a vortex of want and need. I lean into him ready for a kiss when the doorbell chimes to let us know the pizza has arrived.

Once everything is paid for we get ourselves comfortable on the couch. I found plates and we set the box on the glass coffee table. Tobias lifts it and a sweet tomato sauce scent lingers in the room. He flips through Netflix while I set us each up with two slices. He lands on an Adam Sandler movie and the two of us go on a tangent about how much we love his work.

"*Wedding Singer* is number one, hands down," I say.

Tobias shakes his head, a mouth full of pizza. He reaches forward to grab a napkin and pats his face dry.

"As much as I love Drew Barrymore," he says, practically drooling. I let out a snort and he shoves my shoulder playfully. "*Billy Madison* is one of my all-time favorites."

"It's in my top ten, but no one can beat Billy Idol helping him sing to her on the plane. That song gets me every time."

He smiles. "The Broadway version was pretty cool too."

I'm surprised by his knowledge of the show. It wasn't popular and didn't last very long. I never got to see it, because I was so young, but that soundtrack was one of my favorites. We decide to throw on one of Adam's newer movies while we finish eating.

"Thank you so much for today." I lean over and grab my fourth slice as the credits begin to roll.

"I told you it's no big deal. I don't mind it at all. Good pizza?" He chuckles, eyeing the forth slice in my hand.

"Hey, you can't fault me for my love of pizza. Especially you, Mr I-Just-Grabbed-Slice-Number-Five." I pat his stomach. His belly shakes from the laughter roaring through him. I roll my eyes playfully and take a bite of my pizza, moaning.

My phone buzzes, I don't want to check it but do anyway in case it's an update. Francesca's name pops up. I read her message and almost choke on my pizza.

I think I'm in love. Well, I've been for a while but after tonight. The way that man kisses...

A grin tugs at my lips. Tobias leans over, brow raised. His attention lands on my phone. His breath lingers on my ear, raising goosebumps all over my skin. One twist in his direction and our lips will be touching, it sends a throb straight down through to my core.

"It seems you're a great matchmaker." I glance up quickly, lifting the phone so he can get a better look.

He chuckles. "It was pretty obvious she was the girl Sam had been going on and on about."

I laugh. "Was it the way she acted at the brunch that tipped you off? Francesca sure knows how to make an impression."

He backs away, but only enough to take another bite of his pizza.

"He wouldn't shut up about this silly girl that would come visit her best friend at work. He said he couldn't get the girl out of his mind, that every time he turned around, she was there."

Tobias swallows before continuing. "He was afraid to ask her out, because he didn't want it to get weird between the two of you at work."

I finish off my slice and wipe along my lips with a small white napkin. Smiling, I set my phone down and turn to him. "That makes sense. I'll be honest, I've been rooting for them for a while. I saw the way he snuck a glance at her when she wasn't looking. At first, I thought it was because of how she dressed around him, but as time went on it was more."

Tobias leans forward and closes the pizza box. He settles back into the couch and rests his hand over his full stomach. While he flips through some more movies, I take the time to clean up. I have to make sure everything is perfect before Piper comes home. We probably weren't even supposed to eat in here with her perfectly polished floors and white throw rugs.

When I come back, he's curled up on the couch with a sleepy look in his eyes. He pats the spot beside him, and I slide in. He wraps me in his arms and pulls me close. I rest my head on his shoulder. The sleepy sensation I had earlier has returned with vengeance.

"Tonight, was kind of awesome," he whispers in my ear.

"I was thinking the same thing."

His eyes are intoxicating, I could get lost in them forever. He shifts looking over my face as if he's memorizing each feature. "You're kind of awesome too."

I smirk. "Is that so?"

He looks at my lips. Under the scrutiny of his stare, I feel self-conscious. I lick the dryness forming on them, his eyes widening as I do.

"Will you be my date for the Christmas concert at the church?" he asks.

"That depends on who's singing. Shawn Mendes or Tobias Scott."

"We tried to get Shawn, but he had a really busy schedule. So unfortunately, they had to go with Tobias. From what I've heard, he and Shawn have a lot of similarities," he says, with a toothy grin.

I raise a brow flirtatiously. "Oh yeah?"

My face grows closer to his with each passing moment. Like a magnet finding its other half. *Please kiss me!* I want to scream those words, but instead I stare.

"Does he have the same wild hair and dark eyes? And a sexy rasp in his voice when he belts out his notes."

Tobias teases me with a shake of his hips, daring me to come undone. I reach up and without hesitation run a hand through his hair. It's as soft as I expected it to be. I allow my finger to trace the outline of his beautiful brown eyes.

His breath falters at my touch.

"Mmm," he moans.

"Can he sing my favorite Shawn Mendes song?" I whisper, now bringing my lips to his ear. I brush against him. He shivers.

Tobias swallows hard as his Adam's apple bobs. His tongue dances along his lips, prepping for mine to land on his. He hums softly. It takes me a minute to recognize the tune. If I were standing his low voice would bring me to my knees. My cheeks warm.

We get close enough that the top of his nose briefly touches mine. My head tilts and he follows. This is it. I'll finally get to taste him.

"Aunty Kasey."

We both back away from each other. My heart is doing crazy dips and dives and I'm trying so hard to keep it together right now. How did my sister ever have three children with all these interruptions?

Ryan stands right near the couch, his shoulders slumped forward. We had been so caught up in the moment we didn't hear him moving on the monitor.

"I'm scared. Can I snuggle?"

There's no way I'm turning him down. This little boy has been through a lot tonight. I give Tobias an apologetic glance.

Tobias answers, "Of course, you can snuggle with us, little man." He grabs a second blanket that's folded neatly on the top of the couch. He hands it to me as Ryan climbs up on the other side. Tobias reaches out, pulls me close. I let Ryan rest his head on me and wrap an arm around him.

Tobias finds a soft lullaby on YouTube. The music is relaxing. My mind runs through all the almost kisses. It's like I'm sitting on the edge of my seat during an intense movie. I'm wanting to find out what happens, but at the same time I'm scared to find out where it will lead. He presses his lips to the top of my head. With the image of that, I let go and let the darkness of sleep consume me.

CHAPTER 24

I wake to my sister shaking me. I was in the middle of a good dream too, one where Tobias and I finally get that kiss we've both been longing for. The thought tickles my lower abdomen. I'm pulled from my beautiful dream to the sound of Piper's nagging voice.

Tobias stirs beside me. My heavy lids open to see Piper glaring at me with her arms crossed. She's all out of sorts and for her that's saying a lot. I had hoped that she would have been less angry with me, but I should have known that not even a traumatic experience would help our relationship.

"Did you put Ry to bed?" I'm groggy and my voice is hoarse.

"I did." She continues frowning at me like I've done something wrong. The familiar look on her face makes my blood boil, it's the same one my mother gives when I've disappointed her.

"Can I speak with you in the kitchen?" Piper's directing all her fury at me.

What did I do wrong now? I left her house as spotless as it was when we arrived, so she can't be mad at me for that. I stand and Tobias wakes.

"Good morning, Piper. I hope you and the little one are okay," he says softly.

Her curt nod says it all. I've done something without realizing. Hesitantly, I stand. The warmth of Tobias slides away. *Deep breaths, Kasey.*

Piper stands in the kitchen, her arms crossed at her chest. "What the hell is he doing here?" She pivots on her feet and throws me a death stare. I cringe, angling my body back.

"What do you mean? Didn't John or Mom tell you?"

She scoffs and rolls her eyes. "I didn't ask him to watch my kids." She points towards the living room.

Why does this feel like I'm a child in trouble? My knees quake. I hate the effect it has on me. Filled with rage I hold my hands in fists at my side.

"Shouldn't you be resting?" I growl.

Never good enough. I'll never be, for either of them.

"Excuse me? I am a mother and mothers don't rest. I asked you to watch my kids, not him. Plus, cookies?" She swipes the container with leftovers from the island, and dangles the cookies over my head to get her point across.

"What's wrong with cookies? Haven't you ever made Nana's cookies?"

"NO!" she screams, stomping her foot like a child.

I retreat. There are many choice words I want to throw at her but bite my tongue. This is not the time for that. My nails dig deeper into my palms while I wait for her to continue her rampage.

"You could just thank me for taking care of your kids." My body shakes.

"I don't have to thank you for anything. My kids don't need that junk in their bodies, and I do *not* want a man I barely know watching my children. He could be a pedophile for all we know."

"Do you hear yourself?" I snap. "You sound completely insane. You didn't exactly give me much time to prepare. He was my

133

ride." I raise my voice. Tobias will probably never want to speak to me after today. He'll see how crazy my family is and walk away from it all. He deserves normal. This is not even close to how family should act.

"Oh my God. You are one of those parents," I add. The moment the words are out, I regret them. I'm angry and she is ungrateful. A knot forms in my gut and I wrap my arms around my middle to keep myself from falling apart. My palms sting from the force of my nails, but I keep the tears at bay. She can't know how she affects me.

"Oh, so now you're an expert on parenting?" She slams down the container of cookies on the table with a loud thud. Crossing her arms she says, "And how many kids do you have again? Oh, that's right, zero." Her sarcasm bites me.

I release my hands and run one through my hair, tugging hard at the one piece that hangs in front. "John didn't give me anything when he left. He was so worried about you. The only thing he wanted was to make sure the kids were in good hands. And they were! No one was hurt and no one died. The kids were so happy that I was here with them. Maybe you'd see that if you paid more attention."

"Oh, fuck you, Kasey," she says.

We're both speaking out of anger, and I hate all the negativity. I know I shouldn't berate her parenting style, it's not right, but she's belittling me and I'm tired of taking the punches.

I roll my eyes.

"Don't sass me, little sis," she scolds. "You have no idea what it's like to be a parent. So don't act like you do!"

My eyes widen and I open my mouth to say more but the words catch in my throat. There's a lump there and if I speak, I'll cry.

"You can leave now," she says.

"Fine!" I manage.

Out of all the fights with Piper, this has got to be the worst one. Waves of nausea hit me. Leaving things unsettled with my sister could be the balance between having a relationship with Ryan and Marabelle and her pulling them away. I love my niece and nephew, and the idea of not having them in my life gets me choked up.

"Fine!" she yells.

I retreat towards the door. As I start to walk out, I glance over my shoulder and narrow my eyes at her. "Oh, and you're welcome for watching your kids. I hope you and the baby are okay."

I don't allow her to get another word in, I can't. I'm on the verge of tears. They start bubbling up along the bottom of my lid and there's no stopping them. I pass Tobias and John, who are sitting on the couch having a civilized conversation.

"Tobias, we're leaving." I hate how my voice wobbles.

He jolts to his feet and studies my reaction. I can't look at him in fear he'll change his mind about us.

"Thank you, Kasey," John says.

My body sways. Usually, John follows along with whatever my sister says, maybe he realizes that I did nothing wrong. An understanding passes between us.

I withdraw myself from the room. If I don't get out of here, I might lose my mind. I take our jackets from the mudroom closet. Hot tears slide down my cheeks, there's no point in hiding them.

Tobias lingers behind me. I hand him his jacket. As he slides it on, he studies me.

"Hey." He reaches out, but I retreat like a turtle falling back into its shell. A pained expression crosses his handsome face.

"I'm sorry. Can you please just take me home?" I sniff.

"Yeah, of course." His soothing voice causes a wave of chills deep inside me.

As we pull away from my sister's house, I rest my hand atop his thigh. He glances down then back up at me. My chest tightens as he settles his hand into mine. Our fingers slide together, and his touch alone is the only thing grounding me.

For the entire twenty-minute drive I'm able to hold back the sob strangling my chest. The buildup is so painful a sharp wounded cry escapes as he stops at the curb outside my apartment. Embarrassed, I slap a hand to my mouth.

"Oh, Kace. Come here."

My face twitches with each loud sob. When I don't lean into him, he releases his hand from mine and wraps me in a bear hug. His fingers run through my hair as he rocks me in his arms and repeats over and over that I'm okay. The pressure slowly deflates.

"I'm so sorry." Burrowing deeper his grip tightens around my body. I'm safe here in his arms.

"There's nothing you need to apologize for. You did the right thing going over there to help. Those kids love you."

I reluctantly pull away. He keeps me at a short distance but continues to hold on. His fingers gently wrap around my upper arm.

"I'll never be good enough for either of them. I'm sorry you had to witness that, but that's my life and I understand if you want to leave..." I ramble on.

There's a hunger in his eyes. He leans in close enough that the tips of our noses touch. He rests his forehead on mine and lets out a hiss as our mouths get unbearably close.

"Kasey." He looks down at me, his eyes and face stern. "You're more than enough for me. You're everything I could ask for in a partner. You care so deeply for those you love, and when you love, you do it with your whole heart." The fire between us is so strong, but this is not the time to dive in and have our first kiss. We both know it. He backs away slightly, closing his eyes. His breathing is labored.

"Why do you look so surprised?" he whispers, tilting his head so that our noses line up perfectly in sync. "Is it so hard to believe?"

My chest implodes with a hardened sob. He pulls me in, and I rest my head over his shoulder. He flattens my hair with his palm. I dig my face into his neck, inhaling his clean scent.

"You're the most amazing girl I've ever met. If they don't see that – screw them."

His words cut through me, and I grab on, holding him tighter. He grunts under the pressure of my grasp.

Tobias lets me cry it out until I've got nothing left in me.

When the tears dry, he walks me to my door. Like I'm made of glass he gently leans forward and presses a soft kiss to my head. What did I do to deserve this amazing man? He gives me one last hug before departing.

Is it possible to love someone you've never kissed? Because I'm so far down the rabbit hole that there's no turning back. I have no doubt that I might be falling for number thirty-one. Lucky number thirty-one.

CHAPTER 25

Checking in on you.

I stare down at the latest text from Tobias. He spent most of this morning sending me messages to distract me. We have gone from emoji and GIF wars to random conversations. He doesn't bring up what happened yesterday, and I'm grateful for that.

Mom sent me a lovely text this morning to tell me I should apologize. I ignored her and she hasn't reached out since. Then Dad sent one asking why Mom was upset with me. I ignored him too. I need a breather. My focus for the next few days is set on visiting Tobias at school, finishing my manuscript, and the Christmas concert at church.

Francesca plops down on the sofa beside me. She hands me a mug of cocoa. The steam rises, the cup is hot under my cold fingers. She adjusts the blanket and drapes it over us.

"Did you figure out what you're wearing to the concert?" she asks.

"Not a clue," I say, as I blow on the liquid in my cup. Her free hand rests on my leg, a half-smile lingers on my face for a brief second. I haven't given much thought to what I would wear. While all of the family fights still weigh me down, the thought of being with Tobias over Christmas helps give me some relief. "What about you? I'm so glad Sam's coming too."

Her entire face lights up. She's got that dreamy look in her eye. I recall the text she sent while I was at Piper's. I'm happy for them. I'm not sure how much more of them dancing around each other like peacocks during mating season I could take. I've been rooting for them since the day Francesca walked in, causing Sam to trip over a small stack of books, because he was too busy watching her. He was always hyper aware of her presence.

"I'm thinking of the sexy black dress with lace sleeves. That one makes my boobs pop," she says, narrowing her eyes to check out her breasts.

I chuckle. That dress is one of my favorites on her, it flatters her body.

"What about you?" She takes a swig of her hot cocoa, then glances back up. Something catches her eye. She sighs. Her voice turns soft. "Kace, you look so lost, love."

Lost is the perfect word to describe my entire life. The only time I'm not wandering around unable to find my way is when I'm with Tobias.

"I'll be fine. It's nothing I haven't dealt with before."

She tightens her grip on my leg. "It's okay to not be okay."

I meet her stare. "I know." My voice breaks a little.

"Hey, I know the perfect plan, to cheer you up. You and I will go Christmas shopping this week. I mean we actually have really, really cute guys to buy gifts for. We can go out to eat, get a ton of junk food, scour the mall, and have a good old fashioned girls' day out. What do you say?"

She presses her hands together, bringing them to her lips, then pouts. "Please."

"You know I can't say no to junk food."

Grinning widely, she squeals. "Yes! I knew that would cheer you up."

I take in the *Doctor Who* mug in my hand and run my finger over its bumpy surface. Beside me, my phone vibrates. My cheeks hurt from the smile on my face. It's another silly message from Tobias. It's an image of him playing his guitar and one of Shawn Mendes, smashed together using a photo app. *Who wore it better?* I snort so hard that hot chocolate almost comes out of my nose. It burns.

Francesca leans in to get a peek. "Are you sexting?"

"Definitely not." I chuckle. "We haven't even kissed."

I reply "Shawn" and add an emoji sticking its tongue out. I peer up at her through the strands of hair hanging in front of my face. Her eyes grow wide as she stares at me like I've told her I was a virgin.

"You're joking, right? Please tell me you're joking. That man literally undresses you with his eyes. I'm surprised you haven't slid into home yet."

"Who even says that anymore?" I ask, a smile replacing the nagging frown on my face.

She shrugs. "Apparently me."

"Have you and Sam?" I ask, turning the tables.

She hums softly, and her eyes sparkle. A guilty grin spreads from ear to ear.

Shaking my head, I smirk at her. "Ugh. Images. No. He's my boss, just no." I make a gagging noise in the back of my throat. Laughter shakes both our bodies.

"I love grossing you out."

I pretend to shudder, and she playfully hits my arm.

"Tobias and I have tried to kiss. Oh God, the tension drives me mad!" I growl. "It seems every time we're about to do it something gets in the way. The other day when we left Piper's he was trying to be a gentleman. He gave me the space he knew I needed."

"I like him. He's good for you, Kace. The perfect person is out there for everyone. Maybe not in the romantic sense for some, but everyone has their person."

"Is Sam your one?" I ask.

She shakes her head. "Nope. You're my number one. Always." She smirks.

I lean forward and place my mug down on the coffee table. Reaching out I throw an arm over my best friend. We have been there for each other since we were kids. Nothing could ever change between us, she's my rock, and will always be my number one too.

CHAPTER 26

The mall is bustling with Christmas shoppers. It's so crowded that Francesca and I are holding hands, so we don't get separated in the mix. Looking for something to give Tobias is a good distraction. While I hate shopping so close to Christmas, the giggles of children lined up to meet Santa, and carols humming over the mall speakers, brings together everything I love about this time of year.

We slip inside a department store with a ton of ugly sweaters. "Oh my God – Sam would die for one of these. Don't you think?" she asks.

She holds up an ugly green one with a lit-up Christmas tree that says, *Get Lit*. Shaking my head, I snort.

"How about this one?"

I tug a berry-blue one from the rack and hold it up. There's one with Santa that says, *I have a big package for you.*

Her entire face lights up as she steals it from my grasp. "This is *so* him, the saying is perfect..." Her voice trails off as she glances up at me.

"Maybe I was wrong about that one. I just can't think about Sam like that."

She laughs. "Okay, you're right. Look at this one. It's Santa riding a T-Rex, ah – that's perfection. Also, in case he wants to wear it around his family for Christmas, the other ones would be super awkward."

"True. What else are you planning on giving him?"

"I was thinking of going to that specialty coffee shop and picking out a bunch of random flavors. That boy lives off that stuff."

"That's perfect, and it will go nicely with my book-ish gift for him."

"Yes, I love it. Let me pay for this. Holy shit." She holds up the sweater and scowls. "Thirty bucks for a sweater I could probably get my grandma to knit. These people are insane. Anyway, I'm going to pay for my overpriced sweater and then we can go to that shop where they do those engravings."

I know it's late in the shopping season, but I'm determined to find something for Tobias that's personal while not breaking the bank.

Back out in the main corridor of the mall Francesca and I hum to the holiday hits playing. The line for Santa is so backed up that we have to zig-zag through them to get to the store I'm looking for.

The rich scent of peppermint candy canes tickles my senses as we walk by the candle shop. Francesca pauses causing shoppers to have to veer around us. She inhales deeply. Her shoulders fall and when she closes her eyes it's like she's been transported somewhere else.

"Are you remembering the time we ate so many candy canes on Christmas Day that we laid in your bed groaning and nauseous?"

Amusement is clear on her bright face. "Despite our families, you and I had some of the best Christmases together. I think that was the night we watched *The Holiday* on repeat."

Her eyes open, a twinkle of remembrance in them. "Yes! That movie. We should watch it tonight."

She hooks my arm into hers and we start walking again.

"So, this weekend is going to be epic, are you excited?"

"I'm nervous. We talked about spending the night with each other after the concert."

"Oh, and how do you feel about that?" She winks.

I'm daydreaming, my head is in the clouds when I bump into someone. Their bags fall to the floor, and when I snap my attention to the situation at hand, I find myself staring into the deep green eyes of Roxanne. She's about to tear me a new one, her mouth opens ready to yell, but then she stops herself.

"Cassie?"

"Kasey," I deadpan.

"Right."

"I'm sorry, I wasn't paying attention," I say.

I reach for some of the spilled contents of her shiny red shopping bag. Random gifts like men's cologne, T-shirts, and some women's lingerie, then my eyes land on a familiar name engraved into a silver bracelet. TOBIAS. My entire body freezes up with the box in my hand. *Put it back, Kasey. Don't read into it.*

"Thanks for helping," Roxanne says, stealing my attention back.

I throw the gift inside the bag and pretend it didn't crush me to see it amongst her things. Did she have plans on giving it? Were they both exchanging? Did he go and buy her something? I sound crazy. There's no way. He gets all tense when her name is even mentioned – of course he's not going to buy her anything. Right?

"Kace." Francesca grabs my shoulder. I'm not even realizing I'm on the floor still.

Roxanne stares down at me, like I'm a bug that needs to be squashed. Her charming smile non-existent.

I stand, dusting off my leggings.

"I should get going. Gotta wrap these gifts. It was nice to see you, Cassie."

"It's Kace–"

I don't have the chance to finish, she's already walking past me, her hand raised to wave. Hanging my head, I stare at the spotted floor at my feet. *Don't cry, Kasey. Tobias likes you.*

"Come on, let's finish up. And look, the store you need is right in front of our noses," Francesca says, attempting to get me to change direction.

"She got him something engraved."

"What?"

"Tobias," I say, my lip quivering. "She got him a bracelet at this store. And now here I am looking for something similar."

"Your gift is going to be a million times better. An engraved bracelet is so… impersonal."

"I guess. It makes no sense to me, why she's trying to be with him. He's so uncomfortable around her."

"Some girls just can't let go," she says.

We enter the store and I've gone from feeling amazing to back to the same old Kasey with the evil voice in her head. Everything in here feels impersonal or maybe it's the dreadful knot sitting in my stomach after seeing Roxanne.

Something shiny catches my attention on the wall of Christmas ornaments. There's a crowd of people hovering over the section. I squeeze my way through, and reach for the small wooden, beautifully handcrafted, guitar. A trembling laugh leaves my lips. "Perfect. This is just–"

A few rows down a display of comic book related ornaments catches my attention, and when my eyes land on *Thor* I'm sold.

"What's that?" Francesca asks, shoving through the massive crowd.

I glance up at her, my cheeks hurt from smiling. "It's the perfect gift."

Francesca rests her arm over my shoulder. "See, I told you your idea was better."

Back out into the mall, we stop and grab some gingerbread hot chocolate from one of the small vendors and find one empty table left with a view of the North Pole display. I'm feeling much better with my purchases in hand. I watch from our spot as a little girl settles down on Santa's lap, her eyes filled with admiration.

"Should we go sit on Santa's lap?" Francesca asks.

I toss a piece of cookie at her and grin.

"Can you believe we both have men to buy gifts for this year?"

I laugh. "Yeah. It's nice. You think he'll like my gifts?"

"While I don't get what they are, or why it made your smile light up your face, but if you had that reaction, I think he will too."

Smiling, I glance around at the beautiful twinkling lights hanging from the ceiling, and the wooden set depicting Santa's workshop.

"To the best Christmas ever," Francesca says, lifting her drink. I tap mine with hers.

"To the best Christmas ever!" I repeat, lifting the cup to my lips.

"And to the two hot men who love us."

All the liquid I've consumed comes spewing out of my mouth and over the table. Our laughter surrounds us even over the loud murmurs of voices and chaos of Christmas. Even if Tobias and I don't work out, I think the best present of all is still having Francesca by my side, my best friend, my everything. She sure knows how to pull me from a slump when I'm down, and for that I'm truly grateful.

CHAPTER 27

$\mathcal{I}$ pull into the parking lot of the elementary school. Stepping out into the cold I almost forgot how frigid it was with the heat blasting in the car. It's the Friday before Christmas and the coldest winter day yet. An arctic blast is coming through, leaving us with some snow over the weekend. I hope it holds out until after tomorrow night's concert.

I'm buzzed in at the door and given a visitor's pass. The secretary up front has me wait inside a small vestibule. A musty scent stings my nose. It's to be expected; aside from the church this building is one of the oldest in town. The familiar yellow walls haven't changed since I attended as a child. Inside these walls held some good memories, much better than outside of them.

The door opens and I'm met with the most loving smile I've ever received.

"Hey, you." His low rugged voice sends my pulse racing. I'm such a dork for even imagining these things, but this man does things to me that I can't explain.

"Hey," I croak.

"Were you able to get in okay?" he asks, as we walk down the hallway.

"Yeah. No problems at all."

We turn the corner and pass room A15, my smile widens remembering the teacher that once occupied it. Her name was Mrs Powell. She was my first-grade teacher who taught me to love writing at a young age. The minute she broke out the blank hardcover books to write our own stories in, I fell in love.

"Is Mrs Powell still here? Bethany, I think, was her first name."

She was young, probably around my age now when I had her.

"Yeah. She teaches fifth grade. You know her?"

We head through the double doors nearing the cafeteria. If memory serves me correctly, this is where all the specials' classrooms are. Music, Art, and the library.

"She was my first-grade teacher. She's the reason I fell in love with writing," I babble on, talking to the floor in front of me. My cheeks sting. I'm caught up in the memory of how she was always there for me and cheering me on that entire year. It's the most encouragement I ever got from an adult.

"I can take you to see her when we're finished."

My mouth falls open. "Really?"

I have a massive grin on my face. "That would– that would mean the world to me."

I stare up at the man that keeps surprising me with all these nice things.

"It's not a problem, Kace," he says.

We stop at his classroom door, it's decorated to look like a red chimney with smoke, made of cotton, billowing out.

"Class moms." He smirks when he notices my attention on the design. "They don't normally decorate doors for the special classes, but…"

I smirk, shaking my head. "They can't resist the handsome music teacher."

He nudges me playfully with his elbow.

The door squeaks as it opens, he reaches around to flick on

the light. In the far corner near a row of windows is the fake tree he bought at the tree farm.

"Did Sam give you the ornaments?"

"Yes," Tobias says, lifting his chin towards the sill under the windows.

In a neat row are several boxes of ornaments, a few being the extra ones I donated for them to use. I make my way over and scan them.

The music room has pretty much stayed the same too. The posters on the wall have changed, but the piano remains in the front close to the entryway. It's easy to find the spot I occupied during my days here. I can still imagine Francesca and me sitting there in second and fourth grade, it feels like a lifetime ago.

"I'm sorry I can't pick you up tomorrow."

I jump at the sound of his voice, it's close to my ear, his breath dancing along my neck. I turn and take a step back.

I feel much better today, and even if Mom and Dad show up for the concert, I plan on making the best of it. Who knows, maybe I'll finally be able to know how it feels to kiss him.

I'm unable to look him in the eye after the impure thoughts going through my mind.

"Are you, Sam, and Francesca coming straight from the store?" he asks, pulling me out of my head.

"Sam was able get us out early. He's picking us up, we should be there by seven."

Tobias's smile brightens up the room. "Sounds great. Looking forward to it." The tip of his dress shoe bumps into mine. I was so caught up in my fantasy, I hardly realized how close we were.

A knock on the door pulls us apart. He clears his throat and waves the teacher in. Her class flows inside. The teacher lingers just outside the door. Tobias calls me over and introduces me to Ms Goodwin. I just missed having her as a teacher, turns out she started the year after I graduated elementary school.

I take a seat by the tree and the ornaments, out of the way, so that Tobias can do what he needs with the class first.

"Boys and girls," he says, clapping his hands in rhythm to get their attention.

The class mimics the sound, but not in sync. The kids in the class look to be around Marabelle's age. My chest tightens. I hate not talking to Piper, because those two kids of hers mean the world to me. Trying to shake the thought, my attention lands back on the class.

"Class, today we have a special guest. This is my..." He stops for a moment, his words catching me off guard. In my head I'm trying to find the right wording too. We haven't kissed yet, so does that make us anything at all? Are we just friends? Does caring about someone more than friends make them more?

"My girl, Kasey."

I choke on my spit but cover it with a cough. His girl? I've never been referred to as someone's girl. Some would say that's possessive, but the tone in which he said it was soft, and I know that's not how he meant.

"She's here to help us decorate our tree. Who loves decorating for the holidays?" he asks.

All the kids, including me, raise our hands. Tobias turns, a joyful look on his face. The kids start chatting amongst themselves in hushed whispers of excitement. A select few stay silent waiting for Tobias to instruct them on what to do next.

"Before we start, I'm going to quiz you on a few terms. Who's ready?"

The entire class raises their hands again. Even with the side chatter, every single eye stays on him. I find myself glued to him, as well. He gives them all his eye-wrinkling smile. You can tell how much he loves his job.

"What does..." He stalls, while they all sit on the edge of their seats. "Largo mean?"

A little redheaded girl in the very last row nearly throws her arm out of her socket, she raises it so fast. Waving it back and forth she impatiently waits to get chosen.

"Zoey," he calls out to her.

"Loud!" she shouts.

"Yes! Correct!" he says, with a hop in his step. I can't hold back my grin. I'm falling all over again.

"What does it mean to be, piano." He whispers to give them a hint.

Another round of hands shoot up, including Zoey. This time he chooses a young boy sitting front and center. The boy pushes his little round glasses up before speaking. "Soft."

"Beautiful! You guys were really paying attention, weren't you?" Tobias says.

"Of course, we were, Mr Scott," a young dark-haired girl in the center row says. She turns to her friends and they all giggle.

I can't shake my smile. Tobias hops around the room like a bunny while asking them a few more questions. On his way past me he gives a Cheshire grin.

"Alright. Everyone, stand up." He lifts his arms in an upward motion.

Chairs scrape against the cold linoleum as the children all get to their feet. More whispers and giggles carry around the room.

"Let's hear that do, re, mi," he says, settling down behind the piano.

After they finish their warm-ups, I aid Tobias in handing out the ornaments. The kids are eager to decorate. Soft holiday music begins to play in the background. Everyone is chatting, some even come up and ask me questions, and I enjoy answering them.

A familiar tune comes on and all the kids sing along, some using the silly version I remember singing when I was their age.

"Alright, please leave *Batman* out of 'Jingle Bells', and the side commentary out of 'Rudolph'. Let's sing it right."

The kids cackle and one brave soul shouts the line about Joker getting away, and Tobias tries his hardest to stifle his laugh.

I spend most of my morning in the classroom. I understand why Tobias loves teaching music so much, the kids respond well to him. I would stay longer, but Sam needs me at the store. Heading back down the familiar halls we head for the fifth-grade wing. Drawings and projects hang on the walls covering them from top to bottom. Images of me walking down these same halls flash in my head.

"Here we are," he says, stopping in front of Mrs Powell's door. I catch sight of her through the small window. She doesn't look like she's aged a day. There's not one speck of gray in her long black hair.

Tobias knocks. My hands begin to sweat. It's been so long will she even remember me? Standing in front of the woman who opened so many doors for me is overwhelming. I want to grab onto something for support, but before I can, Tobias has the door open and she's staring right at me.

Her eyes widen. "Is that little Miss Kasey Johnson?"

My chin shakes. Swirls of every emotion under the sun circle around me. I don't know whether to cry or smile. She believed in me when I struggled with my words. Sure, in grade one my words were spelt wrong, and my stories were about kittens and bears, but they were my first stories.

Kasey, you are quite the little storyteller, your potential is there, never give up. Her words echoed through my head when I wrote my first novel, and still to this day they are planted there.

Her eyes sparkle with wetness. "Boys and girls," she says, clearing her throat, like the knot is there for her too. "This young woman right here was one of my students when I taught first grade."

She waves me over with a sniffle, attempting to hold herself together for the kids. She throws one arm over my shoulder, with the other she wipes at her face.

"Everyone, say hi to Ms Johnson."

A chorus of, "Hi Miss Johnson," echoes through the room. I give a shy wave and turn my attention back to her.

"Oh dear, your books are superb. I've read them all," she says, reaching for my hand.

"You read them?" I stare at her, blinking my eyes a million miles a minute to clear them.

"I sure did. Your dedication to me was absolutely beautiful." She sniffles.

The eyes of all twenty-something students and Tobias falls upon me. His warm radiating smile heats me up.

"I never would have made it this far if it weren't for you. You encouraged me to keep going, even when I struggled."

Something I've kept to myself was that growing up I was never the smartest kid in class. Reading was a challenge, math was a nightmare, and not retaining information almost kept me back a grade. None of my teachers gave up, but Mrs Powell, she was what pulled me from the wreckage and got me the help I needed.

Her face lights up as she brings me into a hug. Pulling away, she holds me at a short distance. "Why don't you tell the class a little about yourself?" She turns to the kids. "Class, Miss Johnson is an author and has two, almost three, published books."

With a brave face I bare my soul to the class. Every few minutes I examine Tobias's reaction to my struggles, but his grin never falters, not once. There's not even a grimace on his face when I tell them how much extra help I needed to get to where I am today. The love and admiration in his warm kind eyes shouldn't take me by surprise, but it does.

I hope that my story will inspire some of the kids sitting in that room to follow their dreams, no matter how far of a reach they may seem.

Back out in the hallway we head for the parking lot. I'm sad for the day to be over, but I have work soon.

"Kasey Johnson? Is that you?"

CHAPTER 28

I freeze the moment my name leaves the lips of date number twenty-nine. I'm surprised to see Daryl. His long hair is pulled back into a low ponytail. Eyes wide I stare at him. Here under the lights of the elementary school he looks a bit less clingy and a little more like the man I was attracted to upon first inspection.

"Daryl, hey."

Beside me Tobias's hands turn into fists.

"Ah. Tobias Scott. Funny turn of events, huh?" Daryl says as he waltzes over and wraps an unwanted hug around me.

I pat his back gently and wait for the moment when he removes himself from me. His cologne is thick and smells like he bathed in leather.

"How did you two meet anyway?" He pauses for a minute. Realization strikes in his cool blue eyes as he looks at me. "Ah. Stacy. Your mother sure knows how to con someone into a date, huh, Kasey?" He turns to face Tobias. "I mean, Kasey's a catch that's for sure. Am I right?" He nudges Tobias, and it's easy to see he's trying to hold himself together and be professional.

"Wha– what are you doing here?" I ask.

"Oh, this is the part-time gig I told you about, I'm a custodian for a few hours a week. Been here forever."

"What about you?" He's not even hiding the fact that he's taking all of me in, right here in a school. It's making me uncomfortable.

"I was helping Tobias with his music class."

I attempt to smile at Tobias, but he's not having it, his glare says it all. His cheeks are bright and if looks could kill – Daryl wouldn't be standing.

"It was nice to see you again, Daryl, but I have to head off to work."

"Oh right – right, big-time author doing her thang at the bookstore. Keep a tight grip on this one, Tobias, or she might slip from your fingertips the way she slipped from mine."

He pats Tobias on the shoulder. He doesn't say another word to Tobias, nor me as he and I walk out the doors and into the parking lot.

When we're outside I reach for Tobias's hand. "Everything okay?"

"Daryl?" Tobias asks, between clenched teeth.

"I dated him, right before you. One date. It was terrible."

He's still not convinced that everything is okay. His lips are pressed into a straight line, and he's carrying himself tight with emotion. My thoughts immediately jump to everything I know so far about Roxanne. Maybe she cheated on him. Seeing the way his entire body seized up when Daryl reached for me was enough for me to understand what was going through his head. I felt the same way when we ran into Roxanne.

"If it makes you feel any better, I tried to crawl out the bathroom window, only to slip and fall into the toilet."

The side of his lip lifts upwards. "You did what?"

"He was really clingy and I– I panicked," I squeak.

I half expect him to shut down on me, but instead he chuckles.

It's not a full-rounded laugh, but it's something, and the tension in the air eases.

"I'm picturing you attempting to escape."

"If you want to make the picture in your head even funnier, I was wearing reindeer antlers because it was a Christmas theme event at a bar, and there was mistletoe hanging above the bathroom stall. Who does that?"

His grin widens, but not enough to light up his face.

"Anyways, it was bad, and Francesca came to save me."

"The 911 calls."

"Yeah," I whisper.

I hope he's not putting two and two together, that I've dated so many guys prior to him and that every single one was a dud. That I was a dud.

We get to my car, and I lean up against it. What happened prior to Daryl's arrival puts me in an almost dream-like state. I still can't believe I got to see Mrs Powell. I promised to keep in touch, and she gave me her number, and told me to text her when my new book is coming out.

I grab both of his hands and hold on tight. I want him to know that I'm not interested in anyone but him, and how much I appreciated what he did today.

"That was… I can't even describe how it felt to see her again, thank you," I say.

Now I've roped him back in and I've got his full attention. His eyes explore my face, taking in every feature.

"You amaze me more and more every time we're together," I say. "I saw the looks on some of those kids' faces, you helped them see their potential."

For a moment he glances down and kicks the stones on the pavement.

He lifts his head. The love in his eyes has grown significantly. Since our first date he's looked at me as if I was someone special, but it's something more now, like I'm his moon keeping him in place.

"I'm sorry I didn't know what to call us." He averts his gaze again.

"You were worried about that?" I squeeze his hand, and he relaxes at my touch.

"Kind of," he replies.

I want to scoop this man up in my arms and take away the dubiety in his narrowed eyes.

"Your girl sounded kind of nice." My voice dips low into a purr.

His head jolts at the sound, his rigid shoulders loosening. "Really?"

"I like whatever it is we have going on. You're quite honestly the best thing that's happened to me in a long time."

"I couldn't agree more," he says, timidly. "I'm sorry, I got a little weird back there. Daryl's kind of–" Tobias pauses, searching for the right words.

"Over the top? Clingy?"

"Yeah, something like that."

"Well, I don't care much for him. You, Tobias Scott, have my full attention." I grin.

"And you didn't climb out of any bathroom windows," he says, a soft smile growing on his lips.

"No, there was no reason to."

An intense quiet falls between us. I wait for an eye-wrinkling smile, but it never quite reaches. My mind reels because it seems as if he's doubting my feelings for him. Roxanne pops into my head. The bracelet is on my mind, and if I don't ask him about it, I might explode.

"Can I ask you something? Will you promise not to get upset?"

"What's the matter?" Worry lines crease his forehead.

"I saw Roxanne."

His shoulders tense, and brows narrow at me. I slink backward as far as I can go, but I'm stopped by my car.

"I'm sorry, I'm ruining everything by bringing it up."

"Did she say something to you?" His voice is sharp.

"I uh—" Nowhere to go, I'm stuck. I shouldn't have even brought it up.

He brings his hand to my face, resting it gently. "Kace, what's wrong? What did she do?"

"It's stupid."

"Just tell me." He raises his voice in a way I've never heard, and drops his hand to his side, balling it into a fist for the second time.

I wince at his tone. Regret sparkles in his downcast eyes.

"I'm sorry. I saw her at the mall, and she had this present, and it was for you, and – are you exchanging gifts with her?" I pinch the bridge of my nose and shake my head. "I'm screwing everything up."

"No, Kace. No, you're not, it's just I—"

The alarm on his phone goes off and he curses softly. "Shit. I'm sorry, that's my reminder for my meeting. Please trust me when I say there's nothing between her and me anymore. She did some really messed-up things to me. I promise I'll explain, but I can't be late."

"No. It's fine. I'm fine. It's my insecurities again."

He sighs and leans in, pressing a kiss to the top of my head. "Thank you for coming today. I can't wait to see you tomorrow at the concert. You'll still come, right?"

"I wouldn't miss it."

I hate that there are things left unsaid. Today I opened myself up more than I have with anyone, aside from those I grew up with. It was hard, but I hope that in time Tobias can do the same.

"I had a nice time today. It meant a lot that you did that for me with my old teacher. I also enjoyed working with your kids, they seem like a good group. Being here with you, it feels good. I'm sorry I keep bringing up your ex. I can see it's painful, and for that I apologize."

He squeezes my hand. "It feels amazing being with you too. I know I keep asking for time, but would you be okay with a little more?"

"Yeah," I whisper. I lean into him and release a shallow breath.

The heat radiating off him consumes me. I wait for the moment our lips touch, only for them to gently graze the side of my lip, closer to my cheek.

"I'll see you tomorrow," he says into my ear.

I barely get out a word before he walks away. I slip into my car and want to scream out loud or cry. He makes me feel all these things at once, some of it gets me giddy, some gives me impure thoughts, while other things worry me. My world has been turned upside down, and not in a bad way. No one has allowed all these emotions to fill me at once. I just wish the whole Roxanne thing could be resolved.

I turn the key in the ignition and my car makes a strange gargled sound. I knew I shouldn't have brought it today. The cold causes it to freeze up. I wanted more than anything to be here for Tobias, so I took a chance.

There's only one person I trust when it comes to car trouble. Dad. My hands shake as I dial the number. Ignoring my family sounded much easier than reaching out. I'm not going to be prideful, when I can save money by taking it to my dad's friend. He has never once screwed me over.

"Hey, Kace," Dad says, gently.

I tilt my head back against the seat to hold in the tears threatening to fall. Keeping away from Mom was easy, but Dad – it pains me that the idea runs across my mind.

"Dad, I'm sorry to bother you, but I need Nick's number, my car won't start. I'm going to be late for work." My shoulders fall and I rest my head on the top of the steering wheel.

It sounds like Dad is in a wind tunnel, another voice questions who is on the phone, I cringe, he's with Mom. "You know what, never mind, I'll see if I can–"

"Kace, I got it. I'll call the tow truck and Nick. He'll have it fixed in no time. I'll come pick you up, so you're not stranded."

I lift my head and rest it back on the headrest behind me.

"Where are you? I'll be there soon."

I sigh, I hate asking for his help, but cave anyway. I give Dad my location and hang up, then I call Sam to let him know my ETA. I sit in the lot for twenty minutes before the tow truck and Dad pull into the lot. After handing the driver my keys and getting it set up to take to Michael's shop, I get in the car with Dad. It's awkward for the first few minutes while we put on our seat belts, and he starts up his old Toyota.

"So, Mom says you haven't spoken to her." And here we go.

I sigh. "Since when are you and Mom talking?" I use air quotes around the word talking. I can hope it's only that, but the elephant in the car says differently.

"Well, your mom and me…"

"You what?" My blood boils while I wait for an answer. I'm on fire as I grip the soft seat below me.

"We're having an affair, I guess you could say."

My words are zapped into an endless void. So many things I want to say but have to try my best to hold back.

"We want to be a family again, and…"

A crazy sounding chuckle escapes my quivering lips. "A family? Do you have any idea what those two put me through daily? We can never not be a dysfunctional family."

Dad pulls up to the store. He opens his mouth, but I don't let him get another word in.

"Thank you. Let me know when the car is ready."

I bite back the tears and slam the car door. Inside the store Sam's eyes follow me. I try to smile, but he's already caught my frown. As I bend down to put my things in the locker below the register, my phone chimes.

I just saw one of my students. She asked when Miss Johnson was coming back. The kids really loved you (me too). Thank you again.

A swarm of butterflies dance in my stomach, the tears fade, and my heart is light again.

Sam touches my shoulders. "You okay?"

I look up. "Yeah. I think I will be."

CHAPTER 29

*F*rancesca comes bouncing out of her room. I catch her skipping back and forth past the bathroom. She grabs the fabric of her black dress in her fist and lifts her hand in the air, striking a pose. I'm in awe of how her curves look in that dress. Around her neck sits a beautiful Christmas tree scarf she made herself. She's stunning. The subtle makeup job she did looks fierce, yet natural, and her curls sit perfectly tight against her shoulder.

"Damn," I say, peeking over the small makeup mirror. "Even I'd kiss you!"

Francesca chuckles. She lets go of her dress, then takes in my appearance. I'm a mess. I can't even keep my hands steady to put on my makeup. The only two things on my mind involve an explosive kiss, and the other is Mom starting on me. This would be so much easier if the first option was the only one.

"Girl, why aren't you dressed?" Francesca folds her arms at her chest, glaring at me.

"My makeup looks terrible."

I stare at myself in the mirror again. I twist side to side to get a better look. I hate the tiny specks of pimples that have popped up on my right cheek. I tried covering them with a concealer, but it didn't work.

Her footsteps catch my attention and I avert my eyes back to her.

"Why do you look as if you're going to have a panic attack?" Francesca asks.

She pushes my hand away, taking the powder brush, and sits beside me on the edge of the porcelain tub. My makeup mirror is propped up on the closed toilet seat. Standing to put on my makeup was too hard, because my knees are shaking as much as my hands.

I close my eyes as she pats my face with some more makeup.

"Sweetheart, you're shaking. What's going on?"

I place my hands between my legs to get them to stop. She puts the brush down and rests her hand over my bare leg. It's not awkward or weird, we've known each other too long for that. I'm only in my corset and my black lace underwear.

"I've never seen you this nervous before."

I sigh. "I'm afraid I'm going to screw this entire thing up. He was so withdrawn at school, like he was afraid to love me. Then Daryl showed up and you could feel the jealousy rolling off him. What if he's still hung up on Roxanne? I can't go through another Lloyd situation again."

I go to rub my face and pause. I don't have time to mess up the makeup, Sam should be here in twenty minutes.

"Men get scared too. He looks at you with such admiration, he can't pull his eyes away. From what I've heard from Sam is that she would beg him to be with her, he'd fall hard, and then she'd pull back. And it wasn't only once. I mean you didn't hear that from me, but that can really mess someone up. Maybe he's being extra cautious with his heart this time around," she suggests.

Something in my head clicks. "It makes sense, but why can't he tell me that then?"

"Is it easy for you to talk about Lloyd?"

I lower my head, shaking it lightly. "No. Even after all this time, it's still hard to talk or even think about. I don't love him anymore, but that doesn't mean I don't feel betrayed and that I'm not..." I pause. "I'm being cautious too."

"See, give the man some time. Okay? Don't stress. Tonight, is going to be amazing. I mean what Hallmark movie did we step into?" She wiggles her brows.

I shove her playfully.

Her shoulders shake with laughter. "Tonight, you and I are going to have the time of our lives. We're going to celebrate our favorite holiday with two awesome men. Forget about Roxanne, don't worry about your mom. This is your night to be with Tobias. Plus who knows, maybe you'll get that kiss you've been dying to steal from him."

"At church?"

She winks. "Hey, you never know. Now let's finish getting you ready for your prince. Remember, Cinderella's night may have ended at midnight, but your story can rock into the wee hours of the morning."

"Oh my God." I chuckle.

I hold my stomach from the laughter. Everyone needs a Francesca in their life, someone to pull them from diving too deep. Anything is possible tonight. Afterwards, she is going to Sam's, leaving the apartment open and empty for us to come back to. The thought alone sent me into a frenzy this morning. I ended up getting a full wax during my lunch break. I've never done something like that before. It hurt like hell, but I wanted to be prepared for anything.

I glance at the mirror on the back of the bathroom door. It's partially covered with a few bathrobes, but my reflection is still there. It's hard for me to be confident, I've been struggling for years. If I was never good enough for my family, how could I be for someone else? But tonight, there's a small sliver of hope lingering in the girl staring back at me.

I take one last peek at the long-sleeved red dress. I used to be afraid of wearing something so short. My thighs aren't super-model thin, but somehow in these heels and dress, they look perfect.

I step out of the bathroom. Sam's eyes lift from his spot on the couch. His mouth drops as he stands. I've never worn more than regular old jeans or khakis at work. He doesn't look so bad himself, in a simple black tux with a hint of blue peeking out from his button down.

Francesca stands from her spot. In her heels she matches his tall lean body. Her reaction mirrors Sam's, jaw drop and everything. I roll my eyes and allow a smirk to fall through my pressed lips.

"I'm sorry, Sam, but I may leave you for my best friend. Look at her," she says, pretending to drool over me.

He displays a wide grin. "I think Tobias would be pretty upset."

At the mention of his name my face heats up like the Christmas yule log. Francesca takes a few giant strides across the room and takes her arm in mine.

"You two will be happy together. She's my date tonight."

I lean into her, resting my head on her shoulder. Her enthusiasm and excitement gives me all the confidence I need to get me through the next few hours.

CHAPTER 30

*W*e pile into Sam's classic red Mustang. I lean forward between them as we round the corner to the church.

"Where'd you get the nice wheels?" I ask.

"My dad and I built it together. When he passed away it was in his will for me to have it. The car holds many great memories for me."

After all these years working with him, I still don't know that much about his family life. We've discussed college, our love for books, and other likes and interests. We never really dove into our family.

He parks down the street from the church. It's crowded and I'm surprised Sam found a decent spot. It's good he did because the winter chill is dipping down below the twenties tonight.

Once inside we follow the eager crowd to the basement level. The lighting is dim, allowing the glow of the Christmas lights to illuminate the room. There's a small stage and metal chairs set up in rows facing the front. The chairs have red ribbons tied into bows on the backs. Christmas poinsettias are set at the side of each row. In the front corner to the right of the stage sits a small Christmas tree decorated in beautiful white lights.

I scan the room. "It looks amazing in here."

"Tobias did most of it. He and his mom hand make a lot of the decorations," Sam says. He's probably seen it all before, but still stares in awe at its beauty.

Tobias's love and dedication for church, music, and his job fill my heart with a joy I didn't know was missing.

Sam offers to take our jackets, while we go and find ourselves a seat. Francesca pulls me forward, leading me to the front row. I want to tug her back and go hide in the last row, but she has other ideas. She gets us seats to the left side of the stage, right in front. The stage isn't that high off the ground, it's just below waist level.

"Front row?" I ask, raising a brow.

"So he can see how radiant you look tonight and undress you with his eyes." She snickers.

I hush her. "We're in a church." I chuckle.

"Like that would stop me," she says then puckers her lips.

Sam comes over as the thick red curtain pulls apart, revealing Mr Scott. He's as handsome as Tobias, all dressed up in a festive tux, with a red shirt nestled underneath, and a cute Santa tie.

"Good evening, folks, and welcome to our annual Christmas concert. As always, we will begin with some beautiful music sung by my son, followed by our youth choir, then retreat to the hall for a night of dining and dancing. My two favorite things."

The crowd laughs. He goes into a speech thanking everyone who made the night possible. When he introduces Tobias a few people whistle, most just clap. Francesca and Sam hoot and holler, and I can't help smiling at their antics.

My leg shakes as he walks across the stage from the far right. An acoustic guitar is strapped around his shoulder. He takes in his surroundings, his eyes scanning each face on his way over. I'm fixated on the confidence radiating from him. It's a complete change in who he became in the parking lot for those last few seconds we were together yesterday.

When he finds what he's looking for, he's glowing. Dimples form on his cheeks as his lips tick upward into a smile.

"Hello, everyone," he says, a slight pep to his normally deep voice. Did I make that happen?

"I'm Tobias Scott. You might know me from the five o'clock service. I hope it's okay that I play a few songs for you before the real event begins. Let's start with a prayer."

When he concludes, he immediately goes into a rendition of "Silent Night". Candles are being passed around. His voice fills the entire place, giving me tiny goosebumps, not only on my arm, but my entire body.

I'm not the only one affected by his voice. There's a woman a few rows behind me, moved to tears. I catch sight of Mom and Dad on the right side a few rows back. Mom's eyes are shut tight as she sings, like she's praying. I clench my hands into fists, my blood boiling deep in my veins. Francesca's soft touch pulls me from sinking further. I turn, taken aback by the hungry look in Tobias's eyes.

He's captured the hearts of everyone in the room. I wonder how he does that. All he has to do is smile and others gravitate towards him.

For a few seconds he closes his eyes while he sings his heart out. When they flutter open and land back on me, there's a fire in them. Every evil thought that has entered my head, dissipates like a morning fog rolling away.

The entire place erupts in applause the moment he's done.

"I've got a few more songs for all of you. Before I continue, I want to invite someone very special up on this stage."

I gasp, as Francesca grabs my hand, holding tight. Her shriek leaves an echoing ring in my ear, but her supportive action helps calm me. I can't move and I'm afraid if I blink this will all be a dream.

168

"If she's comfortable with it, I'd love to sing it with her. I don't know this song as well as she does, but I've been practicing my heart out for the last twenty-four hours."

Soft laughter fills the room. I'm not sure whether I should laugh with them or cry.

"When she sang this in my classroom the other day, I had to learn it. It's called 'My Song for You.'"

There's an array of awws in the audience. He rests his guitar on the stand beside the mic. My attention lingers on only him. I take in his appearance. A freshly pressed black suit with a maroon button-down underneath. He's not wearing a tie and the top two buttons are popped up, revealing a small patch of chest hair.

Everyone's eyes follow him right to me. He reaches out for my hand. My brain is running on autopilot as I take it without hesitation. When I get to my feet he leans in and whispers into my ear, "I'm sorry. I really wanted to sing it with you. I hope it's okay."

He holds me at arm's length to check with me. My eyes are having trouble focusing that he's so close and everyone is staring.

"I understand if you don't want to–"

I grab hold of his shoulder. Standing on my toes, I whisper, "I want to, because it's with you."

His shoulders loosen below my grip. Christmas keeps looking better and better.

"You know you look absolutely beautiful tonight," he whispers.

As he pulls away his fingers gently glide down the skin of my arm, I shiver at his touch. My trembling hands fold into his.

When I step on the stage, I find Sam and Francesca. Them making googly eyes at each other is far better than having to see my parents.

Tobias picks up his guitar and strums the first few notes. "Just look at me," he says, covering the mic with a free hand. "It's only us."

It takes me a few seconds to get used to all eyes on me. I start off low, but the minute our voices come together I'm able to bring it up a notch. I'm not a professional singer by any means, my pitch is off, but no one seems to care, including Tobias.

When the song ends, he gives me a quick kiss on the cheek. If we weren't standing up here in front of the entire congregation, my parents, and his, I'd have turned slightly to crash our lips together.

CHAPTER 31

*H*e performs four more songs and then exits the stage. The choir goes next. I keep searching for Tobias, but I assume he's helping get everything set for the evening.

When the show ends, Sam leads us through the church towards the cafeteria. It's large and reminds me of a school lunchroom. The decorations are just as immaculate here as they are inside. White lights are hung around the border of the dimly-lit room, and beautiful red and green candles sit in the center of each round table.

Along the back wall is a buffet. An aroma of meats and sweet desserts mix around the room. Christmas music plays softly in the background over the murmuring voices.

As I pull out a chair at a table in the center of the room, someone taps my shoulder. Dad stands behind me with a smile on his face. He looks happy, but there's not a spark in his eyes. My shoulders grow heavy, knowing it's partially my fault.

"You were wonderful up there," he says, softly.

He stares down at his feet, his smile faltering. "Your car should be ready by Tuesday at the latest. I'll bring it to you."

"Thank you."

I appreciate his help, but at the same time I need tonight to be free of my family's problems. My shoulders continue to bear weight. I can't focus on this right now.

"Kace, I'm–"

I hold up my hand. "Not tonight, Dad, please." I'm finding it hard to swallow.

Over his shoulder I catch sight of Tobias entering through the main doors. He scans the room but is bombarded by church members. He looks everywhere but at them.

"You're right. Enjoy yourself," Dad says.

"You too."

He turns and my heart squeezes so tight that it hurts. I hate pushing him away. I have to catch my breath before I look up. Tobias is easy to spot, he towers over the group he's chatting with. I take a few steps forward hoping that maybe he'll catch sight of me.

Somehow through the crowd he finds me. He places a hand on the shoulder of the gentleman he's speaking to, then steps around him. Like a man on a mission, he struts forward, blocking out everything around him, except me.

Within seconds his body crashes into mine. I love how he puts every ounce of his love into his hugs. I never want to let go.

"Thank you for sharing that moment with me." He tickles my ear with his words.

I stare up, unblinking. "I loved being up there with you."

As he opens his mouth, Francesca comes bounding over. "Nice concert, church boy."

"You were great up there, man," Sam comments, holding on to Francesca.

"Thanks. Glad you guys enjoyed it. Do you mind if I steal Kasey away for a minute before we grab some food?"

Francesca's brows raise. "And where are you two lovebirds headed?"

Tobias leans into me, tightening his grip. "I'm taking her for a walk, if that's okay?"

"Yeah, boy, get it!" she says, a little too loud. Some of the guests turn, presenting her with dirty looks.

"Don't do anything I wouldn't do," she teases.

Sam tickles her sides and pulls her away. He glances over his shoulder and mouths *Sorry*. Tobias's shoulders shake with laughter.

"I'm sorry, if you're hungry we can–"

"No," I cut him off. "No. I want to go with you."

We grab our coats at the coat check, then walk out through the back entrance of the church into a small courtyard. When the door closes the distant voices and music vanishes as if we've stepped into another world. The snow falls in a gentle whisper over the grounds of the church. Everything around us has specks of white draped over it like a blanket.

"Wow. This church is gorgeous. You really make this night so special for everyone."

I let go of his hand to explore the small enclosed space. The snow cracks under my feet as I move forward. In the center is a garden, void of flowers for this time of year, but the trees overhanging the area are covered in white twinkling lights.

I look at him, tilt my head back, and let the cold flakes tickle my face. When my eyes meet his, I'm confused by his passive expression. Unmoving, he presses his lips into a straight line. My stomach drops, this can't be good.

"Hey, are you okay?"

I step into the comfort of his warm arms. He nods, his eyes exploring every inch of my body pressed into his.

"I'm perfect. That's the scary part." He laughs.

He lifts his hand and gently caresses the side of my cheek with his thumb. My pulse drums in my ears. Warmth blankets my body from a single touch.

"Scary good or bad?" I cringe.

"Good." The word hardly leaves his lips.

He lowers his head and touches his forehead to mine. Our noses graze ever so slightly. I shiver from his touch.

"So, did I live up to your expectations up there? I mean I'm much sexier than Shawn, and my voice can go an octave higher," he teases.

"And Shawn never would have invited me to sing with him." Amusement dances between us, as he nudges his head ever so slightly against mine. His lips part for me and I'm hungry to taste them.

He takes a deep breath. "I better do this before you freeze to death on me out here."

I don't have a chance to blink before his lips meet mine. I'm rooted in place as I absorb the shock that radiates through me. I'm on fire, I've never felt a flame quite as hot as this. It's only a simple kiss, but it ignites every sensation inside of me. I want to press further, but hold back, because it's not appropriate to shove my tongue down his throat at church.

"Church tongue?" he says into my lips, like he's reading my mind.

Laughter ripples through me. He pulls away resting his head on mine. He takes me back to our Adam Sandler marathon on my sister's couch. Although the night is plagued with bad memories, there are the good ones too. It was the night I truly got to know the man I'd fallen for.

"Wow. That was…"

"Yeah," I whisper.

"To be continued later?"

"Yes please." My voice cracks.

Laughter shakes him. I bury my face into his chest, while he holds me.

"We should get inside. I fear Francesca will start telling everyone we've gone off to do things inside a church that should not be done."

I snort, then cover my mouth, but his smile helps keep the embarrassment at bay. I turn ready to head back inside when he pulls me into him. I wait for him to ignore everything he stands for and just flat out kiss me, tongue and all, but he doesn't. He stares at me for a good long thirty seconds. There's more he wants to say. He's trying to form the right words.

"I more than like you, Kasey." With a free hand he scratches the back of his neck.

"Me too. I mean, I more than like you too."

He closes his eyes and releases a breath. "I'm so glad to hear you say that." His voice breaks.

I straighten myself up and lift onto my toes, planting a soft kiss to his lips. Is it later yet?

CHAPTER 32

$\mathcal{I}$s it cliché to say I feel like I'm floating on cloud nine? Because I totally am. The kiss lingers in my head as he spins me around on the dance floor. I'm in a daze and fear that if someone pinches me, I'll wake.

The small open space between the tables allows for a limited number of people on the dance floor. Francesca and Sam have joined us, but they are stuck in their own bubble of love. Over Tobias's shoulder I catch Francesca doing her signature dance move, the sprinkler to "Rocking Around the Christmas Tree". Sam embraces her wackiness, by mimicking her moves.

I'm surprised Mom hasn't come to steal Tobias away, or to pretend to be proud of my achievements. She and Dad are nowhere to be found. It's sad to say that them not being here gives me some form of relief.

"So, I have a question for you?" Tobias whispers in my ear.

We're dancing along to a cover of a popular Christmas song. There's not many people dancing now, it's getting late, and a lot of folks have left already.

"Yeah?"

"Will you spend Christmas Day with my family and me?"

My mouth falls open. "Really? You want to spend Christmas with me?"

He leans down and kisses me. It's soft, gentle, and totally church appropriate.

"I know I mentioned it before, but I officially want you to come as my girlfriend."

I want to cry and smile at the same time. It's silly, but he makes me feel all these emotions at once. "I'd love to."

His kisses get better and better. He slides behind my back and he dips me. I hold on tight as laughter consumes me.

"And will you come with me to Christmas Eve with my family? As my boyfriend of course."

He lifts me and pulls me to his chest, running his hands through my hair. His lips then gently glide along my ear, as he whispers, "Of course. You're my girl. Right, Kace?"

I pull back, only enough to see his face. I'm blinded by love. Literally. He's all I see in this room full of people.

"Christmas just got a little brighter," I say, meaning it.

I love this holiday, but it's been hard every year. Between my breakup with Lloyd last holiday, and the way I'm treated when my family gets together, I shouldn't love Christmas, but I do. There's something magical about this time of year, and now it just got even more so.

"It sure did. Are you almost ready to leave?" Tobias asks, in a seductive tone.

The edge in his voice sends chills down my spine, leaving impure images dancing around my mind.

"Yeah."

His lips glide across my ear. "I'll go get our coats."

He squeezes my hand and walks away. I drift over to Francesca and Sam, who are slow dancing. Her arm is carefully placed around his neck, and her eyes never leave his. Her mouth moving a mile a minute, and he just watches her with a fondness I've only ever seen portrayed in movies.

"Hey, guys, Tobias and I are going."

Francesca pulls away from Sam, a wide grin taking over her face. I shake my head at her, as if to tell her don't start. I give her and Sam a quick hug as Tobias comes back with our coats. We travel around the room saying goodbye to almost half the guests. Some have their jackets on ready to leave too. I doubt I'll remember everyone's names, but I smile politely and respond to questions.

His parents are at the door saying goodbye to guests as they leave. His mom finds me in the crowd and her face lights up as we step forward.

"Did you enjoy yourself, sweetie?" she asks.

I take in one last view of the room. "Everything was perfect. You both did an amazing job putting it all together."

"Maybe next year you can help us. I'm sure Tobias would like that." She winks at her son.

He shifts on his feet, then turns his attention to me. I respond and he smiles. "What do you say, Kasey? How would you like to be on the decorating committee next year?"

"I couldn't imagine a better way to spend next Christmas."

I mean every single word of it. We hold each other's stare for several seconds before his mom clears her throat. Her smile is radiant.

"That sounds wonderful. We can't wait to have you," she says, as she leans in for a hug. I swallow hard to release a knot that's building in my throat. This is how a mother should be, her love for her son and others has me choked up.

"I'm so glad you could come tonight."

I back away from her and stare up at Mr Scott. He and Tobias are similar in height, but his dad has an inch or two on him. His friendly smile is all it takes for me to feel like he's already accepted me into his life.

"You too, Mr Scott."

"Please, call me William. I hope to see you again soon."

I nudge Tobias with a smile. "That's up to this one." I bump my hip into him. His soft smile and grasp on my body calms me.

"You'll definitely be seeing her a lot. I invited her to Christmas." He's still fixated on me, never straying to look at his parents, while he says it.

His mom claps her hands as if it's the best news she's heard all day. "Oh, Kasey, I'm so glad you are coming. It almost feels like you're already a part of our family. I can't wait for you to meet everyone."

My face burns. "I can't wait either."

Suddenly, every doubt I had about his feelings floats away. His arm constricts, holding on, like he never wants to let go. I could get used to this.

CHAPTER 33

*O*utside the white flakes falling from the sky glisten in the light of the streetlamps. Tobias grabs my hand and leads me towards his truck. He's parked across the street. Thankfully it's not a far walk, because the temperature has dropped, and the snow has gotten a little deeper since we were outside last.

We rush across the empty street. He takes me around to the passenger side and spins me round, pinning me to the truck. I stop breathing at the sight of his starving eyes looking as if he was going to devour me.

He holds my face in his long warm hands and then leans forward. The second his lips meet mine I open my mouth to let him in. Kissing him under the light of the lamp on the darkened street with snow falling is absolutely perfect, almost storybook perfect.

Our heads move in sync, like we know each other's next move. I wrap my arms around his neck, pulling myself up to get closer. Our lips break apart and bounce back several times, needing to come up for air, but only for a second.

"Come on, let's get going. I'm not quite done with those lips yet."

I smirk as he reaches behind me and pulls open the door. I hop inside the truck and with trembling hands clasp the seat belt in place. With a jump in his step, he hops into the truck. He gives a quick glance and smile before turning on the car and pulling out of the spot.

By the time we get back the weather has gotten significantly bad. I text Francesca warning her. She replies right away, saying they had just left and were on their way to Sam's apartment.

Tobias parks near the curb in front of the house. Before I can unbuckle, he's around the other side opening the door for me. We barely make it to the door before he presses me against the outside wall of the house.

His kisses are urgent, like he's been waiting his whole life for this one moment. I sure have been. I've never been regarded in such a way that made me feel loved. One touch from Tobias and the world around us disappears, making everything else slip away.

Once inside, we can't keep our hands off each other. He carefully throws my coat to the floor. I toss my shoes, and trip over my feet. He catches me before I can bring both of us down. Between laughter and heavy breathing, I try to guide him to my room.

He strips his jacket and we stumble together, limbs tangled, messy kisses, all the way to my room. I shut the door with my foot, never once pulling away from him. His mouth tastes fresh, like the first moments after you brush your teeth.

He pulls back, leaving my body cold and untouched. He bends forward and tugs at his shoes.

I glance over my shoulder, pulling my hair up. "Help me undo my dress?" I ask.

With only one shoe he trudges over to me, almost tripping on his way. Toeing off his remaining one, he continues towards me. His fingers glide up the side of my arm. He makes small circles on my shoulder, causing a deep shiver. His hot breath nips at the nape of my neck. I roll my head moaning as he holds on to me with one hand, while unzipping my dress with the other.

A low guttural moan vibrates my chest as he nibbles at my ear. Between my legs becomes a pool of moisture. He starts pulling my dress from my body, shimmying it down my mid-section, then my legs. As he follows the dress down, he kisses every inch of me, up till the panty line near the small of my back.

I step out of the dress and turn to face him. I half kiss, half concentrate on unbuttoning his shirt. I let it fall open, but leave it on, as we crash onto the bed. I almost lose my footing again and he catches me. I giggle, from my clumsiness. He smirks.

"I'm in no rush, Kace. Just kissing you and your body is good enough for me. I'll go as slow as you need me to."

He plants tiny kisses along my jawline, which gets another moan out of me.

"I'm okay with going slow," I whisper, closing my eyes to take in all the sensations that ripple through me.

"We have all the time in the world," he whispers, laying on his side to face me.

"It's not quite how it is in fiction, is it?"

He chuckles. "Nah, but I like it this way. It's not perfect, yet it is at the same time. I love the way your cheeks are always bright red around me." He runs the pad of his thumb over my warm cheek. "I love that you're not trying to be something you're not. You're honest, and lovable."

Carefully he moves his fingers to my stomach, drawing circles close to my panty line. He takes in my black corset, lifting it only slightly to rub the spot underneath, finding his way closer to my swollen breasts. They ache in a way they never have before.

I turn my neck to get a better view. He's got his free hand propping his head up, while his other hand works some magic. I take in his body, it's exactly how I imagined, not overly muscular, but perfect in every way. I run my hand down the center of his dark-haired chest. He releases a hiss and arches so slightly as I dance along the edge of his unbuttoned dress pants.

Eyes ablaze he continues to draw the lazy circles around my lower stomach. His finger slips just under the underwear line. I gasp.

"Is this okay?" he asks.

I reach for his hands, allowing him to lightly place his fingers below my underwear. He tenses, so I pull him back slightly and wrap his arm around to my backside.

"It's fine. Wherever you want to explore me, Tobias. I'm yours."

Our lips meet with urgent kisses.

"You're breathtaking, Kace," he says, his eyes roaming over my half-naked body.

I push into him, his hardness seeping through his pants. What I wouldn't give to just reach down and take him. *My God, where did that come from?* I laugh to myself.

I plant tiny pecks along his bearded jawline. "If every day feels this good, I can't wait to see what our future brings."

"I'll do my best to make you feel this way every day."

I reach out, grab his hand, and place it between us, inside my underwear. His eyes widen as I press his hand further down. My entire body shudders at his touch.

"Oh, Kasey," he moans, at the sensation of how wet I am. "Can I?"

"Mmm," I say, allowing him to create small circles against my center. Bucking my hips, I let out a soft moan as I reach my climax.

"Do-do you want me to help you out?" I ask, suddenly feeling shy.

"Tonight, it's all about you," he says, diving back in and giving me one more pleasurable climax.

"Do you want to spend the night with me?"

A smile crosses his face. "I'd love to."

He retreats his hand from my underwear and grins.

"All the time in the world, right?" I ask.

"As long as you'll have me," he whispers.

I tip my chin and open my mouth to his. Our tongues swirl around each other. I never want this to end. As much as I'd love for him to explore my body more, and how much my body craves it, I need to be kind to my heart. Tobias does as well.

He excuses himself to use the bathroom and while he's gone, I lay there with my hand low on my stomach re-imagining his hand touching me again.

He returns with a smile. His shirt is buttoned back up and I wonder if he plans on sleeping in his clothes. That can't be comfortable.

"Are you going to sleep in that?" I ask, brows raised.

"Well, I only have my boxers…"

"I'm okay with that."

He smirks. "Kasey Johnson, you're something else."

I smile as he unbuttons his shirt again. I prop my head on my hand and ogle him shimmy down his dress pants. He folds them neatly and places the pile on the chair in the corner of the room. His red and green Christmas boxers with the Grinch on them make me chuckle. He looks down at them and back up at me.

"I needed some extra Christmas spirit under the plain black."

He settles in next to me and I throw the blanket over both of us. I rest my head on his chest and listen to the sound of his heart beating as he holds me tight. He doesn't say much more as his breathing slows. I tuck myself in closer to him and he kisses my head.

"I could get used to this," he says.

"How are you even real?"

Embarrassed, I smack a hand against my mouth. His body bounces from his laughter.

"I'm not perfect, Kasey. I can't guarantee that there won't be points in this relationship where you are going to want to kick me in the balls, but I will try to make this worth it."

I crane my neck to get a better kissing angle. I note his heavy eyelids, and relaxed posture. Even with tired eyes he leans down and presses his lips to mine. My entire body quivers from his touch. I can't help imagining what it will be like when I'm ready to have all of him.

I pull away and rest my head on him again. He squeezes me. His breathing calms almost immediately.

"Goodnight, Kasey." It's barely a whisper out of his mouth. The roughness in his voice is sexy and soothing.

"Goodnight, Tobias," I reply, as my heavy eyelids flutter closed.

CHAPTER 34

*U*nder messy sheets, I wake, blinking away the sleep. The scent of a Christmas breakfast hits my nose. I'm consumed with the mouthwatering smell of fried potatoes, sweet cinnamon, and sticky maple syrup. My senses tingle, and my eyes grow weepy, with one of the few good family holiday memories I have.

When Mom and Dad still lived under one roof, Dad would cook an immaculate Christmas breakfast. It was my favorite, and sometimes he'd even let me flip the pancakes. I wipe a rogue tear gathering at the corner of my eye. Only one other person reminds me of breakfast.

I shoot up into a sitting position. Brunch? Tobias? The memories of last night's touches come zooming back into my head. I place my finger where his hand laid only a few short hours ago, and shiver at the image of the memory. Familiar giggles erupt from the other room, and I pull my hand away.

I throw the covers off and shimmy on my favorite pair of black yoga pants with the pink fold-on top with another old boy band T-shirt from when I was thirteen. I somehow believe that Tobias wouldn't care if I walked into the room wearing baggy sweats and an oversized shirt. Plus, he saw me in practically nothing, so I doubt I could scare him away at this point.

Opening the door, I conclude that my suspicions were correct. My stomach rumbles with hunger as I trudge forward towards the new and welcoming scene before me.

Tobias and Francesca are crammed in our tiny kitchen. Tobias is at the stove, while Francesca stands beside him. Her voice is drowned out by the crackles of bacon. She gently shoves him, laughter filling the room.

"Good morning, sleepyhead."

I turn towards the small table just outside the kitchen, and spot Sam setting the table. My cheeks grow warm. Sam, who is technically my boss, is standing in my living room like it's an everyday occurrence. I'm sure my hair shows off that I've endured a wild night. Sam glances up and smirks.

From the kitchen, Tobias and Francesca turn. His face lights up when he sees me.

"What's going on?" I rub at the sleep that still lingers in my eyes.

Francesca comes around the entryway to the kitchen, and stands beside Sam. He pulls her close and when she tilts her head up to him, I swear there's a real spark between their bodies. Their love for each other leaves a warm happy flutter inside me.

"Your boy." She points over her shoulder to Tobias, who is pretending not to listen. Even from the back, I notice the smile, as his ears lift slightly.

"He woke me from a peaceful slumber. Where I dreamt of sweet things." She looks doe-eyed at Sam, then turns back to me. "He asked me what you have for breakfast. Then, because we didn't have your favorite hash browns, he pleaded with me to go to the store with Sam and come for breakfast. Oh, and made us retrieve clothes, since he and Tobias live a block away from each other."

Sam places his hands on Francesca's shoulders and shakes her playfully. She elbows him and he grunts through some laughter.

"It was no problem, Kasey. I didn't mind at all. I was not passing up breakfast, especially when Tobias makes it."

The bacon pops and Tobias curses. He gives another smirk as he turns back to check on the food.

"So yeah, this was all his idea," she says with a yawn. "After this meal I'm taking a nap. At least you got to sleep in."

I run a hand through my unkempt hair, and tug at the small knot at the bottom. "What time is it?"

"Time for brunch," Tobias says from the kitchen.

It isn't a date with Tobias without there being a buffet or brunch. I'm starting to really love brunch.

As I enter the kitchen I notice the time on the stove, it's nearly noon. I haven't slept this late since I was in college. "Oh my God. I'm so sorry…"

He places the netting over the pan and turns to me as he sets the tongs down on the kitty cat spoon holder.

"Why?"

"I never sleep that late."

Tobias chuckles. "Neither do I. I slept until almost ten."

We take a step towards each other. He places one hand around my back and gently kisses the top of my head. The sight of this man standing in my kitchen in tight jeans, a black tee, hair all amiss, and bare feet, I am overwhelmed by a strange pleasure rippling through my body. I could get used to this image.

I take a small step back. "Sorry, I haven't even brushed my teeth…"

His laughter ripples through me. "What are you so worried about? I already told you, you're kind of stuck with me right now. A little crazy hair." He pauses to brush his hands through the strands of hair sticking up. "And morning breath isn't going to scare me away."

The bacon behind him sizzles and smokes. He smiles and

turns back to his cooking. I glance around the room, there's a covered pan with eggs, another one with home fries with all my favorites in it. It's covered in pepper, salt, red and green peppers with onions and it's extra burnt and crisp on the outside. Without even saying anything he finds a way to make my cheeks warm and my heart race.

"Sam, did you pick up my juice?" he asks.

"Of course, it's not brunch without fruit punch."

Francesca snickers as she enters the kitchen and reaches into the fridge to get his juice. "This brand, right?" She holds it high for him. On the wrapper that hugs the container is a picture of the Sesame Street characters and I can't help laughing.

"You had juice on our first date."

Strong arms grasp my waist from behind and he tugs me back into him. I laugh because his hands at my side tickle.

"Something wrong with a man who drinks juice?" he whispers in my ear.

I put my hands around his neck. I don't remember any of my relationships, especially the one with Lloyd, feeling this natural.

"I think it's sexy," I tell Tobias, my lips lingering over his.

He leans forward and kisses me. The taste of bacon lingers on his lips.

"Have you been sneaking pieces of bacon?" I raise my brow at him as I pull away. He rolls his eyes, pretending that he didn't just get caught.

"I need to make sure it's done."

I laugh. "And is it done, Chef Tobias?"

He chuckles and reaches behind him to grab one of the pieces he put on the plate covered in a paper towel and dangles it over my mouth.

"I don't know, you tell me." He lowers it and then pulls it away teasing me. I lightly punch him in the gut, and he grunts and laughs. Then he lowers it enough for me to take a bite and it's so crispy and delicious that I moan the second it touches my tongue.

"Save that for later, will you?"

I smirk. I truly cannot believe how easy it is to flirt with him. There's more than just liking going on between us. Even though it's only been a few weeks I am truly falling for this sexy man standing in front of me.

CHAPTER 35

𝒥'm waiting for Dad to return my car before I head off to work. I lift my phone to check my messages when Francesca comes barreling into the apartment. She was only working until noon, then going to have lunch with Sam. She slams the door hard enough to shake the apartment walls. I jump and stand, catching sight of her angry red eyes and tearstained cheeks.

I race over and wrap her in my arms. She sobs into my shoulder, and I let her cry it out for as long as she needs. No questions asked.

When she seems more stable, I lead her to the couch and sit down beside her, my arm never leaving her.

She shrugs, staring off towards the window. "Maybe he's not my person."

Everyone knows Francesca to be unreserved and outspoken, but deep down there's a girl filled with a lot of insecurities that stem from her crummy childhood. My mom was always on my case, but her mom was never home.

"Oh no, what happened?"

"It was the dumbest fight," she sobs. Her voice teeters several octaves higher than normal. She wipes furiously at her eyes. "I always spend Christmas Eve with your family. It's tradition. You know how I am about that. Then he said he was only planning on taking me with him to his family." She pauses again. "I got pissed because he made plans for me without asking first. I raised my voice, and it all went downhill from there."

She buries her face inside her hands. "It's only our first Christmas together and already we're arguing on how to split our time."

"That doesn't sound much like Sam. Are you sure there's nothing else going on? I've known him for a while and the only time he gets testy is when something is bothering him."

Sam is a gentle soul, and the one time I saw him mad was when he thought he was going to get fired, because he didn't realize until it was too late that a group of teens stole something. It was one of his first days as assistant manager, and he raised his voice at me. He felt terrible afterwards.

"I don't think there is. Everything was going great too. He's liked me for so long and was relieved that I felt the same way. All those years of flirting and all for it to end over some dumb fight?"

I rest a hand on her back and rub gently up and down. "Did you end it?"

"Well, no, but." She sniffles again and wipes her face. "He said he knew," she rambles. "He knew the moment he showed up at the store that day we went on the double date that it was a sign that we were meant to be."

The last time Francesca had a breakdown was when her mom skipped out on graduation. This breakdown is her way of reaching out because she's afraid he'll leave her on her own like her mom. Under all the silliness is a girl who hurts. She was afraid of our friendship failing too. It took a lot of convincing that I wasn't going anywhere, but eventually she just knew that I was her friend for life.

"I... oh God, Kace, I love him. What have I done?"

She hugs herself and rocks back and forth. The doorbell rings, but we ignore it. If it's Dad, he will text me to let me know he's here. I grab her face in my hands ready to comfort her when the doorbell rings several times in a row.

I sigh. "I'm going to get that. Dad's dropping off my car, maybe it's him. Will you be okay for a moment?"

All she can do is stare at me with a blank look on her face. I kiss her forehead, then stand to go find out who is still ringing the bell. Francesca lays her head down on the arm of the couch. The sadness that surrounds her breaks me. I'm worried enough that I'm debating on calling Sam to tell him I'm not coming in today.

I jog down the stairs and pull open the door. I guess I won't have to call him. Standing in front of me is Sam looking as if he'd been to Hell and back. His glossy eyes tell me that maybe Francesca overreacted. He runs a hand through his messy hair.

"Please tell me she's here. She got home okay, right?" He puts a hand over his face, scrubbing hard enough that his eyes turn red.

"She is. She's really upset."

"Fuck, it's my fault." He stares up at the awning and blinks several times. He shifts his weight once or twice, then glances back at me. "Can I? Can I see her?"

I step aside and allow him to go up the stairs first. He takes three steps at a time. His footsteps are loud with determination. I get to the top of the stairs but decide that I should give them some space instead. The last thing I see is Sam on his knees, holding her face in his trembling hands.

I close the door to the apartment and go back down. As I open the main door, two cars pull up, one being mine. Dad steps out and walks around to the sidewalk, I meet him halfway.

"How is she?" I ask.

His heavy eyes blink. He's probably coming off the night shift at the hospital. He works security there.

"She runs like a champ. Needed a new belt and some other minor adjustments. Also got it inspected since it's due at the end of the month."

My shoulders relax. It will be nice to have a nice warm car to drive to work in. I've been relying on Francesca dropping me off during morning shifts, but also walking back home in the cold if she couldn't get me.

"How much?" I ask.

"It's on me."

"Dad," I growl. "I'm not a teenager anymore, I can pay for my own–"

He holds up his hand to stop me. "Look, I know things haven't been great with the family. I'm in no way trying to use this as an apology but let me do this one thing for you. It was a lot of money and I had it. There's no need to worry."

My body tenses. I don't want to rely on my parents for anything, especially when Mom is involved. Having Dad pay for my car would be another way she could take a jab at me. *Kasey, you're a big girl now, if you can't pay for things yourself then maybe you should contemplate getting a real job.* I can hear it now.

"Fine. Did you tell Mom?"

"No."

I close my eyes briefly to calm my throbbing temples.

"Will you be coming to Christmas?"

Let the fighting begin. Dad's face is relaxed. He doesn't want to argue, and I should know this. I get defensive because I've been defending myself my whole life.

"I'm sorry." I don't want to take it out on him. No matter how docile Dad is, he doesn't deserve to be yelled at.

"Darling, I know you and Mom don't have a great relationship, but she does love you."

My jaw drops. Is he trying to convince himself of that? I hate that there's a knot in my throat strangling my words. Most kids would love that their parents have reconciled, but for me, the divorce was the best thing that happened. Now that they are having this affair, I'm convinced she's feeding Dad lines to say, because she wants to get a rise out of me. It's working. She wins.

"Kace." He reaches out and places a hand on my shoulder. I make the mistake of looking up at him. Tears sting my eyes. "She shows her affection differently. Her nagging is her loving you a little too much. You're her baby…"

"That's bullshit! And you know it."

His eyes widen and he takes a step back. He stands there in thunderstruck silence.

"That woman has never loved me," I bite back. "No matter what I did, from the thirty-one dates, to following her every command as a child and teen, nothing was ever good enough. Not even when I became a *New York Times* bestseller. She didn't even congratulate me." I pause for a moment to collect myself. My hands balling into fists at my side. My nails dig in and I hiss from the pressure.

"Kasey."

"Dad, I've accomplished everything I've ever wanted. I did it all on my own. Don't tell me that she loves me, because deep down you know it's not true."

Dad's eyes shine with sadness, and his lips tremble slightly.

"You have always been there, but you've never done anything to stop her snide remarks. So, I'm sorry if Christmas isn't my favorite part of the year."

"I know," he says.

I shake my head. Dad will always stand on the sidelines, because deep down he's terrified of her. Now that they are together, it makes it harder for him to be on my side. She'll use it against me in some way.

"Thank you for the car. I have to get ready or I'm going to be late."

Dad opens his mouth to say something, but I don't let him. I step back and walk away.

Inside the apartment is quiet. Francesca's door is shut. I dress quickly, then leave, not wanting to interrupt them.

I'm trying to shine a positive light on everything. This year I'll have someone who loves me for who I am. He couldn't care less about my flaws and sees the good in me. Keeping that in mind will help get me through the worst day of the year.

CHAPTER 36

ork should have been the perfect distraction before the shit-show known as Christmas Eve dinner with my folks. It's not. I haven't been able to eat, and between the pains of hunger, I'm nauseous. Mom isn't helping the situation. I've received several texts from her to the point where I had to shut off my phone.

If you had a real job, you wouldn't be working these ridiculous hours. I could use your help getting dinner ready for tonight, try to get off early. Is Tobias still coming? Or did you wreck that too?

I want to bury myself in the stacks of books and get lost. It would be easier to escape if Sam didn't look like someone punched him in the gut. He's usually the one to keep me level-headed when I'm down at work.

The store has been quieter than usual. We have had dribs and drabs of folks coming in looking for last-minute gifts, but other than that it's been a slow and painful day. I stare out the window of the empty storefront. Frost and dew creep up the sides leaving a glistening shimmer reflecting off the streetlamps.

"Hey, Kasey, I need your opinion." Sam stands on the other side of the counter. He runs a hand over his face.

"I know Francesca collects charms for her bracelet." His voice shakes. "Which one will she like better?"

He lays out several charm bangles from her favorite designer on the counter. I scan over each one. Wide-eyed I look up. "Are you planning on returning the ones you don't give her, or…"

"I wanted to be prepared. I sound crazy. I'm in this for the long-haul. What I have with her." He stops to bite his lip. "Never mind, you don't want to…"

I reach out and place my hand over his trembling one. "Hey," I say. He peeks up at me, as I study him closely. He has the same distant look in his eyes that Francesca has had since their fight. The love these two possess for each other is unconditional.

"She's *it*."

My lips twitch, an overwhelming surge of warmth riles through me. "Sam, I believe you."

"I want to make things right. I was in the wrong for what I did to her. God, I was such an asshole." He stops and runs a hand through his freshly trimmed hair. "Mom is sick. Her MS is taking a toll on her body. I wanted to make sure I was there for Christmas. Instead of explaining, I got pissed."

I squeeze his hand as we both gaze over the options he's chosen. *Harry Potter*, *Polar Express*, and her favorite Princess Aurora.

"Does she know about your mom?"

"She does. It was still a shitty excuse for how I behaved. I'm stressed, because when I moved away, I never imagined Mom needing me as much as she does. She's got my aunt, but I should be the one, you know?"

"I get it," I whisper. I release his hand and slide over the *Harry Potter* and *Polar Express* charm. "Give her both, you can save the other for her birthday." He blinks down at the options, then glances back up at me. "I won't be mad if you leave my parents' dinner early. I don't expect anyone to stay through that shit-show."

Francesca is the type of friend that never leaves you hanging. Aside from her demons, her outburst was out of pure love for me, her best friend. She understands what I've gone through, suffered through it with me. All we had was each other for so long. She's afraid to let go, because losing what we have would devastate us both. I never want to come between her happiness. She deserves what Sam wants to offer her. A stable and beautiful relationship. I can't ask her to destroy that over my insecurities.

"My family, they're a little intense."

Laughter fills his lungs, and I relax.

"What family isn't?" he teases.

Sam checks his watch, then looks back up at me. "Time to give the ten-minute warning." He grabs the charms and puts them back into a small box beside the register.

"Thank you, Kasey. Francesca and Tobias are lucky to have you in their lives."

I reach over the counter and nudge him. "That makes you lucky too." I smirk.

Sam chuckles, then retreats to the backroom. I'm lighter after my conversation with Sam, but there's still a nagging tug on my heart that leaves me unsettled.

I tie the last ribbon on the gifts for the kids and pack them away in a paper bag. Lifting them I start to bring them towards the door when there's a soft knock. I fumble with my purse and the bags and turn the knob. I'm blown away by the handsome man standing before me. In a pressed green button-down with his hair slicked back with gel is Tobias.

The bags drop to the ground with a thud. I push them aside with my foot and grab at his collar, pulling him into my room.

His hands are on my hips, and in a matter of seconds the door closes, and I'm spun round, my back resting on the wooden frame. He smells and tastes like Christmas – pine and mint – and I want a taste.

I open my mouth, welcoming him in. He shifts slightly, to allow his hardness to press into me, inches below my stomach. The world sways as he runs his eager hands through my hair. Is it possible for this kiss to be a million times more powerful than our first? God, I want him to take me right here against the door. *Where did that thought even come from?*

My insides twitch with want as his hands roam my body. I've lost all sense of the world around me. He rests his forehead close to mine, both of us needing a break.

"Hello to you too. That was some Christmas greeting." His low gruff voice sends shivers down my spine.

"I'm sorry. I might have kind of missed you." I peek up through my lashes but keep still. I love being nestled against his face, with his warm breath dancing along my lips.

He chuckles, releasing me, only to nip at my neck. I hiss and find myself squeezing my legs tight to avoid spoiling my fresh underwear.

"I might have kind of missed you too," he says, in between the soft kisses. He makes his way up my jaw, back to my mouth, and settles them over my lips.

"Skip this dinner with me. We can roll around in my bed all night."

I slap a hand to my mouth. Someone call the fire department, because I need the raging flames shooting out of my body to be put out. I've never had thoughts like this. I've had thoughts, but these are – wow.

His whole body shakes with laughter, as he tucks a loose strand of hair behind my ear. "Why don't we save that for later?"

One last kiss lands on my mouth. I want more, but we have to get going or else Mom will throw a fit. I straighten out the skirt of my red and white polka dot dress. I check my dark stockings for any sign of tears, then glance back up at him.

His eyes roam my face, and he narrows them. "You okay?"

I fidget with the hem of the skirt and keep my focus on twisting the soft fabric in my hands. "There's an awful tug in the pit of my stomach, and I can't shake it. Christmas with my family is intense, but this one is different somehow."

He lifts my chin with his finger. "Whatever happens tonight, it will not alter the way I feel about you. I promise you that."

I rest my forehead on his chest, as his lips brush across my head.

"Hey, are you guys ready?" Francesca calls from the living room.

"Be right out!" I yell.

"I'm glad I came when I did." He chuckles. "Those two were ready to violate your couch."

I reach behind me, turn the knob, and check in on them. They stand from their position on the couch and turn to us. I raise my brow at Francesca, and point two fingers at my eyes, then back at them.

"No hanky panky on my couch. I bought that with my own money," I tease, shaking my fist.

"We were actually contemplating the counter." Sam winks.

"Oh God." I lift my hands to my ears and sing. "La, la, la." Followed by some gagging noises.

Tobias nudges me from behind, his laughter tickling my ear. The smiles on Sam and Francesca's faces give me some hope. I'm relieved that they've made up. With both them and Tobias by my side this night shouldn't be so bad. If only that nagging tug in my stomach would stop, I'd actually believe it.

CHAPTER 37

Sam pulls his car up behind us as Tobias puts his truck into park outside of Mom's house. I grip the seats and hold on tight. I'm not sure I'm ready for this bumpy ride. Tobias shifts to face me. He reaches a hand over and releases my death grip on the seat.

"I'm serious about what I said before. Nothing will change between us. You've got this. Don't forget there are two little people in there who can't wait to see their Aunt Kasey."

Marabelle and Ryan's faces pop into my head. I can't help the tug on my lips at the mere thought of those two. They are what keeps me grounded during family gatherings. I'm here for them and no one else.

"What if I'm the biggest bitch?"

Tobias chuckles. "You? You have the kindest soul, Kace."

A sudden warmth blankets my cheeks.

"Oh. I got them some gifts too." He reaches into the back and pulls our bag of gifts up front. He grabs a second gift, a bottle of wine, likely for Mom. The fact that he got both Marabelle and Ryan something warms my soul.

A loud bang hits the car door. I glance over and Francesca is flat against the window pretending to slide down. I snort, then cover my mouth with my hand. An amused look crosses Tobias's face.

"I'm sorry about her," I joke, pointing over my shoulder.

Tobias laughs. "Everybody needs a Francesca in their life."

That is the truth. Her personality can be overwhelming, but sometimes you need that little bit of silly to change your mood.

"Ready?"

I inhale deeply, then let it go. "I think so."

We step out of the truck and Mom is already standing by the door. Her brows are knit tight as she eyes us walking up the driveway. She holds the door open.

"Tobias, darling. It's wonderful to see you again."

She stops him and reaches up for a hug. Being the kind-hearted man he is, he allows it.

"It's nice to see you too, Mrs Keller. This is for you." He hands her the bottle of wine. Her eyes widen.

"Oh, you just know the way to a woman's heart, don't you?" she says, batting her eyes at him. Tobias's cheeks flush. His smile is kind, but the side of his cheek twitches and the hand holding mine tenses.

"Hello, Kasey," she says in a drab voice.

"Mother," I reply in the same tone.

She hardly greets Francesca and Sam. Sam gives her a kind smile, as she unleashes a fake one, mumbling.

Inside the entryway, Tobias helps me take off my coat to hang. He takes both Sam and Francesca's and hangs them too. Mom has already disappeared somewhere. The sweet smell of cranberry and honey corn bread wafts in the air, causing my stomach to growl.

I stare off at the Christmas tree in the living room. It's not white, thank God, but the ornaments are perfectly arranged the same way they are every year. Presents are neatly piled under the tree. It's picture perfect from the outside. If only it were that way inside too.

A stampede brings me back. Two tiny voices screech out my name. "Aunty Kasey!"

The moment they come skidding around the corner I crouch down to bring them into my arms. They both hit me at the same time. Laughter fills my lungs. It will probably be the only time this whole night that it does. Tobias comes down beside me.

"We missed you guys," Marabelle says, looking between both Tobias and me.

I'm glad I don't miss the gentle smile on Tobias's face that she involved him in that sentence.

"Tobias, watch what I can do."

There's a tiny pocket on the skirt of her red dress. She slips a finger in nonchalantly, but we both notice. Then she reaches her arm out and pulls it back with a quarter in her hand.

"I've been practicing," she says, straightening her shoulders and standing tall.

Tobias gets to his feet, and I follow. He smiles down at her. "I knew you had a little magic in you." He touches her shoulder.

"Kids!" Piper calls, like she knows that they are interacting with us. "Presents!"

"Come on!" Both kids grab Tobias's hand, and Marabelle takes her other hand and reaches out for mine.

When we enter the living room, Piper turns, her face scrunches, and her eyes narrow.

"Over here," she tells them, not even saying hi.

They both glance at Tobias and me. "Go on," I tell them, trying to keep calm.

Francesca lays a hand on my shoulder. I take another deep breath and lean into her.

"Want me to bitch slap her?" she whispers.

I snort. "If only you could."

Francesca and I lead the guys to our favorite little green love

seat, closest to the entrance. Dad walks into the room and immediately heads in our direction. He reaches for me first, and even
though the last time we were together things didn't go well, he
still finds it in him to wish me a merry Christmas. He shakes
Tobias and Sam's hands and gives Francesca a hug. Before he can
engage in conversation, Mom claps her hands like we're all
children.

John comes in last, gives us all a brief hello and then walks to
Piper. He leans in and whispers something in her ear, while eying
me. I clench my hands into fists. Tobias glides a finger up my
arm, causing shivers down my spine. I relax as Francesca and I
plop into the chair. The guys stand behind us.

Mom goes through gifts and hands them out. I hand a small
gift to both Francesca and Sam. I did it so they wouldn't feel left
out. I end up with a small pile on my lap, and Tobias gets one too,
it's from Mom. I've passed out my gifts to Mom, Piper, Dad, John,
and the kids, and give the kids the ones from Tobias too.

Mom and Piper open theirs and throw them back into the box
immediately. The necklaces with their birthstones weren't cheap.
It seems as if I spent more time on their gifts than they had on
mine. I received dish towels from Mom, and random fluffy pink
slippers from Piper. Do either of them even know me? John at
least acknowledges me when he pulls out his Yankees baseball
cap. Dad too, with his Mets tie. The two of them have a "my team
is better than yours" moment, and I actually find myself smiling
over it.

Dad knows me all too well. In my lap sits a personalized
writer's notebook. I'm relieved, since my latest notebook has
three blank pages left. The kids start opening our gifts and the
smile on their faces relaxes me. I bought Marabelle her favorite
book series, Babysitters Club. I used to read them and wanted to
pass on the tradition. Ryan loved his superhero action figures and
pleaded with John to open them. They tear through Tobias's too,
their eyes lighting up. A magic kit for Marabelle, and a set of

comics for Ryan. I watch Piper shove all the gifts from us back away.

"What the hell, Piper?" I stand from my seat.

"They didn't ask for these items," she says.

I clench my jaw to stop it from opening. Tobias grabs me from behind and pulls me back down. Francesca holds my hand. She glares up at Sam. It's time for them to go. I hate that they had to witness this, but Francesca would never leave me hanging.

I stand. "Do you want me to walk you out?"

She shakes her head. "We've got it. If you need me, just call. Okay?"

"'K," I say, the letter barely audible. I wrap my arms around her and then Sam. When they leave, I sit back down on the love seat with Tobias by my side.

Mom claps her hands again. "Dinner's ready."

CHAPTER 38

*I*f there's one thing I actually like about holidays at Mom's, it's the food. Mom is an amazing cook, and her Christmas dinner is no exception. It's like Thanksgiving part two. If I could have gotten something from her, I would have loved for it to be cooking. She never taught me, which is probably why I suck at it. My dad is a TV dinner type of guy, so that could be the reason too.

A large turkey sits in the center of the table. There's cranberry sauce, corn bread, vegetables, salad, it's a smorgasbord of food. There's even a hearty dish of baked ziti, courtesy of Piper. A green vase filled with a fake poinsettia flower sits in the center of the table, matching a hand-sewn red, white, and green tablecloth that Mom's sister, Aunt Sonia, made before she passed. This is Christmas at the Johnsons. The scene before me reminds me of a simpler time, before things got rough and back when our extended family joined us. The house used to be busting at the seams with children and laughter. It's almost enough to erase all the bad, but not quite.

"Tobias," Mom says, turning to him with a smile on his face.

She sits across from the two of us.

"Would you mind leading us in prayer?"

"I'd love to." He agrees with a tight smile. He's stronger than I ever could be, and I admire him for that.

"Lord, bless the meal we are about to eat on a very special day. Keep each one of the people at this table surrounded by your love. Amen."

Amen echoes around the table. Without hesitation everyone starts grabbing for the food. There's light conversation, mostly asking to pass a dish. Tobias helps me fill my plate, as usual he asks me first before filling his. My stomach grumbles as I bite into a soft piece of dark meat.

"Piper, are you going to share your big announcement?" Mom asks.

Why does my sister always have a huge announcement during dinner? Between her college acceptance, her engagement, pregnancies, gender reveal, it's always been about her. Dad clears his throat, shifts in his seat. His attention lands on me. Worry lines crease his forehead.

"First, John got a promotion at work. How great is that?" Her smile visibly reaches her eyes.

Wow. I'm blown away. She's actually showing excitement over someone else's achievement. God, I sound so cynical but I can't help myself. When John first got the job, she turned to him and said, *That's great, dear, but we have much more exciting news to share.* Dad and I were the only ones to congratulate him. Aren't you supposed to be supportive of your spouse?

"Next," she says. Mom stares up at her, a loving gaze in her eyes. "We're having a boy! It's another boy!" She jumps.

Mom stands and rushes to her side. She touches her little round belly and kisses it. Dad's eyes bore into me like lasers, but all I can manage is to stare down at my plate and push around the food on it.

"Kasey, what do you have to say to your sister?" Mom says in that tone you use to speak to a kid.

I mumble my congratulations to her. Then turn to John. "Congrats to you too, John. That's really great news about your job." I say it with the most sincerity in my voice.

"You're acting like a child, Kasey. Your sister has some pretty exciting news, the least you could do is be happy for her. You're over there doing what you always do."

I drop my fork on my plate and wince, the sound ringing in my ear. "And what is that, Mother?"

"Watch your tone, it's Christmas. We should all be kind to one another."

The laughter that escapes me sounds evil. My body is a volcano ready to erupt. The food in front of me no longer looks appealing. Nausea rises in my throat. I'm going to be sick.

"Kind would be thanking me for babysitting your children, while you're in the hospital," I say, glaring at Piper. I don't regret it, not one bit. "And not snapping because I had someone with me, who clearly John saw. Or acknowledging–"

"Oh, stop your moaning, Kasey. We were all happy for you when you published your book. The least you could do is be–"

"Happy for me?"

The strange laugh returns. *No matter what happens, nothing will change the way I feel.* Tobias's words rattle in my brain. I release a shaky breath and stand. "Mom, you told me that being an author is not a real job, that was the first thing out of your mouth when I shared the news. You barely acknowledged it. I was so distraught that I went to my room and cried my eyes out. You do it because I don't fit into who you both want me to be, the cool sister, the perfect housewife living in a house with a fucking white picket fence, and tons of little children for you to mold into who YOU want them to be."

"Watch your language," Piper scolds.

My eyes well with tears. Not even Dad has spoken up to defend me. He's sitting there watching on the sidelines like always. Tobias is quiet, because he doesn't want to get in the middle, and I don't fault him for that. I don't need him to be in their line of fire too. In their eyes he can do no wrong. That makes me angry, and I hate that it does.

"Why do I even bother coming here? No one ever cares about how my day went. No one has ever asked how my writing is going? Or even cares to know that I finished my third book and was asked to write a new series. When I made the bestsellers list not one of you congratulated me or supported me." I stare at Mom. "You go around telling all of your friends, but behind closed doors it's not good enough."

Tobias reaches out for me, but I pull away. My heart sinks at the frown on his perfectly handsome face. I grip the sides of the table.

"I will never be good enough for any of you. I'm realizing now that that's okay." My lips tremble. "Even when Mom set me up on those dates, you weren't doing it for my best interest, you were doing it for you! You've been embarrassed by me since I was little. How could your precious daughter struggle in school? Or work in retail instead of popping out babies. She's not mine."

Everyone is quiet, watching me, including the kids. Guilt presses down on my shoulders, like a fifty-ton elephant. However heavy it may be, it kind of feels good to speak up.

"Marabelle, Ryan, I'm sorry. I'm sorry I used bad language, and I'm sorry for what I'm going to say. I love you both more than you will ever know." Tears spill from both mine and Marabelle's eyes. She knows exactly what's going to happen.

"I hope you all have a wonderful Christmas, but I can't stand here and be a part of it anymore."

I let go of the table, knocking over my chair, bolting out of the room. When I get to the entryway I fall to my knees and sob. A blend of relief and pain surges through me.

"Mrs Keller," Tobias says, calmly. "I know it's not my place to say this, but that woman in there means the world to me. We haven't been together long, but she's something special. I wish you would see that. Do you realize how many readers adore her books? Do you care to acknowledge the fact that getting published is hard? To accomplish that at the young age she did is phenomenal."

I try to hold back the impending sob, so I can listen to the rest of what he has to say. It's quiet enough that I can listen.

"I apologize for my outburst. You are all very lovely people. Thank you for dinner. I do hope that you understand from her perspective how bad it makes her feel. Have a merry Christmas."

Heavy footsteps head towards me. I'm stuck on my hands and knees holding myself together. He kneels next to me. "Let's get you home."

CHAPTER 39

*H*e helps pull me to my feet, then grabs our jackets. No one, not even Dad, stops me from leaving, that right there shows how much they care. More tears fall as we exit the house. Tobias ushers me to the truck, helping me in first.

The door slams shut and his arms close in around me. I grab a fistful of fabric from his shirt, through his open jacket.

"It's okay, Kasey. I've got you."

I cling tighter, trying to fill my body with his warmth. He continues to speak softly to me, encouraging words that at this moment in time are hard to believe. I just walked out on my family and not one of them seemed to care. I can't imagine how I must sound to him right now. The sobs keep coming in waves, they hurt.

"You were amazing. You stood up for yourself, Kace. You should be proud. Maybe this is the push they need."

I try to find the words, but nothing comes out, or anything that's coherent, anyway. He helps me with the seat belt, puts on his own, then drives off, one hand on the wheel the other on me.

When we arrive back at the apartment, he shuts off the engine. "Do you still want me to stay?"

I nod into his jacket. I need a few minutes to collect myself. "I'm so sorry, Tobias." I sniffle.

"Hey, look at me." He tucks his fingers under my chin and pushes up so that I don't have the option to not look. His dark eyes narrow at me. "You are so strong, Kasey. I'm sorry you had to endure that kind of hate in your life. It's not fair."

He tries to wipe the silent tears that fall. I've overcome the sobbing stage, and have entered the *Holy shit, did that really just happen*, stage.

"I will never treat you that way, ever. Even if things get hard and the two of us aren't on the same page. I would never put someone down for who they are. As long as we're together I will always support you."

I wipe my face with my jacket sleeve. God, I'm a mess. I'm sure there's a mix of snot and tears all over my face. He leans down and kisses me softly. We sit there for a few extra minutes, until he leads me out of the truck through the driver's side with him.

Once inside we get ready for bed. Tobias is the most understanding man I've ever met. He was the one who suggested we change and get into bed and relax together. I offer him the bathroom, while I change and use a makeup removal pad to get the residue off my face. He's already seen me at my worst, so throwing on some old sweats, and T-shirt, doesn't bother me.

I crawl into bed, face the door, and wait for him to return. He emerges a few minutes later in black sweats and a matching shirt. Flipping the light off, he crawls into bed next to me. I nestle into his arms as he pulls me further into him.

Even if my Christmas turned into a shit-show, getting into bed with him overrides all the terrible things. I can't help but feel a little lucky this year, even with the family drama, because I found someone who has been slowly fitting back the pieces of my heart, and that is enough for me to be content.

"Kasey?"

"Yeah," I whisper.

The sniffles and sobs have finally subsided, and now there's nothing.

"I love you, everything about you. Being with you is a breath of fresh air. I needed someone in my life to pull me from the funk I was in, and you were the only one who was capable of that." A soft light from the streetlamp glows over his features. "I know it's not the right time to bring–"

"I love you," I tell him.

Wide-eyed he stares at me. The soft glow of the nightlight on his side of the room brightens his face. For those few seconds he reverts to the unsure man I saw in the parking lot at the school. His insecurities are peeking through. I need to show him how serious I am. Loving him was never hard to imagine.

At first, I fear I've made a huge mistake confessing something so big so soon, but then I'm met with a beautiful smile and all of the bad thoughts go out the window.

"What?" My lips tug up. "I love you."

"Really?"

"More than anything in this whole world." I pause. "Okay, so maybe there is one other person who tops that."

He smirks, and I release a breath. I love that he picked up on who I meant. The fact that he gets it makes me love him even more, if that's even possible.

"You don't know how much of a relief it is to hear you say those words. I love you too, Kace." He rests his head beside mine. Our nose gently touched, and it's different from wanting to jump his bones. I feel at ease, like everything in the world is right.

"Tobias?" I adjust myself so that I'm facing him. I'd rather stay where I was, but it's important and I need to get it out. If we're at the stage of our relationship where love has bloomed, then he needs to know why things with my family are so messed up.

His eyes meet mine. He reaches forward to smooth out my hair, and for a moment I relax into it.

"I feel like I need to explain."

"I'm listening," he says, softly.

"Piper was the poster child for everything. She was a straight-A student from preschool through college. She never did anything wrong, and never once tested Mom's patience. Me? I was different. You know most of this story from what I explained in the classroom about my struggles. It bled into our home life too."

I pause to release the knot in my throat. The only other person who knows the entire story is Francesca. She lived it with me. We both lived through our own family horrors.

"I was the kid playing in the dirt, and maybe eating it?"

That earns a small laugh.

"Eventually I became the girl who hid in the closet to write. My sister was made captain of the cheer squad, prom queen, and graduated at the top of her class. I was average. She did beauty pageants too. Then there was me, Mom couldn't get me to sit in a dress for more than ten minutes without me wanting to claw myself out of it."

Tobias smiles. "Did you make mud pies too? I love a heaping sloppy pile of mud pie."

I let out another unexpected laugh.

"She began leaving me out of things. She would send me off with a sitter or to Dad's. She tried to get Dad to take me when they divorced. He wasn't ready to parent a young girl on the verge of puberty. She wanted me gone so bad that she made things worse for me, all because he wasn't ready to handle a child on his own. I resented him for a long time. I'm sorry for dumping this all on you, but I wanted to explain it."

Tobias holds me close, with my head on his chest, while he strokes my hair.

"I'm glad you felt like you were ready to tell me. I want to know it all. The good and the bad. Whoever you were then, shaped you into the beautiful woman you are today. You're perfect the way you are. It sucked you had to go through all of that, but you're so strong. I know you'll be okay."

I lift my head again. He gently caresses my jawline with his fingers.

"You still came out on top. When I met you that day, I wasn't expecting anything. I wasn't ready. I haven't explained, and I'm not ready to go into full detail, but I've been severely damaged emotionally by Roxanne. She played with my heart one too many times. I believed that when she did, it would be different. It never was. When Dad and your mom set me up on our date, you and me, I never imagined it going so well." Tobias is getting a little teary eyed, so I graze my hand over his scruffy cheek.

"I got worried when you said you didn't go to church, but the minute we stepped foot inside and you embraced the entire thing, I knew you'd be different, and I knew I wanted to try."

I press my lips to his. My hunger for him is strong enough for me to almost forget what happened tonight.

"You're the most amazing man I've ever met," I whisper, in between kisses.

"I'm not perfect, Kace. My own insecurities run deep. I promise to try to be the man you want me to be."

"I just want you to be you."

He gathers me in his arms. We lay there in silence listening to each other breathing. I'm positive he's asleep before I am, as his body stills beside mine. I love how easy it is for him to fall asleep with me. I want to stay awake, so I can enjoy every single moment of our time together – but with heavy eyelids my body betrays me, and I find myself slowly dozing off in his soft warm arms.

CHAPTER 40

*E*arly morning sunlight trickles in through the half open curtains. My temples throb at the brightness. Is this what it feels like to be a vampire? The bedroom door squeaks open and Tobias walks in.

He winces. "Sorry, didn't mean to wake you. I was checking in. I'll be right back."

He disappears before I can register the sight of him standing in my room looking all sexy first thing in the morning.

I adjust to sit up and the throbbing grows with each movement. I didn't sleep well. I woke up and cried out in my sleep a few times. It sucked to replay the events of Christmas Eve dinner in my head. All through the night anytime I stirred, Tobias was there. He wrapped me in a blanket of his love. Remembering the way his arms felt allows a flicker of hope that today will be better.

I'm looking forward to meeting the rest of his family and enjoying a nice quiet dinner with them. His brother is coming up from Georgia and Tobias has been talking nonstop about how amazing he is. He's two years older than him and has been in the army since he graduated high school. Tobias says he worries that his brother will get deployed, but also says Dawson is one of the strongest people he knows.

Tobias bumps into the door. I catch sight of the bamboo food tray before I see him. The tray is filled with my favorite bagel, and his, along with his favorite juice.

"Christmas breakfast in bed?" he asks, a single dimple forming on his right cheek.

I smile through the stabbing pain that continues to pierce my temples. I rub at them and moan.

"You okay?" he asks.

I retract my legs so he can place the tray flat on the bedspread. The bed shifts under his weight as he settles in and throws an arm over my shoulder.

"It's perfect. I'm perfect. I'm sorry if I kept you up."

"The only regret I have is that I couldn't give you a perfect Christmas."

I raise a brow at him, and he smiles down at me. "Are you kidding me? Family drama aside, you – you have made this the best Christmas I've had in quite some time. It would have been much worse if you hadn't been there."

His cheeks flush a warm shade of pink under the dark scruff lining his cheeks.

"I see you got your juice?" I point towards the shallow glass of purple liquid.

He chuckles. "It's not breakfast without juice."

"I thought that was brunch," I tease, looking up at him through my lashes.

He tightens his grip on me. I rest my head on his shoulder and he kisses my forehead. We sit in a comfortable silence as we eat the delicious food.

"So, we have some time before we have to go to my parents," he says in between his last few bites.

"Are you implying something, Mr Scott?"

Tobias tips my chin and presses a delicate kiss to my mouth.

His tongue tastes of fruit punch with a slight hint of leftover bacon from his bagel. He pulls away slightly and I lick my lips hoping to savor the flavor.

"First, I have something for you."

He pulls away and reaches down beside the bed. In his hand is a large red gift bag.

"That's an awfully large bag. I could probably fit inside it." I laugh, even though there's a twinge of guilt residing inside me. My gift for him isn't nearly as big.

With his free hand he removes the tray from the bed, placing it gently on the floor, then puts the bag between us.

"They are small, promise I didn't go overboard."

"I like small things."

He chuckles softly, then pulls me close. I reach inside the bag and take out the first box. I unwrap the Christmas tree paper, roll it into a ball, and chuck it at his head. He holds on to me. I laugh as his fingers dance along my hip.

Inside a blue box is a necklace with a book charm on it. Engraved on the book is the title of my series. I stare up at him in awe.

"This is adorable. I love it. Where did you get it?" I ask.

"A good shopper never reveals his secrets."

I push his shoulder and he laughs. He releases me from his grasp and takes the necklace from the box. Twisting my body, I lift the hair off my neck so he can clasp the necklace shut.

I run my hand over the smooth silver surface as his lips graze the back of my neck. Closing my eyes, I release a wavering breath. His kisses trail along towards my shoulders. I toss my head back and moan, letting go of the charm.

I find myself closing my legs to get rid of the sensation, but it's no use as his lips continue to travel upwards. He starts at the base of my neck and then along my jawline. I grip the white fitted sheet and grasp it in my hand. A soft moan leaves my lips as he reaches the tip of my chin.

He gets to my bottom lip when a smile emerges. "Finish opening these first," he whispers.

"Tease," I say, calling him out.

Tobias laughs, a sound I will never get tired of. It's rich and full of life. I never imagined it was possible to crave someone's laugh.

Aside from the necklace he got me a mug that says, *I like big books and I cannot lie*, and a blanket with my favorite Shawn Mendes song printed onto it. It's a soft fleece and I'd wrap it around me, but both of us have other plans.

"I'm sorry it's not much," he says, between our urgent kisses.

"The gifts?" I ask, as he plants several kisses under my chin. I lift my head allowing him to suck harder on the sensitive skin under there.

"Yeah."

"Tobias, they are perfect. You're the only guy I've ever dated who gets me. I love how you personalized each gift. I've been given generic necklaces or some kind of really awful-smelling perfume. Your gifts, they came from a different place." My words come out breathy.

His fingers dance along the edge of my risen shirt. It hangs loosely above my belly button. His touch causes a shiver to rattle me down low.

"I have something for–"

He doesn't let me finish before crashing his lips to mine. My mouth opens, allowing him in. Putting the bad outside of my head I focus on what is happening in front of me. The way his mouth swallows me whole, and how the pads of his fingers against my cheek shoot tiny jolts of electricity to snake through my body.

He tugs at my shirt, and I help him lift it over my head. His eyes roam my body, stopping at my breasts. His eyes widen as he gently cups the right one in his hand and rubs. I moan out his name as he takes the peak into his mouth.

"Holy..."

I grab at his shirt and toss it aside. He lets me place my hands against his chest. I rub over the coarse hairs that cover his body. I love the way his hard abdomen feels under my burning hands. He lowers me, then helps shimmy off my pants. As mine fall to the floor, he begins pulling down his, revealing new Christmas boxers, this time it's dancing Christmas trees. I don't mean to laugh, but it slips out.

I tug at them and peek inside. Glancing up through my eyelashes I blink. A daring look crosses his narrowed eyes. I slip my hand inside and grab hold. He hisses my name and throws his head back. Gently, he pulls my hand away and discards his boxers. I take in his entire body, as I lift my middle and slip my panties off, throwing them somewhere in the room.

He hovers over me, his fingers circling along my middle. I arch my back and yell out. His eyes lower and he smirks. "My God, Kasey." He yells out when he realizes it's because of him.

His low rugged voice is all it takes for me to pull him down on top of me. I'm caught up in the trail of kisses he leaves as he makes his way from my mouth down to my stomach. He sucks on all my most sensitive parts. I arch again.

I reach up and grab hold of his shoulders and roll him onto his back. Our eyes meet and in them they ask for permission. I don't have any doubts that this is the right time for this. My gift can wait. He pulls a condom from his discarded pants. This is it. I'm more than ready.

The moment he enters me the world around us fades. A mutual feeling of love and lust surrounds us. If this is a glimpse of how life will be with him, stop the train, because I'm getting off here.

CHAPTER 41

We collapse onto the bed beside each other when it's over. I stare up at the ceiling listening to the sounds of our heavy breathing. His fingers intertwined with mine.

"We should clean up. Your parents will be expecting us soon."

Time slipped away when we were together. I lost count of how many times it happened. One was not enough for the amount of love that hung in the air between us.

"Come on then, I'll give you a hand."

I twist my head to face him, and he mimics me. I lean forward and press my lips to his.

"Are you trying to get another one out of me before we go, Ms Johnson? Those lips…" he moans. "They are so demanding." The rasp in his voice sends shivers down my spine.

He releases his fingers from mine and rolls on top, a determined look in his dark eyes. I laugh, shaking the bed and him.

"If we move this party to the shower, we could probably still make it before dessert." My face warms and I slap my hands to my mouth. I try to cover the embarrassment of how weird it sounded out loud. Tobias chuckles, and gently kisses my neck, his scruff tickles my skin.

"I underestimated you, Kace," he says, into my neck. He reaches down running his hand over my middle and hisses again. "I think you need a cold shower," he jokes.

I smack his shoulder playfully and he rolls off, laughing with his entire body.

We gather at my bedroom door and peer out into the living room. Sam and Francesca should still be at his parents' house, but to be on the safe side we check anyway. When the coast is clear we run naked across the apartment to the bathroom. I trip a few times, as the two of us laugh and stumble our way over.

Tobias shuts the door and swings me around, pressing me against it. His hungry mouth nips at my collarbone. I can't get enough of how good his body meshes with mine. It's been well over a year since I've slept with someone, but it never felt like this. The last few times with Lloyd felt forced, I hope this never gets to that point.

I slip away from Tobias and turn the knobs in the tub to adjust the temperature. He comes up behind me and grabs me at my waist lifting me into him. I can't stop giggling. Everything that happened yesterday has slipped into the far corner of my mind. The only thing on my mind now is him and the way it felt to be with him.

We get inside the old white porcelain tub. He guides me in with him, reaching for the soap. He suds up his hands, then places them on my body. His hands dig into my skin, and I step back into him.

We take turns washing one another, and I've never enjoyed a shower more.

As we get out, I catch sight of him with a towel wrapped around his waist. I could get used to this. His attention perks up, as he tears his eyes away from his face in the mirror and lands on me.

"Are you blushing again?" He smirks.

Warmth floods my cheeks. Of course I am, he sure knows how to get me worked up.

"Save that for later," he says, the raspy tone returning to his voice.

Inside my room we change into our clothing for today. I never thought a man could look so sexy in a red sweater and gray pants, but Tobias can pull it off. I reach down for my makeup bag to find the small present for him. When I turn, I catch him buttoning up his pants. I don't know where the urge to unbutton it comes from, but the idea warms me.

I lift the bag and hand it to him. "I'm sorry it isn't much, but…"

He takes the bag, leans in, pressing a kiss to my lips to stop me from talking. "All I needed was you, and this," he whispers, planting more along my jaw.

I watch as he opens the bag and stares wide-eyed at the tiny guitar ornament. The moment he pulls out the Thor comic book ornament is when I know I did good. His cheeks turn a soft shade of pink, he's in awe.

"Thor and a guitar." He chuckles. "Seems we both get each other."

"So, you like it?" I ask.

"Like it, Kace. I love it. I'm going to hang this on my tree when I get it home. Thank you." He leans forward, reaching for one last kiss.

He pulls back, holding me at arm's length giving me a once over. "How are you doing today? Be honest."

I sigh. I knew he was going to bring it up. There was concern in his eyes all morning, even when we were in the middle of the most mind-blowing sex of my entire life. He still watched me carefully making sure I was okay.

I wish my answer could be different. Even having the most

amazing Christmas morning didn't fully get rid of the pain of how life will be after today.

"We don't have to stay long if you're not feeling up to it."

I grab hold of his scruffy cheeks in my hand and bring his face down so that our foreheads meet.

"I want to go celebrate with your family. I promise I'll be okay."

"If at any point you're uncomfortable, don't hesitate to tell me and we can leave. I won't force you to do anything that will upset you."

How does someone like me deserve such a great man? All my life I've been told I wasn't good enough. Maybe that's where things have gone wrong in my previous relationships, but Tobias is different. He believes in me and encourages me to be me no matter what anyone else says. Even Lloyd conformed to my parents' way of thinking. He'd subtly leave out newspapers open to the job ads so that I would find them. He also claimed he forgot I had my book signing even when I reminded him that morning. I knew he didn't approve of my lifestyle, and yet I still wanted to be with him.

I hate being that girl and sounding like a stage-five clinger, but I hope Tobias never leaves my side. I shouldn't need a man to make me feel like I'm worth something, but before Tobias came into my life, I felt worthless and unappreciated. With him here, I have the confidence to be me, instead of the person others want me to be.

CHAPTER 42

The home Tobias grew up in is gorgeous. It gives off a well-lived country vibe. A rickety old porch swings around the front stopping approximately halfway back on each side. From the appearance alone, it tells a story of many happy memories. What I love most is that it doesn't look staged like in a movie. Lights are strung on the porch with green garland.

A few extra cars are piled in the small paved driveway. Tobias said his brother and parents were at dinner but the carload doesn't add up.

He holds the door wide open for me. My feet hit the ground as the front door of the house swings open and bangs against the outside wall.

"Brother!" a bellowing voice calls from the porch.

My attention bounces between both men. The similarities are uncanny. The only difference between Tobias and the handsome man on the porch is their hair. Tobias has a long thick mane of black locks, while the other is clean shaven with hardly a spec on his head.

Tobias places a hand on the small of my back and leads me up the path. The guys meet halfway and pull each other into one of those manly bear hugs.

"What's up?" They slap each other's backs.

"Nothing much," he says, pulling away. His eyes land on me, a smile meets them.

"Is this her?" He wiggles his brows. "Bro, you've got some good taste."

Tobias chuckles. "Kasey, this is my annoying older brother, Dawson. Dawson, this is my girlfriend, Kasey."

"The writer." He pauses, pressing a pointer finger to his lips. "Hey, Mom!" He glances over his shoulder towards the house. "You were right. Tobias has good taste in women!"

Make those *three* Scott men who have made me blush. Dawson turns with a devious look on his face. Tobias steps back, returning his hand to where it was. His family is already proving to be more chill than mine.

His mom appears at the door. "Dawson, don't scare the poor girl away!" she shouts at him.

"Wouldn't dream of it, Ma. If Tobias hasn't done so yet, I'm sure she's good." He nudges Tobias in the ribs. "Am I right, Kasey?"

He jogs up the step and Mrs Scott smacks him playfully on the shoulder as he walks up. As we step up onto the porch the scent of homemade tomato sauce wafts out the door. I breathe it in deep and savor the smell.

Tobias lets go to hug Mrs Scott. She reaches for me next and holds on for a heartbeat longer than him.

"Thank you for having me."

"You're always welcome here," she says. "Now come in before you two freeze to death out there."

She waves us all inside. The scent of homemade apple pie and fresh baked bread tingles my nose. The kitchen holds a nostalgic country vibe. Yellow painted walls line the room, and old wooden cabinets with chipped paint are set above and below the countertops. A cookbook with stained pages sits out on a wooden table in the corner.

I love how Christmas joy has spread to this room. Crocheted red and green baubles hang on the cabinets. There are twinkling lights on the window to my right, giving the room a warm bright glow. I've only just stepped foot in here but I love it already.

Mom would have a heart attack if she saw any room in her house in this shape. To me, this is a home. There are pots, pans, bowls, and utensils scattered around. The stove is filled with a large pot and several small ones. Some discarded sauce drips down the side of the stove. His mom has stains all over her Santa apron, but none of it bothers her.

"Dawson, take their coats and put them in the closet for me."

Dawson happily obeys and helps take our things so we can make ourselves at home.

Laughter filters in from the other room. No one is yelling at each other, it's still early, but I can't imagine the type of things that go down at Mom's will happen here.

"Tobias and Kasey are here!" Mrs Scott yells out.

Tobias turns his attention towards a commotion in the hall-way. He takes a step back, awestruck. A woman with similar features stands in the entryway. She's a mix between Tobias and Dawson, but much prettier of course.

"Hey there, little brother."

Tobias blinks and covers a hand over his slack-jawed mouth. "You're. How. How are you even here right now?" His voice breaks.

He rushes over and wraps his arms around her. They pull back, both sniffling and wiping their faces clean of tears.

"I figured Christmas might be a good time to travel home for a while."

Gauging his reaction, I assume the woman is his sister. My heart constricts watching their response to each other's presence. I tug at the strand of hair in front of my shoulder and finger-comb through the piece with force. I don't want to bring my family into this mess and try to erase the sadness I feel over their bond.

Tobias lifts a hand to his face again. "I can't believe you're here." He pauses. "Oh." He turns to me, reaching for my hand.

I step into his arms. "Kasey, this is my sister, Amy." He rubs a knuckle underneath his eye.

"Kasey Johnson." She says my name like she knows me. Two dimples form on her round face. "Bestselling author. God, I love your books. Book one got me through my last pregnancy and the newborn stage." She shakes her head, in disbelief that I'm standing in front of her. "I love you too of course, not only your books. Look at the way my brother lights up when you're around. His cheeks are glowing." She pinches Tobias's cheeks, then taps them lightly.

"Thank you. It's really nice to meet you. Tobias mentioned you don't live around here, I'm glad you were able to come for the holidays."

"Me too. I'm exhausted. Flying from Hawaii to here with kids is a lot, but worth the headache."

"I can imagine. Hawaii sounds lovely though."

"It has its perks." She forgets Tobias and focuses on me. "No more Hawaii talk, let's discuss that book of yours. I can't believe Halia is locked in that awful dungeon. Brythan is going to save her, I just know it. Please tell me you won't kill either of them off." She sets her hands on my shoulder and shakes me lightly.

I laugh. "I literally finished writing book three a couple of nights ago, I'm emotionally drained from it. I'm keeping my mouth shut." I pretend to zip it with my fingers. "You could read it early if you're interested."

She pumps her arms in the air. "Yes! Hear that, Mom."

"Actually, dear, I received a copy early yesterday morning, so I'm ahead of the game." Mrs Scott throws me a grin.

I turn my attention back to Amy. "I'll send it to you when I get home."

"Now if you two would stop fangirling over my girlfriend I want to introduce her to Nonna and the rest of the family," Tobias gently teases.

In the dining room, which has a gorgeous bay window (perfect for sitting in to write) the rest of the family sits around a large oval table. A gorgeous white lace cloth lays over it, and the table settings are well used and yet still somehow look beautiful.

I take in the room around me. There are old handmade Christmas decorations that are on their last leg. Tiny handprints turned into Christmas trees and Santa Claus hang on the wooden paneled wall. The idea that a parent still wants to showcase their children's artwork from when they were younger leaves a heaviness in my heart yet brings me joy at the same time.

His dad stands and makes his way around the table. He hugs Tobias first then pulls me into one. His face glows while he talks to me and turns to the rest of the family members sitting at the table.

"The man sitting over there." He points to the young guy beside a toddler covered in what might be peas. The child sits in his booster and squishes the tiny green balls in his hand. "That's Tim, Amy's husband. Beside him is their son, Ezra."

Tim waves as the toddler flings a wad of mushed-up peas at Tim's head. Ezra's giggle fills the room, making everyone, including the two teens sitting on the opposite side of the table, snicker. They return their heads to their devices. The boy, who I learn is Amy's eldest son, Blake, is playing on a Nintendo Switch, while their daughter, Zoey, is wrapped up in her phone. They both wave before returning their attention back.

"Kids and these ridiculous devices," an older woman with white curls says, as she stands. She places her knitting needle and project on the table, then waddles over to us. Tobias has to bend so far down to reach her. She gives me a once over, her eyes lighting up.

"Oh, she's lovely, Tobias." She purses her lips while taking me in. "I'm Tobias's nonna."

"It's so nice to meet you," I say, as she pulls me into a tight squeeze, like she's not going to let go.

"You're much prettier than the other one. Ohh... I could just..."

"Tobias Scott."

CHAPTER 43

I'm taken aback by the sultry female voice that beckons from behind us. Only one person has that nail on a chalkboard voice that makes me cringe. Nonna retreats, a disgusted look on her face as she glances over my shoulder. A large knot gets stuck in my throat when I try to swallow. Tobias's cheek twitches as he clamps his fingers together.

Nonna mumbles some crazy words. For a small woman, she sure packs a punch. She gives me a sad smile, before returning to her seat. She can't get away from Roxanne fast enough, I'm with her on that.

"There you are, you handsome devil."

I step aside as she reaches him and tugs him into her massive chest. He doesn't move his arms again, but he's being calm, because that's who he is.

"Kasey, hi!" Her high-pitched voice makes me wince. "I think I even got your name right today," she says, gripping me to her chest too.

I'm suffocating in her grasp. Even when she pulls away, her vanilla perfume chokes me like I'm allergic to it.

"I'm glad you're both finally here. Tobias, I have something for you, may I give it to you later?" Roxanne winks and flashes a flirty grin that makes me want to deck her.

Now it's my turn to stand with my hands balled into fists.

Nonna pretends to cough. Roxanne zaps her eyes to the old woman and scowls.

"Is your dad here?" Tobias finally speaks, not answering her question.

"You know Dad, he's in the living room watching football. It's not a holiday party at the Scotts' house without him falling asleep in front of the tube watching sports." She chuckles and smacks Tobias's arm playfully. If I wasn't carefully watching him, I would have never heard the small growl that echoed in his throat.

She reminds me of an animal hunting its prey and she's ready to pounce, Tobias being her target. Saved by the phone, my ringtone lightly plays in my bag that I hadn't realized I was clutching hard. I pull it out for a distraction, Francesca, perfect timing.

From his clenched jaw to his stoic stance, I can tell Tobias doesn't want to be left alone with Roxanne, heck I don't want to leave him alone with her, but what can she do with everyone around? I hope I'm not underestimating her.

"I'm sorry, would you excuse me?" I speak to her first before glancing up at Tobias. His jaw is tightly clenched. I press a hand to his arm, and it zaps him back to life. "Hey, is it okay if I take this? It's Francesca."

"Of course." He loosens up, only slightly and reaches down for a kiss.

It turns out Francesca is having an amazing time with Sam and that they are staying an extra night with his family. She called to wish me a Merry Christmas. It's our first one without each other. The idea is still hard for me to stomach; we've spent every Christmas together since I was old enough to sneak out and ride my bike to her house, even in a blizzard.

After my phone call, Tobias's mom – who wants me to call her Sarah – recruits us all to help. Tobias and Dawson are grabbing anything she needs in the basement, while us girls prep the meal, minus Roxanne who goes to sit with her dad.

Sarah has me rolling dough for the apple pie and Amy stands beside me cutting the apples into perfect tiny slices. Her cutting skills are far better than mine could ever be.

"But come on," Amy says. "I thought he was an asshole when he first approached her." Amy licks her fingers, then glances up to make sure Sarah didn't catch her before she goes back to cutting.

"Agreed. I fell in love with him under the mountain." I laugh as we reminisce about one of my favorite book series of all times, *A Court of Thorns and Roses*.

"Yes! Oh God, I get goosebumps imagining it." She shows me her arm and smirks.

"I don't think our relationship went down that way. When were we under a mountain?" Tobias comes up the basement stairs to our left with some canned goods inside a crate. He places it down beside his mom and she gives him a kiss on the cheek for getting it for her.

Amy rolls her eyes. "Not everything is about you, Tobias."

"So, who is this man you met under the mountain?" he questions, his playful side returning. There's still a hint of apprehension in his smile, but I'm happy that he's calmer than before.

"My book boyfriend, Rhysand," I say, tilting my head back as he wraps his warm arms around my waist. He rests his chin on my shoulder, observing what I'm doing.

Amy snickers beside me.

Tobias turns me, almost causing me to drop the roller in my hand. "The ladies tell me I look like Rhysand. Shawn, Rhysand, I could be either." He straightens his shoulders and wiggles his brow. I laugh at his attempt to be half dorky, half sexy. "They say my wingspan reaches–"

I wave my hands in front of me. "Wait, hold you. You know who that is?"

Amy's shoulders shake with laughter. "I made him read it with me when they first came out. I told him it was hardcore fantasy."

I snicker and stare up at him. "You got the hardcore part right," I joke.

Amy's cackle fills the room. "Now I like you even more. Tobias, this one is a keeper." She smiles.

Before we all settle down for dinner, I excuse myself to the bathroom. I love the old wooden staircase that leads up to the second floor, it squeaks under my feet, like many trips have been made up and down them. On the wall going up are school pictures of each kid through the years. Tobias with braces, Amy in her cheer outfit, Dawson with missing teeth. All my pictures were overpowered by Piper's. I love how each child is displayed for everyone to see their beautiful smiling faces.

Aside from Roxanne's sudden appearance, I'm at home here. I don't have to be someone I'm not, and best of all, they appreciate who I am and love my work. It's a win-win.

As I approach the bathroom two voices catch my attention. I would have used the one downstairs, but it was occupied so Amy directed me up here.

"Why is she even here?" Tobias's voice falls flat.

I press myself against the paneled wall in the hallway and stare down at the newly stained dark wood at my feet. I shouldn't be eavesdropping, but I'm compelled to listen.

"I'm sorry I didn't warn you." Sarah sounds defeated. "You know how your father is. He is a kind soul, and her father has been struggling with work and the loss of Debra…"

"That's not fair, Mom," Tobias slices through her words. "Kasey, she's it for me. She's the one. I feel it in my soul. If I screw this up…" His voice breaks along with my heart.

I rest my head and close my eyes. I imagine he's running a

hand through his thick black hair. Heavy footsteps tell me he's pacing. The image of his face that day at the school comes to mind. He was hesitant to put a title on our relationship and now I sort of get why.

"You haven't told her about Roxanne, have you?" she asks, her tone soft and loving. If she were my mom, there'd be nothing but sarcasm in her voice.

"They've met, I just – haven't told her what she did," he whispers.

"Oh, Tobias."

"Mom." His stern voice makes me want to run, but I'm frozen in place at the sound of his sniffle.

"You weren't the one to mess that up, sweetie. She only wanted one thing…"

"I'm well aware of what she wanted!" He raises his voice, and it shoots through me. This is more complicated than I thought.

Another sniffle from him and his pain shoots through me, like we're connected somehow. If I wasn't sneaking around outside the room, I would have gone in there and hugged him. He's crying and I'd do anything to take that pain away or to make him laugh. Knowing there is someone in the same house who has toyed with his emotions gets me all worked up.

Sarah continues to apologize. The sounds of his light sobs tear me in two. Thankfully the bathroom is the preceding room. I slip inside and very gently shut the door, in the hopes I'm quiet enough to be unnoticed.

CHAPTER 44

*B*y the time I convince myself to leave the bathroom everyone is in the dining room. Some of the food is being passed around, while Amy and Sarah rush back and forth to place more.

Roxanne is standing in the corner talking to her dad and William. There's a sadness in her dad's eyes that I wouldn't have noticed prior to eavesdropping. His smile is a different kind of fake, the kind that says "I'm hurting, but thankful for this moment". I'm weighed down by the guilt of being angry, but knowing she hurt Tobias brings me close to the edge again.

Tobias's sullen face doesn't help my sudden hatred for her. Whatever she did, it scarred him. Tobias leans against the entryway of the dining room. My footsteps catch his attention. He stays there unmoving with eyes ablaze with a mixture of lust and worry. The lines on his forehead lead me to the conclusion that it's more worry than anything.

I stand in front of him, the noises around us fade into silence. I find it easy to block it out when his eyes are on mine. He hooks his hands around my waist then leans down to press his lips to mine. I shiver at the delicate dance his lips are doing.

"Are you okay?" he asks, clearing his throat.

"Hanging in there. You?" I reach up and run my fingers over the dark scruff on his face. He leans into my touch, and I almost lose it right there. *Tell me all your secrets, Tobias Scott.* I want to say the words out loud, but most of all I hope that one day he'll confide in me and explain the rocky relationship between him and Roxanne.

I wish he'd say something. Give me some indication that whatever is between them is over. I know what it's like to hang on – I was holding on tight to my relationship with Lloyd, but when I met Tobias, everything changed.

"Tobias–" The pain in my voice gives him what he needs to know, clarification that I'm not being one-hundred percent honest. He's not being very honest either.

He cuts me off. "Kace." The soft low grumble of his voice and the pain that surfaces there almost brings me to tears, but I keep them at bay by blinking.

I place a trembling hand on his chest as if he were the only thing keeping me steady. "Let's just eat. Okay?"

The roar of voices filters back in. He doesn't argue, only takes me into his arms and leads me to the table where his family is finally starting to all sit for dinner.

We end up on the side facing the kitchen. As we take our seats Roxanne plops herself on the other side of Tobias. I tap my legs in a steady beat to ground myself. *He loves you, not her. Relax, Kasey.*

As his father leads us in prayer, I find myself opening one eye to check on Tobias. It's the first time he's been calm since he saw Roxanne. Ezra, the toddler, catches me with my eyes open and flaps his hands happily. I smile at him, and he squeals.

The food smells delicious as Sarah unveils everything on the table. From fresh grown vegetables to even the canned stuff, everything looks perfect.

Dinner is filled with fun happy memories and conversations that don't lead to anyone getting up and walking out. I love listening to their old Christmas stories, even if Roxanne keeps popping in with her own comments. Tobias did this, and Tobias did that. I suck it up and attempt to ignore each jab she makes at him too.

"Do you remember that, T?"

The way she calls him by a nickname feels so intimate. I place my fork down, my stomach hasn't been all that great and I'm trying not to overdo it.

When he doesn't respond to her remark, she leans over and bumps his shoulder. With no response, she swallows her food and continues anyway, "You were such a baby, because I knocked over your snowman."

The mood in the room is not as peppy as it was a few moments ago, but Roxanne continues anyway, "He was always so sensitive."

My eyes dart all over, first towards Tobias who's giving a smile out of the politeness in his heart. Then at Amy, who snarls quietly in her spot between Ezra and Blake, I'm surprised she hasn't leaped across the table to bitch slap Roxanne.

Roxanne turns her attention to us. "So, Kasey, how did you and Tobias hook-up anyway? I saw you two that day at church, but I don't know your story."

She says hookup so casually as if that's all we are, just a hookup. Tobias chokes on a piece of turkey. He gulps down some water to wash it away. He wipes the corner of his mouth with a napkin, then tosses an arm around my shoulder in a protective way.

"Kasey's mom was the one who approached me at church," Mr Scott says, happily. "She told me she had a daughter who had been on a few dates, but nothing worked out, and she hadn't found 'the one.'"

I cough. A few dates? Try a million.

Amy glances up from her dinner and wiggles her brows. "That was until she met Tobias, right?"

Tobias's arm around me tightens, and he presses a kiss to my head.

"Right," I say, and my eyes meet his.

Instead of getting wrapped up in Roxanne's glare, he only focuses on me. The words that he spoke to his mom pop into my head. *She's the one.* Oh God! My heart lurches in my chest. He literally said that I was the one. Why didn't it register prior to this?

Sarah smiles. Roxanne recoils. Amy gives me a knowing smile. She's trying to find an excuse to shut Roxanne's trap from babbling.

Even through the tension, it's far from the chaos that ensues at my house, and for that I'm grateful. Tobias happily rejoins the conversation when they start talking about music and more silly memories with his siblings. He even gives me a few loving side-long glances that make my heart dance, but there's still that lingering doubt that something is wrong. It feels like that quiet moment before a storm, where you're just waiting for something to happen.

CHAPTER 45

$\mathcal{O}$nce everyone finishes dinner, Amy and I help Sarah bring out the desserts. She went all out. Aside from the apple pie, there are cakes, donuts, fruit salad – you name it and it's there.

Everyone scatters around the house to eat. I settle in the dining room with Amy, Sarah, and unfortunately Roxanne. Tobias is doing the best he can to stay grounded. If it wasn't for his siblings, he would have cracked. Having Amy home for the holidays has been a blessing in disguise.

Dawson too. He and Tobias were arguing over who would play the piano when the family sang carols. Sarah got tired of their bickering and sent them all out to shovel snow, which had gotten heavier since we arrived. Their fighting was playful and nothing malicious like what happened between Piper and me.

"I didn't realize you were an author, that's pretty cool," Roxanne says.

I give her the best smile I can muster. She hasn't done anything to me, and I need to keep calm.

Amy leans into me. "She writes pretty kickass books too."

She's next to me in the same spots Tobias and I sat in during dinner. Sarah and Roxanne are on the other side.

"I'm not into fantasy, but it sounds great," Roxanne says, sincerely.

"This is why we never got along. How can you not like fantasy?" Amy's sarcasm is laced with some venom. Roxanne doesn't seem to notice.

A loud stampede of boots and boisterous men come traipsing into the dining room. Tobias, Blake, Tim, and Dawson are all covered in wet snow. Their boots leave puddles along their path. Sarah glares up at them.

"I don't think anyone is going anywhere tonight," Dawson says. He shakes some snow off his shaved head, and it lands on the table. Sarah gives a scolding look, but in a teasing way.

I glance up at Tobias, not sure what that means for us. His attention lands on Roxanne across the table from me; seeing the two of us together ignites a flame in his eye. He shifts uneasily from side to side. I want to reach out, but Amy is between us.

"Tobias, you and Kasey can stay in your old room. I don't mind having you all over tonight."

Sarah's voice is calm. She seems relieved that all her children will be under one roof again, at least for a night.

Tobias focuses on his mom. The tension in his body dissolves as he analyzes her reaction. "Kace, is that okay with you?" He surveys me.

I'm a little uneasy with Roxanne here, but I wouldn't want to be anywhere else tonight. His family has taken me in and treated me like one of their own.

"Sounds good to me."

"Oh!" Sarah claps her hands excitedly. "Now that's settled, you boys get your asses out of my dining room with your soaking wet boots and dry up. We've got some carols to sing!"

When Sarah says it's time for carols everyone jumps at the chance. Another family tradition that everyone in the household enjoys. Even Blake and Zoey put down their devices to hop in on the action. Dawson and Tobias rush away to get dressed, so they can hurry back down to sing.

Ten minutes later a thunderous boom of running feet charge down the stairs as Tobias and Dawson barrel towards the small wooden piano in the corner of the living room. The bench tips as they playfully shove each other, acting the same as two toddlers vying for that blue square during circle time. Dawson wins, but Tobias doesn't act too upset when he grabs a guitar on a stand beside the piano.

Blake finds his way to Tobias, ogling the guitar. Right away Tobias goes into music teacher mode and begins showing him a few chords while everyone settles down. It's moments like this that make me fall harder. He catches me watching and curls his finger for me to join him. His playful wiggle puts me at ease.

"The Twelve Days of Christmas" is a disaster as Tobias, Blake and I make an attempt to harmonize on five golden rings over all the chatter. The best group ended up being Dawson and Mr Scott who belted out a low guttural baritone on partridge in a pear tree.

Halfway through "Jingle Bells", Tobias hands the guitar to Tim, who plays like he's in a rock band. I'm in awe of how smooth his fingers move over the strings.

Tobias pivots towards me and holds out his hand. "Will you have this dance with me?" He bows, the gesture makes me crack a smile.

Roxanne surveys us as he pulls me into him. I do my best to ignore the jealous gleam in her narrowed eyes. Tobias belts out the lyrics, tugging my attention back to him. I'm plagued with two left feet and find myself tripping over him. At times our laughter overpowered the music.

Once the real singing has stopped, Sarah and I head into the kitchen to prep movie snacks. Another Scott tradition is *A Christmas Story* movie night. I'm looking forward to settling down and taking it easy for the rest of the evening. Sarah must be feeling the same way. There's a heaviness around her eyes, but she still finds it in her to chug forward and smile.

Amy comes bounding into the kitchen with Ezra attached to her hip. He reaches for Sarah, and she scrunches up her nose at him, and talks in a high-pitched voice. Amy hands him over and Sarah dances with him around the kitchen.

I'm filling plastic containers with popcorn and spreading out a bunch of what looks like extra Halloween candy. Amy grabs a handful of candy and places it on an empty tray. "How are you holding up? I know my family can be a bit much."

I laugh. "I'm having more fun than I would have had with my family." I don't want to go into detail tonight, and Amy doesn't push me, even though there's a questioning look in her eye.

She bumps my hip and I spill some popcorn onto one of the trays. "We are pretty awesome, aren't we?"

"Ma! Where's the snacks!" Dawson's voice echoes through the house.

Amy shakes her head and grasps a full tray to try to bring inside. "They're like wild animals scavenging for their next meal. Hope you like to cook, girl; Tobias is just as bad as Dawson. Always hungry."

I crack a toothy smile at her.

She lifts the tray and begins to move it but stops. She turns back to me. "You're really good for him, Kasey. I'm not only saying that because you're my favorite author." She winks. There's a smile behind her pressed lips. "I mean, Tobias's whole world stops when you walk in a room. I do hope you'll stick around with us."

I blink away some phantom tears and glance up at her. It's beyond nice to feel wanted. "However long he wants me here, I will be."

Her face lights up. "Good. Oh." She pauses and grips the tray tighter. "I'm not sure how much you know about Roxanne, but don't let her get to you. Tobias is only on edge because she's been dragging him through the mud since they were in high school. If my father wasn't the pastor, I'd have kicked her ass out of here long ago, but he has to keep up appearances, so he tends to take in strays." Amy stops and takes in my reaction.

"Tobias still refuses to talk about it with me." I stare down at some of the popcorn that escaped the bag.

"He will. Give him time. That was a tough wound to close." She starts to say something else, but Tobias saunters in with his attention on us.

Sarah intercepts his path. "Tobias, help bring some of this stuff in, Ezra wants some Grammy time." She bounces him on her hip.

"Tob!" Ezra yells.

"Yes, Uncle Tobias. I'm the cool uncle, but shh… don't tell Uncle D."

Sarah gives him a playful shove then leaves the three of us alone. Tobias faces Amy and me. His intense glare lands on me, and for whatever reason I can't look him in the eye. The Roxanne conversation with his sister threw me for a loop.

"Everything is fine, little brother, just some girl talk. Now use that giant wingspan and help us bring all this junk inside."

Leave it to Amy to clear the elephant in the room. It still hangs in the air, but much less.

"Yeah, Tobias, stop slacking," I tease.

He raises a brow and smirks. "Slacking?"

On the counter is a can of whipped cream that was left from dessert. He reaches for it and sprays some at me. It lands on my cheek and drips down. I catch it before it falls. Scrunching up my face I step forward and smack his face with the glob. When he tries to spray the can it's nearly empty and sprays everywhere, including on him.

"Now you've done it!" Amy jokes.

I scream as he tries to spray more, but it keeps getting everywhere. He reaches into the bowl of M&Ms beside us on the counter and dips it into the cream still on my cheek, then eats it.

"Save that for later, you two." Sarah chuckles and all the tension in the room vanishes.

"What the heck?" Dawson asks from the doorway, eyeing the situation.

"Your brother wanted to get out of helping bring everything inside, so he sprayed his girlfriend with whipped cream," Amy says.

Dawson chuckles. "I miss all the fun."

"Yes, and now you get to help while they clean up."

Dawson sneers at Tobias, who retaliates by throwing a piece of candy at his brother.

While Dawson helps Amy, Tobias leads me to the downstairs bathroom to get cleaned up. He shuts the old creaky wooden door, then reaches into the closet behind it for some washcloths. Once it's wet, he gently presses the cloth onto my face and starts to remove the sticky white mess. Our bodies automatically move closer, like two magnets connecting.

He rests the washcloth on the side of my face and leans down to kiss me. My body craves him, especially after this morning. With ease he reaches over and locks the door. Then he attempts to pick me up and nearly tumbles, we both chuckle into each other's mouths. He sets me up on the bathroom counter, his center just the right height as he leans into me.

He starts licking my neck right where the cream is dripping. I throw my head back and attempt to suppress the moan building up inside of me.

"Your mom is going to be wondering..."

"Shh," he says, shushing me with his lips against mine.

He presses hard into me. A breath catches in my throat as he thrusts forward.

"Tobias!" Amy's voice carries through the room.

He pulls away and rests his forehead beside mine. "To be continued…"

"I do like cliffhangers," I tease.

"Yeah. Me? Not so much."

A sexy grin lights up his handsome face. I gently caress his cheek. His eyes close.

"I love you so much, Kace. You know that, right?"

"I do. And I love you."

He acts desperate to slip away with me. I hope it's more of him wanting to be with me, rather than escaping Roxanne.

"You ready?"

"Yeah, let me finish wiping up this sticky mess on your face."

CHAPTER 46

*T*obias and I decided to cut out of movie night early. He flips on the switch to his childhood bedroom. The dimmer lights above brighten up the navy-blue walls. I imagine what it might have looked like when he lived at home. Was he a typical teenage boy with dishes piled up to the ceiling, or was his room neat and tidy, like how Mom made us keep ours?

I take a seat on the comforter. The color matches the wall. The light brown dresser is a set with the bedside table, and the bed itself. A large shelf takes up one whole wall. There are so many movies and books, I'm surprised he didn't take some of these things with him when he moved out.

The door clicks shut, and Tobias wiggles his brows. He's calmer than he was earlier. He rummages through the dresser for something then tugs a pair of sweats for himself along with a worn-out black Dungeons and Dragons T-shirt. I snicker.

"What?" He pulls his sweater up over his head.

"So, you're a comic book guitar-playing Dungeons and Dragons guy?"

A deep laughter rumbles through him. "Don't forget, I'm a magician too." He winks.

I throw my head back and laugh.

He crosses his arms at his chest. "For your information D&D is awesome! Lots of role playing involved." His lips pull into a sexy smirk.

"Are you implying you want to role play with me?"

He gives me a seductive wink. I stand, shoving him. His laughter lightens my soul, the bad vibes from earlier vanish. I love this side of him. There's still lingering pain in his dark eyes, but it's mostly forgotten as he tosses his pants away.

I suppress a giggle with my hand. "On that note, I'm getting dressed." As I start pulling my pants down, he rushes up behind me and wraps his arms around me.

He whispers into my ear. "You can be the fairy princess I save, and I'll be the elven king... oh, you could even write a book..."

I bend over, pick up my leggings, and chuck them at his head. He laughs. And throws them to the floor. When his hands are free, he reaches around my back and tugs me hard into his body.

We tilt our heads at the same time. "Kace." His voice is rough as my name leaves his lips. I lean closer, our noses touching slightly. I love how when he presses into me, he rocks his head up and down allowing his face to rub against mine.

"Mmm," I moan.

He turns me so I'm facing forward and steadies me with his hands. With his moist lips he leaves a trail of tiny kisses along my right shoulder, and the side of my neck. My middle throbs, moisture forming in my underwear from only a single touch. His fingers are dangerously close to the edge of my panties. I love how he carefully draws along the waistband before slowly making his way down south.

His whole hand presses up atop the wetness pooled there and he hisses. "Is this what happens when you fantasize about me?" he whispers. His words are unexpected, but I'm turned on so much that it doesn't even matter.

"Yes," I cry, as he nibbles gently on the outside of my ear. I'd never admit it out loud, how I've gotten myself off by the thought of him. I can't even say the words without thinking of how cringy it sounds coming from me.

"Feel what that does to me?" he asks, pressing himself into my back. I moan at his touch and slap my hand to my mouth. I'd almost forgotten we aren't alone. Who knows how thin the walls are.

He laughs, moving me to face him, then gets to his knees and looks up like he's worshiping me. I hum as he tugs on my panties, lowering them to my ankles. The soft touch of his fingers coaxes a moan out of me. His daring eyes peek up as he leaves a trail of kisses up my thighs. My back arches. I suppress a scream by burying my face into the crook of my arm.

I tug at his shoulders, asking him to stand.

He chuckles. "What do you want, Kasey?" His deep baritone voice vibrates my whole body. God, I want all of him, now!

"I need you inside me again." My breath hitches, as he kisses back up over my stomach. He grabs hold of my breasts then kisses those too. I rest my hand over his, pressing his touch harder into my breasts.

"Oh, so that's how you like it."

I'm so turned on by how he speaks to me. I love the way he looks at this angle with his chin tucked down and all his attention directed at me. He gets to his feet, grabs his wallet, and pulls out a condom. I like that he's ready for me.

After a few minutes of me soaring with ecstasy and him trying to get his boxers off without falling, which causes a fit of laughter between us, we finally settle onto the bed. The sensation is as pleasurable as it was the first time, maybe even better. A mixture of dirty words spills from his pale pink lips. I wasn't expecting them, but they make my insides pulse.

I'd love for it to last all night, but both of us have so much pent-up sexual tension to release that it doesn't take long at all.

We climax together and he collapses beside me, a satisfied smile on his face.

"So, how was that for the ending to the cliffhanger?" I ask.

He releases a breathy chuckle. "It was well worth the wait."

I turn my head and he mimics my movement. "See. I told you."

"You're right. I'll never second guess a cliffhanger again."

He reaches over and pulls me close. "I'm going to need a nice shower after that one. My God, woman," he teases. "It's everywhere."

I smack him playfully. "How will we get to the bathroom?"

We do a quick clean-up with some paper towels, then grab half of our clothing we had worn and attempt to put it on to look somewhat presentable, like we didn't just have mind-blowing sex right above a pastor and his family. Oh God that just sounds dirty. My cheeks warm as Tobias sticks his head out the door. He check-searches the hallway like he's a spy. I bite the back of my hand to suppress a giggle.

He waves his hand and together we tiptoe through the upstairs hallway like two naughty teens trying to not wake our parents. Inside the bathroom we lock the door. We scrub each other down and I even get a second round of him.

CHAPTER 47

$\mathscr{I}$ find it hard to sleep. There's ice spitting against the window and a frigid winter wind whipping the tree outside. It's not the weather keeping me awake, it's the replay of the dream I had. Flashes of it play in my head of Tobias and Roxanne kissing and me catching them. It's the Lloyd scenario all over again, and even though I know it's fake, it still feels incredibly real.

"Kasey, are you alright?" Tobias's voice catches me off guard. I didn't realize I was being a nuisance with all my tossing and turning.

After our shower it felt like a dark cloud loomed over his head again. I held back asking him as I don't want to ruin the one Christmas Day I've actually enjoyed, but I don't think I can any longer.

"Sorry to wake you. I'm having trouble falling asleep."

"Oh. What's on your mind? Did you not have a nice Christmas?"

I roll over. In the darkness I find his face and press my hand against it. "No. That's not it at all. You made this Christmas one of the best I've ever had. Despite my awful family, and… and…" I stop myself from saying her name and focus on the positive. "There's honestly not many I can remember that stand out as good, but being with you changed that. I don't know how I got so lucky meeting you."

"But–"

If he insists, I'll just bare my soul. "You still won't talk to me about things, and I can't erase awful thoughts. I blame my last relationship for messing with my head."

"I told you, I have no feelings at all for her. I wish you'd stop with that." There's an edge to his voice, and I'm sorry I even brought it up.

Dropping my hand, I turn so that I'm facing the window again. I close my eyes and attempt to sleep. After a few long beats of silence, he sighs.

"She did things to me, like tell me that she loved me, and then two days later she'd be with another guy, no warning. Then when things didn't work out, she would crawl right back to me. I allowed it for far too long."

When I don't respond he continues.

"The last one was bad. It wasn't the first time I'd caught her cheating, but it was *who* she cheated on me with that pissed me off. She knew how I felt about the guy but did it anyway."

Something clicks into place in my head. It's a small town, anything is possible. "Daryl?"

Tobias is quiet, and that's how I know I've hit a nerve. "I don't know what else I can do or say to make you understand that I want nothing to do with her. I'm tired of explaining that."

"I'm sorry, I'll never ask again. Goodnight." Silent tears fall, but I don't let him know.

He releases a harsh breath, then snakes his arms around me, pulling me to his chest. I gasp from his touch.

I hold on to his warm arms, not wanting to let go. He swipes my hair from my shoulder, and gently places a kiss against my neck and cheek. I can sense that the love he has for me is real, but I can't help wondering how much our previous relationships will affect what we have. The fear of it bringing me back to the place I was a year ago frightens me.

CHAPTER 48

*T*he soft morning light peeks through the curtains and dances across the comforter. My hand reaches out, touching the space beside me ready to crawl into his arms, but it's empty. After a sleepless night it was one of the things I'd been looking forward to.

I don't dwell, instead I head downstairs where the fresh aroma of coffee permeates. The kitchen is empty, car engines are rumbling to life outside. Peeking out the window above the sink I find Tobias bundled up. In one hand is a shovel, while the other is frantically moving around in frustration.

Lifting on my toes, I attempt to get a better view. My hands dig into the countertop as I lean in. My chest aches. It's Roxanne. His posture is stiff as he continues to flail his arms around, and I can't tell if his red cheeks are from the cold or out of anger.

"Morning," Amy says, bouncing in with freshly wet hair.

My hand slips and I almost lose my balance but hold on.

"You look wrecked. Everything okay?" she asks, coming over to fill one of the mugs left on the counter with coffee.

For a mom she barely looks bothered by the early morning and appears well-rested. She steps beside me and peeks out the window. "She's gotten him riled up. I'm going to have to go out there and give her a piece of my mind."

I rest my back against the edge of the counter and stare off across the room at nothing.

"Hey, Kasey. Tobias is in love with you, don't let Roxanne get under your skin. I know I said that last night but I mean it. She's always meddling in things, and he lets her, he always has. He wouldn't do anything with her though, not when he's with you. He's not that kind of person."

I take another moment to stare quietly, then turn to Amy. "Would he break up with me first?"

My lip quivers and I hate it. I don't want to cry in front of her, but Lloyd never waited to break up with me, and look where we ended. I'm not sure I could handle another relationship where someone cheats on me. It makes me believe that all those other dates, the ones that didn't work, were actually because of me, not them.

She sets the coffee mug down, and steps in front of me. Her hands touch my shoulders and with narrowing eyes she stares deep into mine. "Kasey, I know my brother, and I don't think breaking up with you is on his mind. I'll admit when Mom said he was dating again I was worried. Worried for the girl he'd drag into his drama with Roxanne, but then Mom said he'd started to perk up, ignore her, and she felt like her son had gotten his life back."

I wipe at the wetness pooling at the corner of my eyes, unable to stop my lip from trembling. Without question she embraces me in a hug and holds on tight. I want to push her away, afraid I've already grown attached to not only him but his family.

The door opens with a loud thud and the two of us jump apart. Tobias stomps through, boots dragging snow with him. He doesn't stop to ask what's happening, only keeps trudging forward, leaving a trail of wetness in his wake.

Dawson clears his throat from the doorway. Amy and I turn

our attention there. "Whew, that woman is a piece of work." He kicks off his boots, but instantly regrets it as he walks through Tobias's mess. He hangs his head, then finally turns his attention on the two of us. "Oh. You saw that, huh, Kace?"

"Mhmm."

He sighs, makes his way over, gripping my shoulders. "He needs you. You're already his shining light, but he truly needs someone like you to pull him from this darkness. You have the spark that just might do that. Go check in on him, he might need you."

"You think?"

"No. I don't think, I know."

Upstairs I slowly enter the bedroom. The wetness trail going all the way to the bed where Tobias is sitting at the edge with his head in his hands. Without a word I sit beside him. It's a tense silence that feel like hours, but it's only minutes.

"Are you ready to go?" he asks.

"Yeah."

His eyes are dull. Something is different, like she took that spark that Amy and Dawson spoke of and tore it out. His hand slips into mine, but a thick fog of uncertainty hangs in there between us. I hope that whatever spark she took from him, I can bring it back. If I can't, I fear this relationship will go up in flames.

CHAPTER 49

*S*am's been whistling and dancing around the store for the last few days. I swear I caught him moonwalking across the sales floor. Francesca's witty ways have rubbed off on him for sure. If he starts leaning over the counter to talk to me then I'll know he's lost it.

We're at that halfway point between Christmas and New Year's where no one has a clue what day it is. This point in the year is like limbo. It's that "I better eat the last of those cookies before my new-year new-me" resolution starts on the first. My only resolution is to resolve how I've gone from being sick over not being good enough to having gut-retching pain from walking away.

I hope Tobias and I are okay, but he's been distant. I miss that excited Christmas morning feeling he gave me. When he dropped me off after we left his mom's house, there was some unresolved pain lingering, that he tried to hide. Tonight will be our first night out together since then and I want it to go well. Last night on the phone we talked for hours, everything felt okay. Hopefully it's only my mind playing tricks.

My phone buzzes in my pocket and with the store empty of

customers, I pull it out to check. Tobias's name lights up my screen. Bile sits in the back of my throat, burning so bad I struggle to swallow.

"Sam." My voice breaks.

He stands from his spot on the floor. He'd been rearranging some lower shelves near the front of the store. He peeks his head around the large shelf.

"Can I take this in the backroom?"

He waves for me to go. Before I reach the door, I answer. "Hey." I try to sound peppy, instead of worried.

"Hey." Dread fills me at the sound of his monotone voice.

The door slams shut behind me and I jump at the sound. I settle myself in the far-right corner of the room and slide down the wall. This isn't going to end well.

"I'm sorry to do this," he says. "I have to head over to Mom's. Her car won't start, and Dawson wants me to pick up some parts for him to see if it will work. Dad isn't home, he's working on something for a retreat in January. So, it's up to me."

I tuck my knees into my chest and hug them with my one free hand. "Mmhmm." I rest my forehead on the top of my kneecaps.

"Kace? Are you okay over there?"

I don't respond, so he calls out my name again.

"Fine. Yeah. I'm okay." *No. I'm not okay*, I want to scream, but I don't. How can I push him for answers if he's not ready to give them? Trust is the hardest thing in a relationship. I trusted Lloyd and he broke it. Would Tobias do the same?

"I really have to go, there's a backup on the expressway."

"'Kay." Kay? Now he's definitely going to suspect something is up, I've never said that before. I've used okay, but never shortened it.

I count the number of heartbeats in the silence between us. There are ten.

"I'll call you later if I can." His words are quick and snappy, like he doesn't want to talk at all.

"Bye." I press the end call button. I drop the phone carefully onto the floor, then wrap my other arm around my leg. I pull them towards my chest and squeeze.

I won't allow myself to cry when there is nothing to cry over. There's nothing wrong, I'm overreacting. We had a nice Christmas despite his ex showing up, and I'm not going to ruin those memories with my sadness that mostly stems from my insecurities. If I was strong enough to tell off my family, I'm strong enough to deal with boyfriend drama. I'm twenty-four for Christ sakes.

"Kasey, Tobias told me to…" Sam stands in the doorway. His forehead creases as he peeks at the text then back down at me. "He told me to check on you."

"I'm fine." I stand and grab my phone, waving him off.

I slip it back inside my jean pocket and wipe at my dusty pants. From the looks of it Sam is contemplating calling Tobias.

"Really. I needed a second, that's all."

He raises one brow imitating The Rock. An unlady-like snort flies out of me.

Sam smirks. "Real classy, Kace."

"Sorry, you looked like The Rock for a second, or it was a sad attempt." I snicker. Sam grabs a knitted hat from our overstock trend wall and throws it at me. I catch it and laugh. Sometimes a friend is all someone needs to laugh again. Tonight, for me, that's Sam.

"Are you sure everything's okay?"

I can't hide the worry. Sam knows me too well. The fact that Tobias asked Sam to check on me has to mean something. I'm reading way too deep into what's going on, everything will be okay.

"We're all locked up. I just have to count the register and then we are good to go." He hesitates by the door, probably waiting for me to break down. Before he can continue his phone goes wild with several beeps. He lifts it to check, and his eyes go wide.

"What's wrong?" I ask, my voice wavering this way and that.

"It's uh… it's nothing."

"That's not nothing, Sam. Is it Francesca? Is she okay? Your mom?" I shoot several questions at him. I step back when his neck flushes. If it's his mom I hate the guilt that's rested on his shoulder because of my nagging.

"Francesca and Mom are okay. It's Amy. I mean Amy texted me. She's fine. Fine." Two more texts pop through. My pulse drums in my ear. I didn't even know Amy had Sam's number.

"Sam, what's going on? Is it Tobias?"

I fight the urge to cry. He just told me there was a traffic jam. *Kasey, breathe.* What if he… my thoughts drift to every awful scenario.

Sam interrupts my thoughts. "He's not hurt, in a physical sense."

"Then what?" I wince at my sharp tone.

"He had a run-in at his mom's house with Roxanne. She was there picking up something for her dad and Tobias flipped."

I stare off at the floor. He wasn't heading to his mom's. He was already there. He must have called me after. I'm used to men lying to me but coming from Tobias the sting hurts so much I have to hold my middle to keep myself from crumbling. I was trying to give Tobias space in regard to Roxanne. The fact Amy is worried scares me.

"He canceled our date." My eyes don't leave the laces on Sam's sneakers.

Sam shakes his head. "It's not what you think."

"And what's that? He obviously still has some sort of feelings for her, if being around her affects him so much."

Sam strides across the room and once in front of me gently places his free hand on my shoulder. "Do you trust me?"

Sam has never given me a reason not to. "Of course."

"I never thought he'd find someone to be with again. He struggled for months finding a girl, he bailed on a ton of dates, including a double date well before the one we all went on. Then he met you and, Kace, he would never hurt you. Not intentionally anyway. Let him work through his shit and once he does then you can seek him out."

Deep inside my nose an itch builds. I try to stop it with a sniffle, but that only makes it worse.

"I'll check in on him for you, okay?"

"'Kay," I say, voice tight.

Sam sighs. "Count the till for me, and I'll make a quick call. Tonight, Francesca and I are going to show you a good time."

"I can't intrude on your date…"

"Are you kidding me? If it's hanging out with you and Francesca, I'm more of the third wheel than anything." He laughs. That makes me smile.

"True."

"Okay. I'll be on the sales floor in a minute. I'm sure he's fine."

CHAPTER 50

J don't drink coffee often but being that it's New Year's and my sleep cycle has been thrown off, I brew a cup in Francesca's machine. The taste doesn't appeal to me, even doused with an unhealthy dose of sugar and some vanilla creamer. I pour it into a travel mug as I prepare myself for work.

I haven't confronted Tobias about lying the other night, but he's been texting as if nothing was wrong. I'm not buying it. Amy has been distracting me with funny sightseeing pictures. Sam gave her my number the other day and she's been texting nonstop since I sent her a draft of book three, she's already more than halfway through. She's upset that I've had to work every day this week and have not been able to join her and Tobias, but with the holidays and Mr Ruppert's post-holiday schedule I couldn't ask for time off.

I grab my coat and keys, and the gross concoction of coffee I made, and head downstairs. I turn the knob and when I swing the door open Dad is standing on my front step. His hand is raised, ready to knock.

"I'm sorry to barge in on you, but you haven't been answering your phone."

I squeeze the warm mug in my hand. "I don't have much time."

"I'll make it quick."

I sigh and step outside, locking the door behind me. "Okay."

Dad quietly stares down at his sneakers. I don't want to have this conversation. It can't lead to anything good. We keep going around in a circle, I tell him how I feel, he tells me he understands, then crawls right back into Mom's lap like a lost puppy.

"I should have reached out sooner, but I wanted to give you space." He doesn't blink as he observes my reaction.

A crazed laughter races through me. Space was the one thing I could have done without. Deep down I wanted them to follow me out of the house and beg me to come back inside. They would tell me they were sorry, and things would be normal, but that's not how it went down, and space was what hurt the most.

"Kace, I should have stood up for you more." His breath hitches.

My jaw drops. He should have said this years ago. I hate that he was Team Kasey yet stood by Mom's side.

"I came to tell you that I left her, again. On Christmas Eve moments after you walked out, I did the same. I hoped that you'd still be outside and when you weren't I figured you needed time to sort through what had happened. She is your mother though, and I think..." He pauses when he catches the flabbergasted look on my face.

I blink furiously attempting to hold the hot tears that threaten my eyes. I woke up tired, but with hope that since it was New Year's, things would be okay. Clearly, life had other plans.

"I'm so tired of the disappointed look on her face. I dated thirty-one guys for some kind of validation that I was good enough. Even when I brought Tobias home, she still had the audacity to throw my insecurities in my face." My voice catches in my throat, and I have to pause. "It hurts to walk away from my family, but until I'm shown respect and not ridiculed at every gathering, I will keep my distance."

Dad wipes at the corner of his eyes. "Forget my opinion. I hate that you're hurting and if I could take away all that pain I would. I doubt me saying anything to her will ever make her change. She has to want it."

"And she doesn't," I whisper.

"Have I ever told you how proud I am of you? Not only for how you stuck up to your mother, but for everything you've accomplished. You paid your way through college, worked hard, and published two amazing books."

He reaches out for me, and I follow through. He sandwiches my hand between both of his. "Honey, you don't have to feel like you've failed, because you have done the complete opposite. If Mom doesn't realize that, then it's her fault you walked away. I'm sorry it took me so long to say these words to you."

"I hate that it hurts." My voice squeaks, and I lose it right there in front of the house. As if life wasn't throwing enough curve-balls, it pitches Dad right at me. He wraps me into his arms, and I stay there. I can't recall a memory when Dad hugged me, and it wasn't just because we were saying goodbye.

"If she doesn't realize what an amazing young lady you've turned out to be, then it's her loss."

I hold on. I haven't been this close to him since before he moved out. Sure, he'd been in my life, but we'd give a casual side hug or a wave. He's ready to fix things between us. I'm more than willing to mend my relationship with Dad. His apology means a lot and the fact that he's walking away from her solidifies that.

"I'm sorry for everything."

He hushes me while brushing my hair to calm my nerves. "You have nothing to be sorry for, Kace."

When my tears have dried, I give Dad one last hug before settling down in my car. The weight of one problem releases some tension in my shoulders. Before I pull out of the driveway, I check my phone. I have quite a few text messages. They're mostly Francesca talking about tonight, but the two that make my heart speed up are the ones from Tobias.

I'll be at your apartment by 7pm. Taking Amy to the airport.

The second text is a picture of the two of them on top of the Empire State Building with a sign that reads:

Wish you were here, Kasey.

My stomach flutters, but upon further inspection, his eyes seem distant. His smile doesn't reach them, nor does it make them crinkle. I rest my head on the steering wheel, needing a few minutes to breathe. I stick my phone inside my bag and vow not to check it for the rest of the day. If I do, I'll make myself crazy.

Work has been quiet today. We had a few midday rushes but nothing that was too overwhelming. New Year's has always been hit or miss. We finally close in twenty minutes and Francesca has been hanging around for an hour waiting. She helped me organize some Valentines titles to prepare for the post New Year's holidays.

Sam is working on starting closing procedures. He's already shut down the second register and has moved onto the till. Francesca lays her body over the counter, and props her head on her hands, her elbows planted firmly on the surface.

I'm knee deep in special orders and organizing them so they are ready for the opening manager to call the customers to let them know they are in. Sam and I have the afternoon shift and

Mr Ruppert usually comes by and helps us close out the day, even though it's another short one.

Francesca picks at her glittery blue and gold New Year's nails, then turns her attention back to me. "When is Tobias coming?"

"He said he's coming around seven. He's taking Amy and her family to the airport."

I retreat and continue working on the orders. They've gotten me through the past hour. The day went by fast, but the past hour has dragged. I'm anxious over what will happen with Tobias. My chest has felt tight since late this afternoon and every breath takes all the energy out of me.

"Kace?"

I glance over the writing on the sheets to make sure the phone numbers are clear, then run through the alphabet in my head so all orders are correctly placed in the box. Albert, Boone, Buscemi. The neater they are the better. I find a few out of place and fix them.

A hand on my arm catches my attention. I glance up, blinking at Francesca. Had she spoken to me?

"I'm sorry did you say something?"

Francesca squeezes my arm. "I just wanted to know what Tobias wanted from the Chinese place, I'm going to go order now while you two close up."

"Oh. Um…" Holy crap, I don't even know what kind of Chinese food he eats. I put my finger up to my lip and lightly nibble on the nail.

"Pork fried rice and dumplings," Sam cuts in.

"Great, thanks." Francesca smiles at Sam, then peeks over at me.

I've lost myself, gone back to the place I was a year ago. Francesca knows where my head is and is urging me to come back. Francesca and Sam have both been my rock this week. I love having Sam around, as much as I love Francesca. If it weren't for them, I don't know what I would have done.

Sam comes around and gives Francesca a kiss on the cheek. "We'll be over in fifteen minutes. You have everything written down?"

"Yup, yup," she says, as upbeat as she can be. With the amount of worry in her eyes I'm surprised she's able to throw a smile at Sam. "I'm excited to spend the night with my favorite people and slip into my Pikachu slippers."

I perk up and face Sam. "You let her wear those?"

His eyebrows rise. "I don't know," he says, tickling her ear with his lips. "She looks kind of sexy in them."

Laughter fills my lungs making it surprisingly easier to breathe. Our plans for New Year's are the perfect way to end the year, snuggled up at home in our comfortable clothes with the people we love the most. I hope the image in my head of how the evening pans out is correct, but the sinking feeling in my stomach begs to differ.

When Francesca leaves, I slip a quick text to Tobias, praying it will help put my mind at ease.

Hey, can't wait to see you in a little while. Tell Amy I'll miss her.

His text comes through right away.

Same. Love you.

I wait for the text to light me up with joy, but it never ignites. His automatic response felt robotic.

Sam pulls on his jacket and begins to shut off some of the lights from the panel on the wall near the stockroom. "Are you ready?"

"Yeah. Let's go." My voice doesn't sound as convincing as I want it to.

He zeroes in on me, giving me the "I'm here if you need me"

wide-eyed look. I throw on my jacket, but keep my arms around my center, not only is it cold but if I don't hold on, I may just fall apart.

CHAPTER 51

Cold Chinese food sits in open containers on the small brown coffee table. The three of us are on the couch, Francesca in the middle, Sam and me on the ends. We've eaten so much food that I'm thankful for my sweats. They have the right amount of elastic to fit perfectly after a large meal.

It's close to midnight and we are still waiting on Tobias. I stare at the cartons of food that were meant for him – I swear it's mocking me. I attempt to pull myself out of wherever my mind has wandered off to and put myself back in the conversation.

"Right, do you remember that?" Francesca nudges me lightly in the ribs, her laughter ripples through the room.

"Yeah. You were such a nerd." I stick my tongue out at her.

I'm finding it hard to focus on their conversation. *You're stronger than this, Kasey. Enjoy your time with friends. He'll come around, and if he doesn't you can exist without him, you have for twenty-four years.* I try to believe that no matter what happens tonight I'll always have the girl beside me, who is snorting like a pig at our old memories.

Sam throws his head back dramatically and laughs. "Francesca, a nerd?"

I smile at Sam. I hope more than anything that he'll remain a constant in my life too, just as he has been since I was sixteen.

"She was Hermione from fourth grade through middle school and would make me role play Harry Potter with her," I say.

He's laughing hard enough that his face is bright red. She gives him a playful tap on the arm and rests her head on his shoulder. He throws an arm over her and holds on tight. Their relationship has blossomed into something amazing. There's a slight pang of something tugging at my insides as they snuggle close to each other. I gaze down at the ground and away from their intimate moment. I catch sight of the container and close my eyes, needing a second to recollect myself.

Sam wipes his eyes from the tears brought on by my laughing. "I can't picture you as Harry."

"I was Harry. Every time."

"No." Francesca shoots up from her spot. "Remember you played Ron too."

Sam loses it when we tell him. He grasps his stomach. "How did you get stuck with all the male characters?"

I reach around Francesca and shove his shoulder too.

"Wait," he says. "Does that mean if you played Ron, did you two…"

"Oh God no!" we shout at the same time.

He laughs so hard his body shakes. He holds his hands up to defend himself. "Oh man, I'm being ganged up on. Where the hell is my backup."

My laughter fades. One minute it's vibrating through me, the next there's nothing but silence.

Sam tosses me an apologetic glance and clears his throat. "I'll be right back."

He swipes his phone off the coffee table and strides away towards Francesca's room. I'm not in the mood to talk, so I excuse myself to go to the bathroom. Francesca would never push me, but I need the silence and the privacy to catch my breath.

I lock the door and rest my back up against it, checking my phone for a missed call or message. I pull it from the front pocket of my gray sweatshirt. The last from him was the one he sent at 6:17pm.

"Hey. We're getting worried about you." Sam's voice carries through the paper-thin walls of our apartment. I don't mean to eavesdrop, but Sam's voice is so loud I can't help it.

"What? Are you nuts? No, but you need to get here soon. Not good, man." Anger rages through him, it resonates in his loud voice.

"She's over here waiting for you. She keeps staring at the damn cold container of food she ordered for you like it will magically make you appear." He pauses. "Dude."

There's a giant plot hole in my life, and I don't know how to edit it to have it make sense again. How could we go from fooling around on Christmas to this? Was it something I did? If he was still hung up on Roxanne, why would he start something new? This has to stem deeper than some old love.

"I know I'm your best friend, but if you hurt her." He pauses. "I'm not sure I could forgive you for that."

I press a hand to my chest, like the pain is real. There's nothing physically wrong with me, except for maybe the impending panic attack building up under my hand. The sharp sting brings me to my knees. I rub at my throbbing temples and wish the night was over.

I turn the phone back on, there's only twenty-five minutes until midnight. There's really no point, he's not going to make it in time. As much as I'd love to stick around and cheer with Sam and Francesca, I've suddenly lost the urge to celebrate.

I get to my feet and step out of the bathroom the same time Sam comes out of Francesca's room. He freezes in place and his cheeks flush. I shake my head and head back for the living room.

"There you two are," Francesca says, bouncing up onto her knees.

She senses right away something is wrong.

"Happy New Year's." My gaze shifts between them. "I'm not going to stay up. I'm exhausted."

They stare at me with pity in their eyes. I swallow hard as Francesca throws her arms around me. Sam comes from the other side and joins in the hug. I'm half laughing and crying but holding back the tears.

"Happy New Year's," Sam says, as I retreat to my room.

I close the door softly behind me. Inside the darkness I crawl into bed. The pillowcase beside me still has his pine scent from Christmas. I breathe it in and hold on to it while quietly crying into my pillow, making my eyelids heavy with sleep. I cry it out until the blackness of sleep begins to take over. Happy freaking New Year's.

CHAPTER 52

The bed shifts under me. I open my eyes to a blurry figure sitting on the edge. It's Tobias and he's staring down at something in his hands. His head hangs low. I stay quiet.

The part that scares me the most is that he hasn't taken off his jacket, and he's still in regular clothes. He's not planning to stay. A soft whimper leaves my lips. He watches me, and I can't tell if it's from the night light, but I swear his eyes are red.

I blink away the sleep and tears. I'm horrified by what he's holding. I sit up. "Where did you get that?"

"It must have fallen out of your purse. It was left in my room at my parents' house."

From the soft glow of the streetlamp outside I can see exactly what page he's on. It doesn't look good for Tobias and me. I get why he's angry, if I found a book of women my boyfriend had dated with weird labels, I'd freak out too. It looks like the new year is going to start off exactly how last year did, with me crying and alone.

He's quietly scanning the page, the one with his name on it. I should be angry at him for going through my book. It's not like I'm secretly dating the men in it.

"So, I'm the one who took you to church, huh? Is that a metaphor for something? I'm right up there with the one who burped the alphabet and underwear guy, and..." He pauses, face void of emotion. "Daryl," he says, his voice edgier with each passing moment. "Fucking Daryl, I was what... two spaces after him. I'm lumped in with the one person who I can't stand the sight of." He shakes his head.

"No, Tobias you don't–" I need to explain that none of the men in that book mean anything to me. Especially Daryl. When I had written Tobias's name in there, I didn't have the slightest idea on where we'd be today.

"Number thirty-one, was it just a game to you?"

I reach for the book and try to get it from him, but he pulls it back slightly.

"What *is* this, Kasey? Something for your next novel?"

"What the hell, Tobias? Am I really that shallow? I thought you knew me better than that."

He sighs and runs a frustrated hand through his dark hair. His cheek twitches and I hate that it's my fault.

"Maybe I don't really know you. It's only been a month. I knew I wasn't ready, but my father told me to give it a chance... clearly, I walked right into another trap."

A crazed laugh leaves my lips. "You don't know me? You're the one keeping secrets, Tobias. You saw Roxanne that day you went to help your mom and when you called you were already leaving and upset about something Roxanne did. You lied! So don't fucking turn it around on me!"

He jumps to his feet. The thud of his boot sounds louder than it is. The soft throb from earlier has become pronounced and shoots through my brain. He narrows his cold eyes at me.

"What is it that you want me to say, Tobias?" I throw my hands in the air. "Do you want to know why I went on all those dates? I'll tell you, because unlike you I never lied." I get to my knees on the bed and cross my arms. "I started going on those dates in hopes that my mom would have a reason to love me. If I found the perfect guy, she'd accept me for who I was and be proud of me. The joke was on me when I fell in love and she still didn't care. By that time, it didn't matter, all that mattered was you."

"And I just happened to be the sucker who bought into the blind date."

Anger ripples through me. I nearly face-plant off the bed, but steady myself once on the ground. I grab a whole chunk of my hair and start tugging as hard as I can. It only makes the pain in my head worse, but I need the stimulation.

"You were the only man I didn't crawl out of a bathroom window to run away from. You knew I'd been dating around, so why does this come as a shock?"

He stands and turns to me, his jawline set tight. "Because I didn't expect to have a tagline near my name, like some goddamn TV episode. Maybe it's better that we didn't dive any further into this—"

"Any further?" I cut him off, my voice squeaking. "I spent the holiday with your family. I hugged your mom and felt at home. For once there were people that respected me, and I had a man who helped me realize that I am worthy to be loved. I never felt like I was worth loving, because of my family, but you helped me gain that confidence I was missing."

I stand and when I get too close, he backs away. His eyes shimmer in the dim light and a single tear slips down his cheek.

"I'm sorry, Kasey. I can't do this anymore. Roxanne made me realize that I wasn't ready…"

"I get it. You're still in love with her. So why carry on with us if you did? Huh?"

He shakes his head. "I'm not in love with her anymore, but this whole situation made me realize that maybe I wasn't emotionally ready to dive back into something serious."

"That's bullshit, Tobias. It's bullshit and you know it!"

I step forward and this time he doesn't move. I grab a hold of his shirt, hanging on, pretending he's my last lifeline and if I let go, I'll fall. I sound pathetic. Is this how Mom views me? The pathetic Kasey who is holding on to a man like it's the only thing keeping me together.

Tears slip from my eyes and blur my sight, distorting my image of him. I tell myself that it's okay to let go. I'm better off alone and this was all a huge mistake for me too.

"Fine. You don't want to be with me… then go. I wish I'd never gone on that date! I was done." I pause and put the back of my hand to my mouth. "I was so done and then there you were to sweep me off my feet." My voice breaks and my lips quiver.

My chest aches, feeling as if I've been punched dead center and the sensation has stolen my breath. My lungs deflate. It's Lloyd all over again, but no matter how short of time I've known this man compared to Lloyd, the pain almost physically hurts.

Tobias doesn't move, so I throw my arm out and point to the door.

"Get out!" I growl.

He stands his ground. I march around him and throw open the door. Sam and Francesca both look up from their spot on the couch. Their wide sleepy eyes watch in horror.

I point towards the front door and yell again. "I SAID GET OUT!"

I wrap my arms around my middle trying to hold myself together.

"Here's your notebook." His voice is eerily calm, and I almost change my mind. I desperately want to grab his shirt again and pull his lips to mine, but I have to be stronger than that.

He hands me the book as he departs from my room. Francesca's mouth hangs open, and Sam shakes his head, a disappointed scowl on his face. I don't want to come between them and hope that Sam picks his side over mine.

I stare at the back of Tobias's head and follow him to make

sure he leaves. When the front door closes, I take the notebook in my hand and chuck it. The thud is loud enough to make me cover my ears. A primal scream escapes my lips. I catch Francesca giving Sam a nod. He doesn't hesitate and flies after Tobias.

When Sam leaves, reality comes crashing down on me, jolting me awake.

"Oh my God." My body shakes and I fall to the floor in a dramatic heap. Francesca is by my side in seconds. She lifts me to my feet, and we start to head for my room.

"No, it still smells like him."

She doesn't ask me any questions, only changes course and heads to her room instead.

Francesca's loud whisper bleeds through the door, waking me. In hushed tones she and Sam speak as if I'm not here. I hate that they are talking in whispers around me, like I can't handle it.

I throw off her black comforter and sit up. The light hits my eyes, and it stings. They are still raw from a night of tears. I've got that hangover sensation, with a throbbing head and sensitive eyes. My stomach isn't so great either, like I'm on a ship at sea in a wicked storm.

I give myself a minute before standing. There's a chill in the air this morning, even inside. It was probably the landlord downstairs who thinks it's summer year-round. I shuffle across the ugly beige carpet and open the door. They turn towards me, lowering their heads. They've been caught.

"You're awake."

"Yeah, can't sleep with the racket you two are making out here."

I squeeze past and start heading for my room. Francesca playfully smacks Sam and whispers, "Told you that you were too loud."

I open the door to my room when unfamiliar rough hands graze my arm. He pulls back for a second then reaches out again, placing his hand firmly in place. I concentrate on the hardwood floor below my feet.

"I got you covered at work today..." Sam says calmly.

I face him. "I wanted to work." I hate the snip in my voice.

"I know. Take the day and relax."

I tug my arm away and hold it to my chest with the other hand. Sam looks taken aback by my gesture. "I needed to go to work. I can't sit here in this apartment and ponder all the things that went wrong last night."

Francesca steps forward. "It was my idea. Not Sam's." She turns to him briefly, then back to me. "I figured we would do what you did for me." She shrugs.

"I appreciate you both trying to help, but I can handle putting on my big girl panties and moving on with life."

I glance between them and try so hard to not let the building sob escape. I cover my mouth with my hands and step further into the threshold of my door.

Francesca sighs. "Kasey..."

I keep my eyes trained to the floor and shake my head. I hold myself tighter and without another word retreat to my room. I guess I have all day to figure out what went wrong. I don't want to argue with them. When I slip inside and shut it another rush of tears hits me. They are silent and burn my cheeks as they fall.

I don't want to cry over this. I already spent the week before New Year's last year locked in my room crying over a man who I thought cared. From here on out I will not go on any dates, and I will most certainly not fall in love. The only thing I care about at this point is getting book three ready for publication and writing my new series.

I stand and walk over to the window. I wish I was going to work all day, being cooped up in here is going to drive me crazy. I could try to work on my new book, but I'm not sure if I'm in the right mood. I want it to be perfect.

Francesca knocks on the door. She peeks her head in before I answer. "I'm sorry."

I'm standing in the middle of the room facing the window, wiping my eyes furiously, willing the damn tears to go away. They won't stop and I can't control the tightness in my chest either.

"It's okay to cry."

"I'm so tired of it."

She comes over and takes me in her arms, then helps lead me to my bed. "I know, sweetheart."

She holds me tight and lets me cry into her shoulder for the one thousandth time. I hate that this is affecting me so much, it shouldn't. He's just a guy and there are plenty more out there.

"Sam was here to drop off some cake from Holly's Bakery, if you want to binge."

I laugh through my tears. "Is it the one with the crumbles of cookies on top?"

"What other cake would it be?"

I retreat from her arms and sit up. I take several deep breaths to clear my mind. No matter how heartbroken I am I can't let a perfectly good cake go to waste.

"Cake sounds perfect," I tell her.

She smiles. "I thought so."

CHAPTER 53

I take a moment to collect myself as I pull up to the high school. Sarah sent me a text the day after New Year's asking if I'd still be interested in speaking to her class. I couldn't say no, even with the way things were with Tobias. I'm a professional when it comes to my work and won't back out of a commitment unless there's an emergency.

It's been two weeks since Tobias and I have split. I've officially put on my big-girl panties and ventured out into the world. I could do this, no matter how much it hurt. I've been keeping myself busy with my editor and trying to churn out everything so we can do a December release.

I step out of the car wrapped up in the warmest clothes I have. It's a brisk morning. The cold wind makes tears spring to my eyes. I'm not convinced it's from the cold, but I'll blame it anyway.

I only spent one whole day in bed, because I knew I had to move forward. I spiraled after Lloyd, and I didn't want to land in the same boat. I need to prove to myself that I can be strong. A man shouldn't be what keeps me grounded, only I can be the one to build my confidence. I wish I'd realized that sooner.

I ring the buzzer and the door clicks open. Inside, a lady behind plexiglass greets me.

"Hi, I'm here for Mrs Scott's class. I'm the guest speaker, Kasey Johnson."

The woman who appears to be in her late twenties stares up at me almost star-struck.

"You're THE Kasey Johnson. I heard you were coming today. It's such a pleasure to meet you. I'm a big fan of your work."

I love knowing that someone is so excited about my books.

"Thank you so much." I reach in my bag for one of my cute little bookmarks. The artist who drew the character nailed them. It's one of my favorite drawings, it portrays my two main characters out in the snow staring at each other in a daze. Before I hand it to her, I sign the back with the pen left for visitors, then slide it through the glass. She stares down at it wide-eyed.

"Thank you. This has made my day," she says then grins. "When is book three coming?"

"I hope to have it out by Christmas. It's going really well, and I think you'll love it."

Her cheeks swell with a held-back smile. Like she's trying not to show too much of a reaction while she's working. "I haven't read a series in quite a long time, but yours helped reel me back in."

I see my reflection dimly in the window. There's light in my eyes again. It's nice to see. There's been a darkness clouding them since my breakup. "I'm glad to hear."

She shakes her head trying to get her thoughts together. "Let me call down to check if she's ready for you."

With a wide smile she makes the phone call. I'm presented with a white visitors' pass sticker. She buzzes me into the lobby and as I open the door Sarah comes walking around the corner. Her smile is enough to light up any room. I thought this would be easy, but the lump in my throat returns. I swallow hard and look away to clear my head.

The moment she's within reach, she wraps her arms around me. I wasn't expecting to be swept up into her hug. I blink to get rid of the tears. Sarah is "home". She holds on tight, and I almost hope she's never going to let go. Pulling back, she stares at me. There's a glossy glow in her eyes, and it kills me.

"The kids are really excited to meet you. These are my seniors."

I'm relieved she doesn't bring up Tobias. She grabs my arm and leads me to her room. I remember these halls too. It wasn't long ago Francesca and I were traipsing through here on our way to class.

We head upstairs where the English classes are held. The room she stops in front of fills me with memories of ninth grade. Ms Garcia was the teacher then. She named me editor of the school paper and I spent many long hours at the desk, which still sits in the back corner near the closet.

As I step inside the kids are anxiously awaiting my arrival. The boys not so much, but the girls – some of them already have my books perched on their desk.

Sarah introduces me and I step up to the small wooden podium. In front of all of them I forget about my broken family and heart. My books and writing in general always brings me happiness, no matter how shitty things are.

After a thirty-minute discussion and several rounds of questions, a few of the girls who had my book come up and ask me to sign them. I spend time chatting until the bell rings. They look disappointed and I kind of am too. It was easy to lose myself in the books.

As they all file out of the room, the pain rages back on. I don't let it show as Sarah walks me back down to the main office. She grabs her coat in the classroom, so I expect she's walking me to my car.

"You did great there with them. Those girls have been talking about this for a while."

I let out a soft laugh. "I love meeting people who have read my book. Veronica has a great premise for her story. If you want to give her my email, I wouldn't mind reading more for her."

Sarah smiles and places a hand on my back as we reach the car. "She would love that." She stays silent as I dig for my keys.

Once I've beeped my car, I face her. A melancholy look draws on her face.

"I'm so sorry, Kasey." Her voice breaks, and it tears me in two.

I should have expected this. Sarah is the type of mom who hurts when her kids hurt. She's the mom who scoops you up after a serious fall and tells you everything will be okay.

"Is he... how is he?"

You would think with the way he threw those accusations at me that I wouldn't care, but I'm not that person. He was hurting and I understand that. I wish our first fight wasn't the one thing to tear us apart.

She shakes her head and the tears spring to her eyes. I may not be a parent, but I can understand how it must feel when your child is hurting.

"You look so well compared to the zombie that's crashing at my house." She wipes some tears from her eyes.

The thought of Tobias taking this hard, hurts. I imagine him in that classroom putting on a brave face when deep down his heart is one shattered piece away from exploding. There's still some anger lurking in me. I hate that he held on to that book for a whole week before confronting me. He made me think everything was okay, when in reality it wasn't.

"I'm sorry for bringing it up," Sarah says. "That was awful of me..."

"No," I say. "You're mama bear and you care about him. It must be awful to not be able to comfort your child. I'm sorry it came to this. I don't..." I pause to collect my thoughts. I hang my head and take a breath. "I think it was a big misunderstanding and more than anything I wish I could fix it."

A thoughtful expression lingers in her eyes. "I like you, Kasey. You're so good for him. I'm sorry that you had to find out about Roxanne the way you did. My husband has a kind heart and she and her dad aren't doing well. With the loss of her mom and their housing situation, we just wanted to reach out to them. I still haven't forgiven her for what she did to Tobias. She dragged him around for so long." Sarah puts a curled fist up to her mouth and holds it there for a moment. "I somewhat feel like this is my fault–"

"No, it's not," I interrupt.

This is what a mom loving her son is all about. I wish I had that.

"He was very hesitant to go on that date, but then he did and… he loves you more than he's loved anyone before."

I wiggle my itching nose. My eyes sting with tears.

"I'm sorry…" She swats her hand in front of her. "Forget I said anything. I should get back inside. I have another class in a few minutes."

She tries wiping her eyes with her cold hands. To calm her frustration, I wrap my arms around her, and for the first time in a week I cry. Sarah runs her hands through my cold tangled mess of hair. Her soft coo calms me as she tries to tell me it's going to be okay. "I'm so sorry," she says.

"I've been both angry and sad. There were moments where I wanted to call and yell at him, but I also wanted to cry and be sad. I don't hate him, in fact if he wanted to, I'd have a conversation to go over what went wrong. I'd be happy to talk to him to make things right."

She places a hand on my shoulder. "You have a heart of gold, Kasey. You care so deeply for those around you. You're a beautiful young woman and whatever happens between you both, I do hope you keep in touch. I wish he would have talked to you. This whole thing could have been avoided. He's so sad, Kasey."

I wrap my arms around her and hold on tight. There's a possibility I'll never get to hug this woman again or share a meal with her family during the holidays, but I do know that no matter what I want to keep her in my life.

"I hope to see you soon," she tells me.

"Of course."

She starts to walk away, but then stops. "Kasey?"

I glance over my shoulder.

"Happy early birthday."

I smile and say thanks. She walks away and when I get in my car for the first time all week, I don't have the urge to cry, like it's all been dried out by that last burst.

CHAPTER 54

I raise my hand to ring the bell, but retreat. I've been standing on Mom's doorstep for five minutes contemplating whether I want to have this conversation with her. It's weighing me down and if I don't try to make amends it will eat me alive.

I could walk in, I have a key, but I've chosen not to. After my morning with Sarah the other day I longed for some kind of contact with Mom. Sarah showed me what a mom should be and from that I felt I needed to give mine one more chance. Does she deserve it? Probably not, but I have to do it for my sanity.

My finger lingers over the bell as the door swings open.

"I saw you on that Ring thing your father installed. It's cold, get inside." Her belligerent tone has me clenching my hands. I'm already regretting my decision to come here.

I step inside the house. The decorations have swapped from Christmas to neat hand-crafted Valentine's Day decor. A beautiful heart filled wreath hangs on the closet door, and a sign with the letters L O V E arranged side by side hangs on the opposite wall. She's never once put tiny handprint Valentines or drawn hearts on the wall, not even from her grandchildren.

She turns back to glare at me. "Are you going to hang your coat or what?"

"I'm not staying long."

Her eyes narrow. "Then what did you come here for?"

Coming was a mistake. I'm here to try to be the bigger person, to work things out, but as usual she's making it difficult. She's my mother and even through all the crap she's put me through, I still somehow love her.

I squeeze my eyelids together and take a few deep breaths. If I don't remain calm this will blow up in my face again. She'll turn it around and call me out as the bad guy. She taps her heel on the floor impatiently.

"I came here because I hated how we left things. I thought by coming and talking we could come up with a way to be in the same room without hating each other."

She crosses her arms and clicks her tongue. There's a fire in her eyes that not even I can extinguish. "Is that what you think? That I hate you."

My chest heaves. "I don't know how I'm supposed to feel." I start off quiet, while I try to get a hold of myself. "Ever since I was little you and Piper have put me down. When I struggled in school you told everyone I was just dumb. When I was to become a published author, you told me it wasn't a real job. Even when I got into college, it wasn't the school you imagined me going to."

"I never said you were dumb, Kasey. Where do you come up with this stuff? You're trying to start drama between us so that it makes you feel better." The tapping of her foot becomes louder, as she picks up the pace.

"Are you even listening to yourself? What do you want from me, Mom? I went out on all those dates for you. You wanted me to find a man and when I found him, it still wasn't good enough." I don't talk with my hands often, but they are moving like I'm directing an orchestra. The more worked up I get the less I know what to do with them as they flail around.

"Found as in past tense. I heard that it ended already." Click, tap, click, tap. Her heels are starting to drive me mad.

I stomp my foot and it echoes around us. I look ridiculous, but there's no getting through to this woman. I need to let go. The question is, how do you let go of a parent? No one should have to walk away from their family. All I wanted was respect and love and it's time I realize I'm not getting either. I should have let it go at Christmas.

"Do you want to be single for the rest of your life? Tobias was a good man. Maybe it's for the better, he'll find a woman who has her priorities straight."

The eye roll at the end of her sentence makes me lose it. My jaw clenches and I grind my teeth together. *Kasey, just do it. Rip off the Band-Aid and say goodbye.* I straighten my shoulders and stand tall. I expect there to be tears, but my eyes are bone dry. I've cried too many times over this woman, I'm done.

"What does it matter if I'm single or divorced, an author or a sales associate? If I'm happy and doing something good with my life, why should it matter? Other than this." I point between us. "I'm happy with who I've become. I don't need a man or anyone else to tell me how to be happy."

"Good for you." Her tone is sharp and full of anger.

My jaw drops for a single moment. For my mental health this will be it. I have all the people I need to make me happy.

"You might be my mother, but I'm done with this relationship. I can't have someone in my life who lets me down. It's become unbearable to the point where your hatred towards my life has become my biggest insecurity. I won't allow it anymore." I can't believe how calm and rational my voice sounds. "Goodbye, Mother."

Her laughter takes me by surprise. "Oh, sweetheart, you'll be back. You said you were leaving after Christmas, yet here you are."

My lips pull into a straight line. I'm void of any emotion. Instead of engaging her, I backtrack towards the door.

"Don't you dare walk away from your mother!" Her voice wobbles, but I tell myself it's for show. She doesn't mean it.

Without another word I slip out of the house and gently close the door. My shoulders drop as I step out into the driveway. A sense of freedom settles over me, like a huge burden has been lifted. She says I'll be back, but I won't, not this time and maybe not ever.

CHAPTER 55

he second I walk into my apartment my phone rings. Piper's name pops up. I could choose to ignore it, but I need to tell her myself. This call will hurt the most. It's not because I want to make up with my sister, it's Marabelle and Ryan. I hate that I have to leave them, but if I'm going to walk away unscathed, I have to do it.

"What?" There's a weird calm in my tone.

"Why is Mom crying?" Piper yells.

Her words make my heart lurch, but then I remember all the horrible things she's done, and the moment vanishes as quickly as it arrived.

"She's being overdramatic."

I toss my keys on the small round table we keep by the door for the mail. The keys fall right into the wicker basket. I plop down on the couch and listen to her drone on about how I should show Mom respect and that I'm an awful human being. I let her ramble on for a good three minutes before she takes a breath.

"Can I talk now?" My voice falls flat.

She's never going to let me talk or let me live down the night I babysat for her. She'll never be the sister I need her to be. I'm not asking her to come over so we can braid each other's hair, I'm looking for a normal sane relationship that doesn't involve fighting. I want her to be my go-to person, like Amy is for Tobias and Dawson. I'll never get that though and it sucks.

"You should apologize," she growls.

I twirl around a small loosened thread on the couch and tug.

"I'm not going to apologize." I sigh. "What I'm going to say is going to hurt me more than it will you or Mom for that matter. I need time to heal from the damage…"

Her temper sparks. "Damage? Are you listening to yourself, Kasey? Stop being so emo, you're not fifteen anymore."

"Damn it, Piper. Let me finish!" I stand up and pace the room. The sadness has washed away into anger. "I don't care anymore. I'm doing this for me, for my mental health. This year has put me in a dark place and I'm tired of being swept away by the guilt of not being good enough."

She snorts.

"The only thing I care about is Marabelle and Ryan. I will send them their birthday and Christmas gifts, but that's it for now. I'm stepping away entirely. Please let them know that I love them and it's nothing they did."

She'll never say a word to them. They'll think I abandoned them, but for now it is what it is. There's no turning back and there's no getting through to either Mom or Piper.

"You're so childish."

I have nothing left to say. My heart and my mind need a break. There is finally some light at the end of the tunnel over my breakup with Tobias, and I need to do the same with this.

"Goodbye, Piper."

She screams at me not to hang up, but I can't listen to it anymore. I press the end call icon and fall back onto the couch. I throw my phone as gently as I can to the floor. Francesca's door opens, I don't have to turn to know she's heard the whole thing.

"I'm proud of you, that took a lot of guts. You should be really proud of yourself. I wish I could tell my mom how awful she makes me feel too."

I'm numb. There are no tears, no sadness, and no anger left. I'm afraid to speak, worried I'll cry, but now my eyes are as dry as a desert. I blink in her direction. Out of all the bad things in my life, I'm so glad Francesca and I have each other. Her mother was absent without a care in the world. We kept each other afloat when our families hadn't.

"So, about tomorrow night." She's trying to distract me.

She curls her legs behind her on the couch and faces me. There's a devious smile on her face and I'm scared to know what for.

"What have you done now?" Clearly she's planning a birthday that I didn't ask for. My plan was to work the morning shift, come home and chill, but Francesca had other ideas.

"You deserve a night out, plus Sam already made reservations for your favorite sushi place. So there, you can't back out now." She sticks out her tongue.

I shove at her shoulders, a small splinter of a smile on my face. "How can I resist sushi?"

She grabs a hold of my shoulders and shakes me. "That's my girl. Now cheer up, you old fart, you're gonna be twenty-five. Phew."

It's crazy that we're at the point in our lives where we are supposed to know how to "adult". I'm not sure I'll ever get used to that.

I laugh. "Twenty-five looks different than I imagined."

"Yeah, but you deserve a fresh start. I promise we'll make it worth every minute." She winks.

I'm not sure what to do with the little wink at the end. I trust her, but when she and Sam have a plan, it usually ends up with some kind of surprise. When Tobias and I split, Sam brought the cake, and then one other night they nearly bought out the entire shelf of Ben and Jerry's at 7-11 to cheer me up. In fact, there are still ten containers left.

There's no doubt in my mind that the two of them have something up their sleeves, I just hope my heart can handle it.

CHAPTER 56

"I can't believe you're working on your birthday. Lame!" Francesca playfully rolls her eyes.

I laugh. She's perched in her usual spot beside the counter, picking at her sparkling red nails in honor of Valentine's Day in a few short weeks.

I go back to pulling out some books that arrived in a shipment earlier today. It's the last box and once I'm done it will be time to celebrate. If my birthday had been a week or two ago, celebrating would have been the last thing on my mind. I'm slightly less angry with the world, and almost like myself again.

"You're different today," she says, eying me suspiciously.

I find it easy to smile. Missing Tobias sucks, but it's getting more bearable with each passing day. Sam says he'll come around and that he's the type of guy who needs time and distance to sort through whatever is happening in his head. I'll give him all the space in the world if it means we can fix things.

"I feel a little different," I say as a few customers enter the store.

I greet them with a smile. "Hi, how are you?" I scratch at the base of my throat, liking that my voice doesn't sound intertwined with sadness anymore.

They find me and wave, then go off into one of the aisles on their own. I miss Tobias and there will always be a place in my heart for him. I'll wait and if we're meant to be then it'll happen. I have to believe that.

Francesca's face lights up and she reaches for my hand. She holds on tight. "You know what? We should party it up old-school style. Oh… remember that club we used to go to?"

I shake my head as I dive into the memories of our college days. Fridays and Saturdays were club nights. I don't know how we managed to spend hours dancing, then hit the TGI Fridays next door. If I did that now I'd be passed out from exhaustion before I even made it to Fridays. When did I become an old lady?

"I'm happy having a quiet night with my two amazing friends."

"Awe, I'm your friend now?" Sam comes strutting up the dimly lit aisle, a wide grin on his face. He hops up the step behind the register and I lean back into him. He squeezes my arm in a friendly manner.

"The best there is." I smile. I'm thankful for the friendship that has blossomed between Sam and me over the years. Lately, we've grown closer and having him in my life has been a blessing.

"Hey." Francesca pouts. "What about me? I thought I was your number one." She crosses her arms.

I blow her a kiss and she smirks.

"See," she says pointing at Sam. "She loves me more."

"Yeah, but can you provide her with all the book porn?" He raises his brow and sets some new releases on the counter.

Eyes wide I flip over each book one by one. He knows me all too well. They release on Tuesday, but I always sneak a peek before they release.

"That's not even a thing, you can't use book porn like food porn," she insists.

He swings around the counter and wraps his arms around her. He's oblivious to the family of five who are wandering around close by, because he only has his sights set on Francesca. She squeals and gives him a gentle kiss on the tip of his nose.

My heart twists at the thought of how different tonight would have been if Tobias had been here. I miss the daring look in his eyes when we'd flirt or how he'd watch me as if I was the only one in the room. My lips quiver and I try to hide it by lifting the book I'm reading in front of my face.

"We should get going. Mr Ruppert said we can head out. Yanni is here to take over the sales floor," Sam says.

Yanni, one of our co-workers, comes out from the backroom. He's a newer employee and offered to come in early, so we could start our night sooner. He's always looking for extra hours, so it worked out perfectly.

I take several deep breaths before I pull the book from my face and place it with the rest of the new releases under the counter.

"I can hear the sushi calling me from here." My stomach rumbles loud enough that Sam turns to give my stomach a glance.

We say our goodbyes to Yanni and head out.

CHAPTER 57

The sushi place is only a few stores down, so we walk there from Once Upon a Storybook. Someone holds the door open for us when we arrive, and the scent of miso spills out into the street. Inside, the young male host finds Sam's name then helps us to our table. It's a Friday night around peak hours, so the restaurant is crowded. I'm glad Sam reserved us a table or the wait would have been at least an hour.

The man takes us through the dull-lit restaurant. One side is set up hibachi style, the other is a small, darkened corner without the entertainment. Sam thankfully has reserved a spot in the quiet section. I love hibachi but tonight I'm flying under the radar and in need of relaxation.

We slip into a cozy booth by a window that looks out onto one of the side streets. It's not the nicest view, just an alleyway and a brick building on the other side. I don't mind because I love the atmosphere here, the darkened room gives it such an intimate setting. Around us there are couples, my chest tightens at the sight of them. The hibachi is mostly filled with families and large groups. Maybe that would have been better. The high I'd felt earlier is somehow fading to oblivion.

Francesca and Sam sit on the far side, and I face them. Behind them there aren't any other booths, only a wall with a portrait of cherry blossoms. A waitress comes over with a basket of edamame and water. She tells us she'll be back to take our orders. I open the menu to browse through as Sam immediately dives into the edamame basket.

"So, ladies, what are we watching tonight? *Harry Potter* or *Twilight?*" Sam asks, peeking over the menu at me.

"We should do *Hunger Games* or maybe *Maze Runner*," Francesca suggests.

As much as I live for *Twilight*, I'm not really in the mood for a dreary love story, especially *New Moon*. I'm on the verge of bouncing back from the breakup but watching Edward walk away from Bella, although fictional, might be too much for me to handle.

"What about *Divergent*? I haven't seen them yet but I think the movies were never finished. Theo James though." I threw the suggestion out there because I love the actress that plays Tris too.

Francesca slips an edamame into her mouth and hums. "I did hear that about *Divergent*. Hmm... I'm leaning towards the *Hunger Games* and could use a little Gale in my life."

Sam lowers the menu and glares at her.

"What?" She laughs. "Hey, if you're allowed to make googly eyes over Hillary Duff, I'm entitled to some Hemsworth action every now and again."

Sam puts the menu down and wraps her in his arms. He kisses her cheeks and along her jawline. I lower my eyes back to the menu to find out how much my favorite sushi is, even though I've memorized the price.

"She should have ended up with him," Sam pipes in.

Now it's my turn to lower my menu and glare. "Wait, I thought you said you never read the books?"

Sam starts talking about how he picked it up last month and couldn't put it down. He's mostly into high fantasy, so it's rare for him to read something else. My eyes wander around the room. Sam proclaims his love for Haymitch in the book. He's really into the conversation. It's weird that he's getting all worked up over a teen dystopian but seeing this side of him is fun. Every few seconds Francesca nudges him and he sends her a sideways smirk.

I've done well spending time with them through all their lovey-dovey moments, but suddenly being trapped in this restaurant is making my chest ache for what could have been.

My mind clears and I finally chime in with my thoughts. "I agree about Haymitch, that would have been more interesting than Snow."

"Exactly." Sam mumbles with the edamame he stuffed into his mouth.

The waitress comes back over, and we put our orders in and hand her the menus. She returns a few minutes later to serve us each salad with my favorite ginger sauce.

I stare out the window as Francesca and Sam bicker playfully. The conversation has moved from teen dystopian to the annoying way Sam eats his popcorn during a movie. Outside everything looks cold and depressing. The high of the Christmas holiday has faded, leaving a dark bleak street, lit by only the softly faded streetlamps. In two short months it will be spring and five o'clock won't be so dreary, but I'll have to try my best to get by till then.

"She fell asleep during that one, remember that?"

My attention shifts to them. Eyes wide I stare blankly because I missed their whole conversation. I'm not sure when we went from Sam's eating habits to whatever it is they're talking about, but something tells me the conversation had been over for a while.

"I was telling him about the time you–" Her voice shrinks, as her eyes land on something behind me.

Confused by the bug-eyed look on her face I crane my neck to check what the fuss is all about. I suck in a breath. The intensity of the moment catches me off guard. I place my hand over my heart to control the unsteady beat.

Pinch me, is this a dream? Tobias is standing in the restaurant with a small gift wrapped in shiny metallic blue paper. His appearance reminds me of our first date. He's dressed in dark clothing and his hair is perfectly combed back stiff with gel. There's only one difference, his pleading eyes glance at me, asking for forgiveness. The sadness consumes him like a grim cloud looming overhead. His eyelids are heavier than normal. His usual bright charm is nowhere to be found. Worry lines crease his forehead.

"Hey, man, you came," Sam says.

I whip my head back to the two of them. They were cooking something up and it was Tobias. I grip at the fabric of my navy-blue dress where my hand lay over my heart. Knowing they told him to come and that he did means... My thoughts are interrupted by Sam standing and reaching out. I pivot in my seat only to find the back of Tobias's head bobbing away through the crowded restaurant.

No! I want to cry out, but my voice is gone. I grab at my throat, then glance up at Sam, waiting for him to tell me what to do next. I stare at Francesca next and lift my shoulders.

"Go," she whispers. "He wanted to be here. He was the one who asked."

I tilt my head to meet Sam's eyes. He nods.

Tobias wanted to be here, and I lost my nerve to talk. This whole time he thought I didn't want him.

"He asked what was happening for your birthday and if I thought it would be a good idea to–"

I don't allow Sam to finish that sentence, I'm up and out of the booth before any more words come out of him. I lose my footing and thank God that Sam is there to hold me up. He urges me again and I race after Tobias. I hope it's not too late to get to him.

Knowing Tobias and his good luck he found a parking spot right out front, and he's already gone.

I maneuver through the tables and catch him as he is walking out the door.

"Tobias!" The door closes behind him. *No. Shit no! Come back.*

I push my way through and find him walking towards the bookstore. "Tobias!" This time I yell loud, causing other heads, except the one I want, to turn. "Tobias, please wait!" I'm closer and this time he stops.

I wait until he faces me before I take the extra few steps. There's a huge gap between us that I hate.

"Happy birthday, Kace." His voice is barely above a whisper. His Adam's apple bobs, and I stare at it.

Through blurry vision I meet his eyes. "Where are you going?" I'm shaking, and I'd blame the cold, but that's only half of it.

He shrugs and I hate the defeated look on his handsome face. God, I wish I could reach out and touch him. What if he doesn't want me to? I start to take a step back but hold my ground.

"Honestly, I thought I could handle it, but it hurts too damn much." He blinks several times staring up at the dark early-evening sky.

"It doesn't have to hurt anymore. Talk to me, Tobias. Please." The break in my voice piques his interest.

He presses his lips together in a straight line. A shiver flows through me, I forgot my jacket inside in the rush to get to him. I'm an idiot for wearing a short-sleeve dress in the dead of winter. To be fair I never imagined I'd be standing on the sidewalk attempting to reconcile with my ex.

I have to be brave, the quiet between us is killing me. I need his warm hand in mine. When our fingers lock, he gasps for air. His hand slides from mine and retreats. All I can focus on is the idea of him walking away again. The idea of it hurts worse than the night we broke up.

He tucks the gift box into his jacket and shimmies out of it, then drapes it over my cold body. His hands stay locked in place around me and the jacket.

"Talk to me, Tobias," I plead.

"I don't want to ruin your birthday," he says, flatly.

I grip his hand again, this time I won't let him slip from me. We need to have this discussion. There has to be a way I can fix what happened between us.

"If getting closure is what I get on my birthday, then so be it. I need something. I hate how we fought and that things were left unsaid. Mostly I hate how we broke up over a silly fight. If we weren't so wounded from our previous relationships, maybe that fight would have gone differently. It sucks not having you around." I wipe the edges of my eye.

"I hated it too." His words are quiet. Guilt makes his shoulders fall and I wish I could release the pressure for him. I'd do anything to see his eye-wrinkling smile again. He sniffles and catches a few stray tears that fall.

"If it's too much and all you want to do is wish me a happy birthday, then I'll have to accept it. All I want is to clear the air. I'm not mad anymore, I'm just..." I pause. "I'm sad."

He takes a deep breath. "I'm sorry I accused you of being fake. The day I found your book, Roxanne was at my parents' house. I was in my room, and she cornered me. She tried to kiss me, said that she loved me more than you did, that she and I were meant to be." He stops for a moment so his brain can catch up with his words. Even from the outside, his mind is reeling. He scratches right above his brow.

"She got so close to kissing me and I lost it. Then I found your datebook and it triggered my insecurities. I'm so sorry, Kasey. I'm sorry that I almost cheated and that I got bent out of shape over a stupid book. The idea of almost kissing another woman killed me. I was angrier with myself than anything."

I catch a glimpse of regret in his eyes. "You were still hurting when we started dating, weren't you?"

He rubs at the bridge of his nose and gently rocks his head up and down. "I didn't want to admit it, but I was still very much in love with her and angry all at the same time. Then you came along, and everything changed. You made me whole again. When I saw that book the first thing on my mind was that you were going to do exactly what she did. That I was one big joke…"

"I'd never hurt you, Tobias. Not intentionally."

The hands that still rest on the jacket around me squeeze tighter. I move in towards his body. Being this close, having him hover over me like he's my shelter from a storm, feels so good I could cry happy tears.

"You were never a joke. When I wrote those, I was under the assumption that it would be another date that would fail, but then I saw you again and knew it was more than that. I did it to prove to my mom that I was something, so that she'd love me. Now I've lost so many people, more than I can handle." A sob leaks from my trembling lips. I'm trying to hold myself together, but all I really want is for him to take me in his arms and never let go.

"I hate myself for going on those dates. I don't know why I thought everything would end up like a fairy tale and all the pieces of my life would suddenly fit together perfectly like the ending of some book. I was only fooling myself. I'm sorry I hurt you, so very sorry. I never meant to…"

"I know. I know that now."

People walk around us, most look annoyed as we stand in the middle of the busy sidewalk. I don't care, the only thing I want is for him to forgive me so that we can move on. Whether we're together or not, he has to know how I feel.

"I wish there was something I could do to make it up to you."

His cheek twitches with such anxiety that I find myself reaching for him. I press my hand to his cold scruffy face. Being this close makes my body ache. From this angle all I have to do is reach up ever so slightly and his lips would be on mine.

"You can come inside and have sushi with us and then watch some really long marathon of a movie series based on a book. We still haven't decided which. Your friends miss you." I stop to gauge his reaction. "I'd really love it if you spent my birthday with me, it would mean the world to me." I try to smile through the tears and light sobs that rattle my chest.

"Do I even deserve it?"

His words break me. With the hand resting on his cheek, I tug him closer, then I reach up on my toes and brush my lips over his. I've missed his warm skin touching mine. He sighs into my mouth and releases a shaky breath.

"We both had a lot to think about after that night," I say. "We said things that maybe we didn't mean in the heat of the moment. You walking out that door, even though I told you to, hurt more than walking out on Christmas Eve dinner. I'm willing to start over. The only reason I didn't reach out was because I wanted to give you space to figure out what you wanted."

He leans forward and rests his forehead against mine. Slowly, he rolls his neck back and forth and closes his eyes. A tear falls and lands on my hand. When he opens them, they shimmer, the sadness washed away with hope.

"Has anyone ever told you what an amazing woman you are?"

Now it's his turn to lean in and graze over my lips with his.

"Maybe this one guy." I roll my eyes playfully.

"Oh yeah?" he questions, pressing in for a kiss. His eyes crinkle at the sides and I almost let out a squeal of joy.

"Yeah. He is pretty amazing."

"Kace?"

"Yeah?" I whisper.

There are no words, only his hungry lips pushing to open mine. They are hot and moist just as I remembered them. The heat of the moment forces warmth to rise in my cheeks as his tongue reaches out for mine.

He pulls back. "God, Kasey, I love you so much."

"And I love you, Tobias."

We rest our heads together. We might be in public, but this feels so intimate, as if we are hidden from the crowds on the street.

"I'll come have dinner with you."

I smile. "You will?"

"I wouldn't miss it."

I chuckle softly into his mouth as I mash my lips to his again. This time he slowly invites me in. The kiss doesn't last long and that's okay because I'm willing to take this as slow as possible. We both have obstacles to overcome when it comes to our feelings, which have been hurt by our pasts, but want to move forward. It will take some time, but I'm willing to put all my effort into this.

"Good. Then you can make me breakfast in the morning."

His laughter takes me by surprise and warms my entire body. "We'll call it breakfast-making 101. I'm the teacher, you're my student."

I wiggle my brows. "Are we role playing now?"

His laughter fills the street and people walking past us stare in our direction. He throws an arm over me and together we walk into the restaurant, over to our friends who are patiently waiting for us – like they knew it was going to work out.

I know what he meant when he told his mom I was the one. Deep in my heart I feel it too, but only a matter of time will tell. I don't know if I'll ever make up with Mom and Piper or if Dad will ever be strong enough to stand up to her for me. What I do know is that here on my twenty-fifth birthday, I have everything I'll ever need to get me through. I can't wait to spend a lifetime of Christmases with Tobias. I'll figure out the other stuff along the way.

EPILOGUE

TOBIAS

I pace back and forth through my tiny apartment. I'm fully aware that the neighbors downstairs are probably going to complain any minute. Sam watches my antics but doesn't say a word. Laughter breaks the incredibly long silence. He holds up his phone.

"Why is there a picture of my girlfriend's ass in yoga pants on your phone?"

Sam chuckles, and I glance at the name of who sent it. Francesca. That girl drives me insane, but I love her in a total platonic sisterly type of way. She's not only dating *my* best friend, but she's also my soon-to-be-fiancé's best friend.

This year has been amazing in so many unexpected ways. I don't want to ever lose that feeling or the girl who provides it. I've known she was the one since the moment I brought her into that church on our first date and she didn't bolt. Making the decision to get over all the insecurities I faced after my on-again off-again relationship with Roxanne was the best thing I could have done.

"She and Kasey are doing yoga before the signing. She says it's their pre-signing ritual."

Kasey's book signing is today for the third and final book of a series she wrote called *The Beauty of Frost and Flames*. It's a fantasy novel about a human turned Fae Queen. I'm not one to read a fantasy with romance elements, but my girl killed it. I'm not saying that because I love her, she has thousands of fans to prove it.

Sam's phone goes off and he answers right away. "Yes, Mr Ruppert. Oh, wow! That many, huh? Alright yeah, of course I'll be there in a few." He hangs up and stares up at me.

"There are over three hundred fans in line for the signing. That was Mr Ruppert, he says he needs some help."

"So, it's time?"

"Go get your girl," Sam says.

"She's going to say yes, right?"

Sam chuckles and stands. His hand lands gently on my shoulder and he squeezes. "You got this. I'll be there with you every step of the way."

"You really think a flash mob is Kasey's style?"

I really wish I would have thought this one over. Maybe just a dinner for two in a dark candle lit restaurant or Christmas Eve, I could have done it right here in front of my tree. This is all over-whelming.

"Are you kidding me? This is something she's going to remember for the rest of her life. Girls are saps and it will be something you'll see her smiling about years later. You'll ask her, *Kace, why are you smiling?*" He says this in a deep voice that I guess is supposed to be me. "And she'll answer, *Oh I'm remembering the time you proposed with some of my biggest fans and your sexy voice singing to me.*" His voice goes when he attempts to talk like Kasey.

I chuckle and it melts away some of the nerves. The pulse in my neck throbs so hard that it's probably visible as it beats under my skin.

Sam grabs his coat and hands me my leather jacket. I hesitate to take it, but I have to, because the woman who I'm close to asking for her hand is my everything and she needs to know that.

I live on the border of town, one street over and I'd be in the next town. I like living here, but it's time for a change of scenery. This small one-bedroom one-bath apartment has served me well, but it's time to move on. On my quest for the perfect ring, I've also been searching for the perfect house. There are a few on the market right in the village and within walking distance of Kasey's bookstore.

I don't want to push everything on her all at once, but I'm also ready to leave this lonely bachelor pad behind for something more spacious to share with the woman I love.

I drive Sam and me to the store. He is technically working the signing, but everyone is in on the big surprise, including her dad. He's the only family member Kasey talks to after a fall out last year. I hate that her family made her think she wasn't good enough. She didn't deserve to be treated that way. She still gets the look in her eye when she's with my family. I can tell she misses *hers*, but to be fair they haven't even tried to fix their relationship with her. So, I'm not too worried about them missing out.

When we pull up to the store, seeing the amount of people waiting with my own eyes has me in awe. The signing doesn't start for a while and according to Sam. Kasey won't be showing up for at least another forty-five minutes and it's already wrapped around the block.

We enter the store and we're greeted by Yanni, one of the employees working today. Christmas is everywhere, including in the string of twinkling white lights along the walls. It's the perfect scene for a holiday engagement. Kasey loves Christmas, and I want her to know that every one she spends with me will be much better than all the ones in her past. I want to show her the love she deserves.

There are some regular customers browsing around the store

like it's a normal day. To them it is, but to me it's one of the biggest moments of my entire life.

I sit down at a table up front in the corner of the small shop. It's where Kasey will be sitting and where a group of fans will do a dance to her favorite Shawn Mendes song, before I come walking out to sing "Grow Old with You" using my guitar.

Sam brings over the girls that are going to be involved with our flash mob. I never thought I'd be one of those clichés, but here I am staring up at Kasey's adoring fans who are willing to do it for us. This engagement was six months in the making and led to late nights and Kasey wondering if things were okay. I was so distracted with trying to make this perfect that my mind drifted. Thankfully Sam was able to help keep that storm at bay.

We practiced while Kasey was off from work two nights ago. It was a simple dance. The girls who volunteered are all either dance teachers or professional dancers in other aspects. Living close to the city it was easy to find most of them. There's only around ten, it would be hard to have any more due to the amount of space we're working with. The plan is to have most of the fans file through and an hour or so in to make a chaotic scene.

The bell rings and I glance up worried she's here, but it's only her dad. He walks right over to me. A smile radiating his round face. When I came to him asking for his daughter's hand he was thrilled.

"You look pale, son."

I chuckle. "Just a little."

"Are your folks coming?"

"Yeah, they should be here soon. My mom is going to video chat with my sister while it's happening. I think she's the most excited."

After last Christmas my sister, Amy, and Kasey ended up growing close. It's a big change from my previous relationship where they never got along. I'm happy they bonded, especially since Kasey's not close to her own sister.

"Before you take the plunge," her dad says, "I want to tell you that getting to know you this past year has been a pleasure. You are just the man I imagined my daughter marrying."

I stand and when I do, he pulls me into a hug. We both slap each other's backs. I pull away and my eyes land on Kasey. Shit. Her eyes narrow. I hope she doesn't suspect anything. She slowly makes her way over to us. She's early, I wasn't expecting her yet. Sam's behind her scrambling to get the fans to follow him somewhere else for the time being.

"That was weird," she says, staring at me.

Her father laughs. "What, you've never seen men hug it out before?"

Her brow lifts at her father and I worry we've blown our cover. She presses her lips together, studying both of us.

"I want a hug too," Francesca says, bouncing over in between us.

She throws an arm over Kasey's father and me, and stares back at Kasey.

"Are you ready for your big day?" Francesca asks.

I nudge Francesca with my hip. She shoots me a look and I do the same back.

"I mean the signing. Dude. There's a lot of people out there. Remember your first signing. This is crazy."

Kasey's face pales and I quickly scoop her into my grasp. She rests her head quietly against my shoulder.

I'm confused by the strange look on her face as she lifts her head and stares back up at me. "You okay?"

"I'm good. I didn't sleep well last night."

I pull away slightly to get a better look at her. She's definitely not sleeping. I can tell by the purple bags that linger under her beautiful brown eyes. She glances out the window and a small smile stretches out on her face.

She looks back over, her eyes wobble with tears. "They're all here for me, aren't they?"

"They are, Kace, you did that. I'm so proud of you."

Her smile grows wider as Mr Ruppert comes walking over. He straightens his slouched shoulders and gives Kasey a look. "Are you ready for this?" he asks.

"Of course. Bring them in."

I watch as she settles down in the seat I occupied a few minutes earlier. I step aside near Sam and Kasey's father. As they let some fans in, Mom and Dad come. She was expecting Mom to show, so I'm pretty sure she doesn't suspect a thing.

As the time ticks away, the nerves start to get the best of me and I excuse myself to the back to prepare. Behind me Francesca follows me into the stockroom.

"You okay, church boy?"

I laugh it off, because of course I'm okay. Asking her to marry me is beyond the scariest thing I've ever had to do. I don't want to screw this up. That girl in there deserves the world and I want to give it to her.

"Look." She places both of her strong hands on my shoulders and shakes me lightly. "She's my best friend and from the minute I met you I knew you'd be the one. No matter what happens out there she's going to say yes. That girl is so in love with you I don't see this going any other way. Could there be a double wedding in our future?"

Francesca holds up the small diamond on her left hand. Sam proposed to her after only six months. He knew from before they even kissed that he was going to ask her to marry him. He would always tell me that he would one day marry the girl who hung out at the bookstore.

"As much as I love Sam, you two should have your own special day."

"We already do." Her face lights up.

I'd forgotten that through all the chaos of my proposal that she and Sam went out to pick out a venue yesterday.

"Sam didn't say anything…"

"Yeah, well he wanted today to be about you. We're having a June wedding."

She smiles happily as she stares down at the sparkling ring on her finger. Since she's gotten it, she's never stopped looking. "So, best man, let's discuss the bachelor party…"

Sam peaks his head through. I know exactly why. It's now or never. Over the loudspeaker of the store through the partially open door the sounds of Bruno Mars' "Just the Way You Are" is playing. It's low and over the rumble of the fans inside, but Kasey is well aware it's playing. She mouths the lyrics while she signs and chats with her fans.

For a moment I'm caught up in her beauty. I love the way her nose scrunches up when a fan makes her laugh. I love when her eyes widen as she speaks about the characters she created. Then as someone compliments her – whether it be regarding her book or a personal time in their life that Kasey helped them get through with her writing, her face glows.

I pull my head back into the room and take a few deep breaths.

Sam watches me closely. "Do you want me to send the fans in?"

I release a long flow of air. "Let's do this."

"Now you know how I felt." Sam laughs.

My mind flashes back to the summer when we all went to the beach. It was Francesca's favorite spot and our last day on our getaway out east in the Hamptons. Kasey's job was to make sure Francesca was on the beach at the right moment, as the sun was setting. That night I couldn't believe how perfect the sunset was. It was a huge orange ball in the sky and the reflection off the water made for a beautiful picture – taken by me of course.

"It's rough."

Sam pats my back. "Yeah. You got this though, she's all yours, man."

Sam walks away and Francesca hands me my guitar that leans

on the wall near the door. She opens the door enough so I can watch the first part of the proposal. Dad has his phone up pretending to check email, but really, he's starting to film as the fans file in. Mom has Amy on the video chat, but has it turned round, so Kasey doesn't notice.

I love the excitement in her fans' voices, and I love how authentic it sounds, because they are her real fans.

"We made a dance for you. Can we show you?"

I watch as she looks up at Mr Ruppert. He's in on the whole thing too. He gives the girls the green light as Sam secretly changes the song behind the register. The song starts and I watch Kasey's face. Her smile turns down for a moment as she looks around, and then it perks back as the girls start dancing for her.

I'm not sure what's going through her head. Part of me wants to jump out and say, *Hey it's me*, but the other half wants her to not know until I appear. I avert my eyes for a moment to the dancing girls and they're killing it out there.

The song is going way too fast. Before I can even process what's about to go down, I hear the ending beats as the song starts to fade. When it does Kasey stands and claps. The girls file back over to her and get their books signed. I wait as it takes them a few minutes to go through. She's telling them how amazing they were. I think she has an idea that something's going on, because every few seconds while chatting her eyes scan the room – like she's looking for someone.

Sam stares over at me and pauses the music so that nothing else comes on. Mom points the phone in my direction and play-fully I stick out my tongue at my sister who has tears streaming down her face.

Francesca turns her head, looking over her shoulder at me. "You're on."

In that moment for a brief second, I panic. I close my eyes and take another breath. Yanni standing at the door holds it closed for a moment so no one else comes in. Kasey looks relieved to take a short break. She reaches for her water as I start strumming the chords.

Her eyes widen as she sets the drink back down without even putting it to her lips. I step out around the register and her face reddens. My favorite thing about her is anytime I'm around she gets small splotches of pink along her cheeks. Mom starts crying and she notices and then turns back to me.

Francesca is crying too. Her whimpers are loud behind me as I walk forward.

Kasey's hand flies to her mouth to cover it. Water fills her eyes and sticks to the tips of her lashes. She looks around at everyone standing there watching this moment. The fans outside are eagerly observing through the window.

Francesca runs over and reaches out for her to stand. She follows along, takes her hand, and brings her to the front of the table. The song is about to end as her dad steps up and holds out the box. I finish singing in front of two crying women. I stare at the one I want to spend my life with and hand the guitar to her dad in exchange for the ring.

Francesca steps back into Sam's arms and watches from her usual spot perched next to the counter. I fall to the floor on one knee while looking up at Kasey. Her whole body is shaking with happy sobs.

"Kasey Anne Johnson. There is no one in this world I'd rather grow old with. From the moment you came into my life I knew this was it. You were the one when you walked into that church with me and sat down with my young friends in the choir. You fit right into my life like a missing puzzle piece."

She removes her hand from her face allowing me to catch a glimpse of her tear-stained pink cheeks.

"Kasey, will you spend the rest of your life going to brunch with me?"

She smirks. Her head bobs up and down. At first, she's at a

loss for words, but then very faintly she says, "Yes." A steady stream of tears rolled down her glowing face.

I slip the small diamond onto her finger and my entire body warms knowing this is the woman I'm going to spend my life with. Wetness touches my cheek, and I somehow missed the fact that I'm crying too. I get to my feet and take her beautiful face in my hands.

"Kace…"

For a moment she's silent as she looks up at me. I hope she's not second guessing. She holds my stare. "I'm pregnant." She swallows hard.

"You are?" I hold her tighter. My eyes wander down to her stomach and I'm overwhelmed with love.

"I am. Is – is that okay?"

"Okay? Baby, this is the best day of my life." I can't help the smile on my face at the thought of her carrying something we created together.

"Really?" Her voice squeaks higher than normal. Slowly, I lean down and place my wet salty lips atop hers. Her confession explains all the early bedtimes and restless sleep, the stomach aches and extra glow on her face.

"Really." I pause. "I love you so much."

"I love you."

Kasey glances upwards, a grin crosses her face. I check to see what she's smiling about when my eyes land on some mistletoe. Our eyes meet, and with a determined look, she grabs the back of my head and presses her lips hard against mine.

The people in the room shout their congratulations, and even the crowd outside roars with excitement. I wish I could hold her for longer, but I have my whole life to do that. Her fans are patiently waiting to meet her.

"We'll celebrate later, okay?"

She nods. "Yeah. Sounds perfect."

She turns to walk away, and I pull her in and kiss her. She

giggles softly under the touch of my lips. My body shivers like there's an electric current running through. She pulls away and gives one of her killer smiles.

When she goes back to finish her signing, I can't help but stand there for a few minutes and watch her. She wipes her tears and begins signing again. I get a ton of congratulations from fans as they pass through.

Sam comes over and pats me on the back. "You did it. Congrats."

I give Sam a quick smile before focusing back on Kasey. After thirty-one dates she finally found me. If it weren't for that crazy number, I never would have met her. She glances up for a moment and I take it all in.

I've always loved the holidays, but with Kasey, it makes it that much more special. I cannot wait to spend them all with her.

Here's to the next chapter of my life with... my one lucky Christmas wish.

THE END

ACKNOWLEDGMENTS

I wanted to give a big shout out to all of my family and friends who have been so incredibly supportive of this new journey. And to all of my readers, from the bottom of my heart, thank you. And, of course, to Bloodhound for making this dream a reality.

A NOTE FROM THE PUBLISHER

Thank you for reading this book. If you enjoyed it please do consider leaving a review on Amazon to help others find it too.

We hate typos. All of our books have been rigorously edited and proofread, but sometimes mistakes do slip through. If you have spotted a typo, please do let us know and we can get it amended within hours.

info@bloodhoundbooks.com

www.ingramcontent.com/pod-product-compliance
Lightning Source LLC
Chambersburg PA
CBHW050523110726
47899CB00005B/1573